# Three Fifty-Seven A.M.

*Timing is everything*

Also by Kendra Norman-Bellamy

*For Love and Grace*
*More Than Grace*
*Crossing Jhordan's River*
*In Greene Pastures*
*One Prayer Away*

# Three Fifty-Seven A.M.

*Timing is everything*

Kendra Norman-Bellamy
&
Hank Stewart

**URBAN CHRISTIAN**

*www.urbanchristianonline.net*

URBAN CHRISTIAN is published by

Urban Books
1199 Straight Path
West Babylon, NY 11704

ISBN-13: 978-1-60162-990-6
ISBN-10: 1-60162-990-7

First Trade Paperback Printing March 2007
First Mass Market Paperback Printing May 2009
Printed in the United States of America

10 9 8 7 6 5 4 3 2 1

*This is a work of fiction. Any references or similarities to actual events, real people, living, or dead, or to real locales are intended to give the novel a sense of reality. Any similarity in other names, characters, places, and incidents is entirely coincidental.*

Distributed by Kensington Publishing Corp.
Submit Wholesale Orders to:
Kensington Publishing Corp.
C/O Penguin Group (USA) Inc.
Attention: Order Processing
405 Murray Hill Parkway
East Rutherford, NJ 07073-2316
Phone: 1-800-526-0275
Fax: 1-800-227-9604

# Hank's Dedication

I want to dedicate this book to my son, **Austin O'Connell Stewart** ("Austin Boston"). You are my best friend, and I thank God for giving me the best SON in the world. I LOVE YOU THE MOST.

# Kendra's Dedication

This book is dedicated to the memory of my dear sister-in-law, **Valeria Bellamy Bryant** (1970–2005). You lived a beautiful life wherein you were an angel to all you met. By God's grace, you earned those wings, girl. FLY!

# Acknowledgments

I want to thank my family: To my loving mother, **Ruth Stewart,** who has reared five wonderful children; my two awesome sisters, **Bobbie and Valerie** and my two incredible brothers, **Bernard and Marshall**; I dedicate this book to all of you. Special tributes also go out to all of my **cousins, aunts, uncles, nieces, and nephews**. To ALL of my **friends**, I have too many to even begin to call names (please understand). But you all know who you are, and I thank you for being a part of my life.

I will forever be indebted to **Kendra Norman-Bellamy**, the most talented sister of the pen that I know. You are a jewel. I really enjoyed working on this project with you, and I'm looking forward to the next one (smile).

I dedicate this book to my other brothers, "Five Men on a Stool," **Antonio, Ken, Leonard, and the best band in the land.** I know my mother didn't birth you all, but you are truly my family. Speaking of which, my spiritual family at **Antioch Baptist Church North** in Atlanta, thank you for ALWAYS being there for me, and to my pastor,

**Rev. C. M. Alexander,** for being a father to me and keeping me on the straight and narrow.

And finally, I dedicate this book to my **Lord and Savior, Jesus Christ**. I don't know why You bestowed this gift on me, BUT I'm GLAD You did.

With humble gratefulness,

*Hank*

# Acknowledgments

To my **Lord and Savior**, thank You for the gift You've given me and for allowing me to use it for Your glory. To my husband, **Jonathan**, and daughters, **Brittney and Crystal**, thank you for your unconditional love and support. **Bishop & Mrs. H. H. Norman**, thank you for being wonderful, godly parents. I endeavor to always make you proud. To my siblings, **Crystal, Harold, Cynthia,** and **Kimberly**, thank you for believing in me.

Hugs and kisses to my **extended family members** who wish me well, and to my dear **godparents and godchildren. Terrance**, my "bestest cousin," I treasure all that you do for me. I'm so blessed to have you in my corner. To each and every one of my **dear friends**, you are invaluable gifts from God, and your continued support is appreciated more than I can ever express. To my spiritual family at **Revival Church Ministries**, thanks for the prayers you've whispered on my behalf. I know God is listening and answering. To the leaders and worshippers at **Total Grace Christian Center**, thanks for keeping my spirit in "rejoice mode."

**Hank,** of all the gifted writers you could

have chosen to help you bring your famed poem to life, you chose me, and from the bottom of my heart, I am grateful. Thank you for the challenge of *Three Fifty-Seven A.M.* I feel blessed to have worked with a mind as spiritually grounded and as positively creative as yours.

To all of the **readers** who will enjoy this book and the **book clubs** who will gather to discuss it, thank you. Without you, this project could not be successful.

From my heart to yours,

*Kendra*

# Chapter 1

## *Saturday Afternoon: 12:20 P.M.*

The Bible says that there is a time and a season for everything: a time to be born and a time to die, a time to plant and a time to pluck that which has been planted . . . a time to weep and a time to laugh . . . and so forth. The first few verses of the third chapter of Ecclesiastes are almost poetic, and its familiar words had been read only a few hours ago through reading glasses that sat on the tip of a broad, freckled nose.

"I always did say that timing was everything," Essie said when she ended her morning devotion.

The Bible also says that God is no respecter of persons, and if God's Word says it, then there's no question that it's true. But somehow, when it came to metropolitan Atlanta, the sun appeared to shine brighter, the streets seemed to be cleaner, and the flowers bloomed with just a little more color in Alpharetta than anywhere else. That wasn't to say that God liked the people of Alpharetta any more than

He did those who lived in other areas of Atlanta, but there was no denying that the grass really did seem greener on their side of the city.

Spring had arrived only a few days ago, but hints of it had been growing on tree limbs and in flower-beds for weeks prior. The sounds of singing birds and the sight of the blossoming garden that encircled the trunk of the weeping willow standing in the yard of 216 Braxton Way represented signs of life to the keen ears and aging eyes of seventy-seven-year-old Essie Mae Richardson.

When Essie was just a child, her mother talked to her about the sensitivity of her ears. Especially during those times when her schoolmates would tease her and make her feel somewhat self-conscious. Often-times, Essie could hear the sounds of light rainfall outside, the humming of bees in a hidden hive, things no one else could. Sometimes she could even hear the whispers of her older sisters as they huddled in a corner and exchanged stories about the boyfriends that their parents had no knowledge of.

"Girl, you got the ears of a blind man," her mom would tell her. "God give you them strong ears for a reason, so you sho'ly better use them to listen to whatever He got to tell you."

Growing up in Alabama, Essie had quite a number of friends, but now she could be described as a loner of sorts, not doing much outside of her home, other than going to church for worship. But she was happy and contented, and although her footsteps had shortened and her eyesight had dimmed over the years, her hearing remained as sharp as ever.

Essie had been a member of the Temple of God's Word for the past forty years, and she occupied the left end of the front pew every Sunday morning, rain or shine. The church was only two miles from her home, and as much as she despised driving on any stretch of road in Atlanta, she would push her reservations aside long enough to drive herself to morning worship and back home every week.

"It's the least I can do for the only somebody who loved me so much that He died for me," she'd been known to say. That response would almost always be followed by a thoughtful chuckle.

Essie had been a widow since she was a teenager. Her husband had died serving in World War II, and she never had the desire to remarry, despite several opportunities and the urging of her parents and sisters.

A lot of people had a tendency to forget that Blacks served in the military back then (if they knew at all), but Essie Mae Richardson remembered all too well that they did. The only man she'd ever loved had been sent to North Africa in 1944 to join the Allied Forces there. He left on a plane and came back in a box.

Every now and then, she still got teary-eyed when she thought of Benjamin Richardson. In a way, he'd died for her too. He and hundreds of men like him had died for a country whose leaders wouldn't even allow them to vote. Ben would always be a hero in her eyes, but even the price he paid was no match for what Jesus had done.

Daily prayer and Sunday worship at Temple of God's Word were two of the things that kept Essie going strong. Tomorrow, it would be time for her to crank up the old '67 Chevy for her Sunday morning ritual, but today was a day to sit on her front porch with her knitting and watch the happenings of the outside world.

With the weather so pleasant, the children of families in nearby houses played together on the sidewalks and in the grassy clearance across the street. For some of them, it was the first chance to show off the new clothes and toys that they'd gotten for Christmas nearly three months earlier. Some were on skateboards or rollerblades, riding up and down the sidewalks, while others rode bicycles. Those who didn't have the luxury of wheels to take them where they wanted to go just ran alongside those who did, and seemed to have just as much fun. The energy and excitement that came with being young was something that Essie remembered well, and was now admiring with fondness.

The sound of an approaching engine took her interest from the children and brought her eyes to the four-way stop just a few feet from her house, which occupied a corner lot at the mouth of the community.

It was Mason Demps driving one of three cars that he'd purchased inside of two years. As was the case with most of the residents of Braxton Park, Essie didn't know Mason personally, but recently she'd spoken to his wife, Elaine Demps, in passing. Elaine jogged somewhere in the neighborhood every weekday morning, claiming she was keeping in shape, but Essie sensed that it was more of a means of relieving stress.

Elaine, a freelance writer who worked from her home, started her morning jogs as soon as her husband left for work, and Essie had seen enough discord in her lifetime to know when couples weren't getting along. The day before, Essie was sure she'd seen tears in Elaine's eyes when she mumbled a heartless "Hello" as she strolled by her house. There was some type of friction going on in the

Demps' household for sure, and as Mason turned the corner in his new BMW and headed toward his house, Essie was almost certain that his collection of expensive toys had something to do with it.

The blanket she was knitting wasn't earmarked for anyone in particular. *Maybe I'll give it to Elaine to make her feel a little better.*

"Hey, Ms. Essie!" one of the neighborhood children greeted from a distance.

"Hey, baby. Y'all be careful, you hear? Watch out for them cars."

"Yes, ma'am."

Essie pushed her spectacles up on her nose and released a soft laugh. Spring break was just a few days away, and she was looking forward to seeing the children play like this throughout the week instead of just on Saturdays. Somehow, all the children in the neighborhood knew her name, but she knew very few of theirs. To her, they were just "baby," "sugar," or "honey." The little girl she'd just had the exchange with lived one street over, on Braxton Lane, but she played on Braxton Way because that was where her friends lived, the empty lot on the corner across from Essie's house being a perfect spot for their afternoon recreation.

Braxton Park used to be more of a retirement community, but in recent years, the houses had been renovated. When the face of the area had been lifted, the cost of living there went up too. Because a childless, elderly white couple she'd cleaned, cooked, and cared for years ago had died and left her their small fortune, Essie was capable of remaining, but many of the original residents were not able to afford the increased costs. The vacated houses had been reoccupied, and some had even been purchased by younger families who worked so much that they hadn't time to build personable relationships the way Essie and her former neighbors did. Sometimes Essie wondered if these contemporary families even knew the members of their own households, let alone their neighbors.

"Jerrod, where are you going?"

It was more of a demand than a question, and Essie had heard it more times than she could count over the past two years. The call was coming from the house directly to her left. She wasn't sure of the mother's name, but because she'd heard the boy's name summoned frequently, she was familiar with it. Today, the call caused Essie and a few of the children playing near the road to turn and give attention to the young woman, but it got little notice from the boy it was directed toward.

"Out," Jerrod responded as the front door of the house swung open and he emerged, bounding down the front steps, two at a time.

His mother fished for details while following him. "Out *where*?"

"Why you all up in my business?" he retorted, clearly irritated by her questioning.

"You ain't but fourteen, Jerrod. You don't have no business! Your room is a mess, and I didn't see you do any homework. You know the rules around here. It's homework before anything else."

"Whateva," he said with one side of his top lip curled in disdain. "It's Saturday, Ma. It ain't like I got to go to school tomorrow. I'll get all that junk done later. I gotta go."

"You don't have to go anywhere, Jerrod. Get back in here! I'm not playing with you!"

"You trippin' for real now." Jerrod flipped his wrist

in her direction as though her command meant nothing. Pulling his bicycle from the side of the garage, he straddled the seat and began pedaling.

"Jerrod, I *know* you hear me talking to you!"

Essie shook thoughts of picking up the potted plant beside her chair and throwing it as hard as she could at the ill-mannered child, but she knew that would be extreme. The least she could do was speak up and tell him to mind his mama, but in the back of her head, Essie could hear her own mother telling her to mind her own business.

"If I told you once, I done told you a thousand times," she remembered her mother saying to her as a child when she'd become meddlesome. "Stay out of grown folks' business, Essie Mae. If people don't ask for your input, then you keep it to yourself. Don't make me take a switch to your narrow behind about your fast mouth."

In addition to the remembrance of her mother's orders, Essie also recalled the scripture she'd read earlier that morning, the one about "a time to speak and a time to keep silent." She bit her bottom lip as she watched the boy ride away in spite of his mother's constant calling.

*Timing is everything*, she reminded herself, at the same moment hearing the house door slam as the boy's mother went back inside in aggravation. *Lord have mercy*, Essie thought. *I can't even imagine how raw my backside would be if I had ever flat-out disobeyed my mama like that. Times sho' done changed.*

Her heart went out to the mother, who didn't look much older than a teenager herself. She must have been pretty young when she had Jerrod. (Essie had never seen the boy's father.) Involuntarily, she shook her head in a mixture of anger and pity. Raising a boy as a single mother must be a chore. Raising *any* child as a single mother had to be challenging. Maybe when she finished the blanket, she'd let it be a gift to her next-door neighbor. Perhaps it would offer some comfort for the mounting frustration that her son was causing.

"If that blanket is for my baby, I'll close my eyes and pretend I didn't see it."

Essie looked up from her task and broke into a wide grin. She may not have known many of the people in her neighborhood, but she knew Angel Stephens. In fact, she'd named her when she was born twenty-seven years ago. Angel's grandmother, Thelma, had been one of Essie's dearest friends back when the neighborhood was full of people her age. Thelma had passed away a few years earlier and her son, Angel's father, had moved away from the neighborhood even before that. Shortly after Angel got married three years ago, she and her husband, Colin, moved into the house on Braxton Circle where Angel had been born.

"Look at you!" Essie put the knitting aside and stood to embrace the girl who had been the closest thing to a daughter or granddaughter she'd ever had. "Girl, you look even bigger than you did three days ago. You 'bout ready to go down any day, ain't you?"

"I have another six weeks," Angel said, beaming and glowing with expectation. "Ms. Essie, I've never been so ready to drop a load in my whole life!"

Essie laughed heartily and hugged Angel again before offering her a place to sit on her porch.

"No, this ain't a blanket for your baby, and if it was, it wouldn't be now that you done seen it. You had an appointment on Thursday, didn't you? Was the doctor able to tell you what you were having?"

"I want to know so badly, Ms. Essie." Angel shook her head and rubbed her swollen stomach. "The doctor keeps saying that he can't tell because the baby is always positioned wrong. One time he said it was a boy, and then another time he said it was a girl. Finally, we gave up and told him we'd just wait. It was too frustrating. Colin says it's a boy. He said he's going to be the first one to give both our parents a grandson. I want a boy too, but as long as the baby is healthy, we'll both be happy."

"If you really want to know, Angel, I'll tell you."

Angel laughed at Essie's words. "What? Are you getting ready to lay one of those old wives' tales on me? Am I carrying 'high,' Ms. Essie? What does that mean . . . a girl or a boy?"

"Laugh if you want, but there's a lot to them fables," Essie said. "But this ain't no old wives' tale that I'm talking 'bout. When your mama was pregnant with you, I told her she was having a girl and she did. It's a gift God gave me. I ain't never been wrong. Not one time have I been wrong."

Angel wasn't laughing any longer. She looked at Essie as if she was trying to decide whether she really wanted the woman to predict the sex of her child.

"Well, do you or don't you?" Essie asked, precisely judging the young woman's thoughts.

Angel gave in. "What do you think it is, Ms. Essie?"

"It ain't what I think, it's what I *know*."

Angel smiled and used her hands to hold both sides of her belly. "Well, whatever it is, it sure has a mean kick. What is it, Ms. Essie? Tell me."

Essie's face lit up. For months she'd been hearing

Angel and Colin voicing their desires to know the sex of their child, but since they hadn't asked her, she held what she knew to herself. She figured the doctor would tell them soon enough, but now Essie took extreme pleasure in the opportunity to be the one to give the official word.

"You tell Colin that if he done went out and bought any clothes or toys meant just for a little Junior, he can take every one of 'em and open 'em up 'cause y'all definitely having a boy."

Angel rose with excitement from her seat as though Essie's words were the law. Raising both her hands up in the air like a winning field goal had been made during a football game, she let out a loud shriek and then hugged Essie tightly.

"Are you sure, Ms. Essie? Are you really, really sure? I want to tell Colin, but I don't want to tell him if you're not sure, you know what I mean? I should have asked you if it was a boy a long time ago. I know you're always right about these kinds of things, but I still want to be certain. I don't want to get his hopes up on having a son if you're not sure," Angel babbled.

"I'm as sure as them flowers is a-blooming 'round my tree. You can tell him just what I said. Y'all got a son on the way."

Looking at the watch on her arm, Angel headed for the steps. "He's going to think I'm crazy when I tell him that you told me what the doctor couldn't, but I'll bet he'll be happy just the same. He was 'sleep when I left the house for my walk, but I'm sure he's up now. And if he's not, I'm gonna wake him."

Essie laughed as Angel's voice faded while she continued to talk and walk away at the same time. It was good to see some happiness among the grownups in the neighborhood. Angel and Colin had a solid marriage, and they were young people who loved God. Essie was proud that Angel's parents had raised her to be a respectful woman. She looked up at the sky above and smiled. Essie was sure that Thelma was somewhere up there, looking down and beaming with pride at the way her granddaughter turned out.

"Well, I guess it's safe to say for sure this blanket ain't for the baby," Essie mumbled with another soft chuckle while looking at the pink knitting. "It's for somebody, though," she added, looking up in time to see Mason Demps drive past her house in the Range Rover he'd purchased last summer. "It's for somebody," she repeated. "I don't know who, but time will sho' 'nuff tell."

# Chapter 2

## *Saturday Afternoon: 2:00 P.M.*

Saturday was generally one of the days that Elaine didn't do her outdoor exercise. In the normal scheme of things, jogging was a Monday through Friday ritual to help her clear her head before sitting at her computer and typing out the next short story to submit to whatever magazine was soliciting her talent. Exercise wasn't just good for her body; it had become imperative for her sanity.

By now, on any other day, she would have long-ago finished her run and would be working passionately on a project she'd be proud to see in print. But today she had a severe case of writer's block and couldn't stay focused.

It wasn't often that Mason had a day away from his job as a truck driver. The job took him away from her for at least sixteen hours each day, and by the time he made it home at night, he was too tired or just too uninterested in doing much of anything else, other than sleeping or lazing in front of the television, snacking on roasted peanuts. His job paid well, but Elaine felt that the money wasn't enough to cover the true cost of it all.

The problem didn't lay in how many hours he spent away from home or the checks he received twice a month. The issue that was draining her was *how* her husband used the free time he did have and *how* he spent the money he brought home. Every two weeks, Mason was given a weekend off from work, but instead of him making time with her a priority, he chose to squander those days unnecessarily "juicing up" the vehicles that he insisted upon purchasing, and showing off the finished products to his friends.

Just a few minutes earlier, he'd come from a barbecue at the house of one of "the boys" and was only home long enough to change clothes and switch vehicles before he was off again to pick up a few friends and cruise the streets of Atlanta. At thirty-two, Mason seemed to still have a need to impress his friends, but cared none at all about pleasing his wife.

Recollection of the recent dispute caused a throbbing in Elaine's head. She rubbed her temples, trying to massage away the increasing pain. She had tried to approach the subject of his constant absenteeism with some refinement, but Mason's insensitive attitude had pushed her over the edge once again.

"So you're just going to leave regardless of how I feel. Is that it?" Elaine followed him around the bedroom as he searched for the keys she'd intentionally tucked under his bed pillow.

Between the two of them, Elaine was, by far, the more vocal. For the most part, Mason was a man of few words. He'd been that way for as long as Elaine had known him. In the earliest years of their marriage, she'd thought of his placidness as a positive trait. It gave her a chance to vent without interruption. Now, when Mason shut down, it just felt like he was ignoring her.

When he didn't answer her question, Elaine reached forward and grabbed him by the arm. "Do you hear me, Mason?"

"Dead people can hear you, Elaine," he shot back, snatching his arm from her grip. "You act like I'm catching a one-way flight to New York or something. I'm just going to run to Ace's house to see what he wants. I said I'd be back in an hour."

"So, I guess whatever it is that Ace wants to talk about is more important than what I want to talk about." Elaine placed her hands on her hips and stared straight up into Mason's eyes. No new words exited her lips, but her body language dared him to give the wrong response.

"I don't have time for this, Elaine," he said, pushing past her. "I'm sure my conversation with Ace won't be nearly as exhausting as whatever you have to talk about. Let me get this visit over with, and I'll reserve the energy for when I get home and have to deal with you."

Elaine couldn't have been more insulted. "*Deal* with me? I'll tell you what. Why don't you go ahead and catch that one-way flight to New York. Then you won't ever have to *deal* with me again!"

It was at that moment that Mason lifted his pillow and discovered his keys. The expression that immediately made its way to his face showed suspicion at how the keys had gotten there. "Don't tempt me," he mumbled just before walking past her again and heading for the front door.

The whole argument had lasted for less than five minutes, but the disturbing memories of it still lingered an hour later. Exiting the house, Elaine closed the front door with more force than was needed. She loved Mason, but being married to him was getting to be more of a chore than an honor. Locking the door behind her, she dropped in her sock a single key that would allow her back inside once she was finished with her exercise.

Fortunately, spring had ushered in perfect temperatures, allowing her to run at this time in the afternoon without the threat of getting overheated. Pacing herself, Elaine began slowly. It was a strategy that she'd taught herself, finding that she could run longer if she didn't start out too quickly. Not many of her neighbors were out and about, it seemed, but she had to cross the road to the vacant sidewalk on the other side to avoid the children who were playing and had no intention of clearing a path for her.

"Running again?"

Elaine turned to her right and caught a glimpse of the elderly woman, sitting on her porch and knitting.

"Yes, ma'am," she responded through a light pant. "Gotta keep in shape."

She knew the woman only as Ms. Essie, just like everybody else. Elaine had never held a real conversation with her, but sometimes she had the urge to. There was something about the lady that made her feel both comfortable and uncomfortable at the same time. Essie had beautiful, trusting eyes and a maternal spirit, but sometimes Elaine got the feeling that the eyes peering through the reading glasses could see right through her. Still, Elaine found herself drawn to the woman who sat on her porch daily. She figured that at Essie's age, she must have experienced a lot in life. No doubt, Essie had gone through marital problems and could probably shed a little light on how she could handle this situation with Mason.

Elaine considered the idea of picking Essie's brain for a bit of insight, but not today. She was in no mood for talking. Mason had ruffled her feathers too much for her to try to discuss it with anyone right now. Today, she'd just run it off. One mile up the road, and one mile back home. She was certain that it would be enough to take the edge off for now.

Just as she approached the sign that identified her subdivision, Elaine thought of her Walkman that she'd inadvertently left behind. Music always made her run easier and made the time pass more quickly. It was too late now. She didn't want to backtrack just to get it. This would be one time when she'd have to keep herself focused without the crutch of having the latest R&B rhythms drumming in her ears. Cars whizzing by with elevated sound systems were all she had to use as substitutes.

The cool air that still lingered from the winter chill felt refreshing on Elaine's face as she tackled the hill that, at one time, had been too challenging for her to complete without breaking her stride. One thing for sure, as unfortunate as her reasons were for taking on this habit, doing it so often had heightened her level of fitness. Elaine had never been obese, but ever since her miscarriage three years ago, she had been struggling with weight gain from the eating binges that her depression had brought on.

It was her third miscarriage and the most difficult one of all. Whereas her body had disposed of the first two pregnancies within their first trimesters, the third one had entered its fifth month when she suddenly lost the child that had been progressing without any foreseen difficulties. That third miscarriage was the starting point of the decline of her seven-year marriage.

Whether it was his intent or not, Mason was making her feel as though the last loss was her fault. Elaine knew that her husband wanted children, but she couldn't control whatever it was that was hindering her from giving them both what they desired. Mason had six brothers and two sisters. All of his siblings were either married or "playing house," as Elaine liked to call it. Whatever living arrangements they had, they all had children; having babies in the Demps family was like a badge of honor. Elaine supposed that in Mason's eyes, she was impeding him from getting his award.

Beads of sweat, not minimized at all by the sweatband that she wore around her head, broke through her skin and began to run down her face. Although thoughts of the day's heated discussion still lingered, Elaine was beginning to feel better already, and she still had another block to go before turning around and heading home. Her pace quickened as she reached the top of the hill and began her downward slope on the other side of it. Every time she mastered that rise in her outdoor track, she felt a sense of victory.

"Hey there, my Nubian queen! Every day you run past here, you just look better and better."

Elaine heard the slightly accented declaration coming from the Goodyear tire shop, but she disregarded it.

"Running so hard must make you thirsty. We have fresh cold water over here, if you want some," the voice offered.

As dry as her mouth was, it was almost enough to curb her determination to continue ignoring him, but Elaine kept her mind focused on the traffic light that was less than a quarter of a mile down the road and continued running. Once she made it there, water would be accessible to her.

"Okay then," he called out with an unbroken spirit. "If you change your mind, I'll be here when you're on your way back!"

When Elaine knew she was no longer in view of the stranger, a withheld smile broke through her lips.

It had been a long time since a man had spoken words to her that hinted admiration. It had been years since Mason had. Over the past twelve months, Elaine had gotten a new layered hair cut and lost fifteen pounds, but her husband didn't notice either one of the physical improvements. They still shared occasional intimate nights, but those moments were becoming fewer and felt as though they were carried out because of obligation instead of desire. And the open flirtations and sweet compliments that he used to give her in the earlier years of their marriage had long ceased. Most likely, the mechanic who'd just broken away from his job to entice her was grungy and stinking from the chores his employment entailed, but his words sounded good just the same.

Finally reaching her one-mile marker at the entrance of another subdivision, Elaine stopped to catch her breath. She used the sleeves of her shirt to wipe away the accumulated perspiration and then paced in circles to keep her heart rate from completely plummeting. When she suddenly realized that she'd forgotten to tuck away the two dollars in her pocket that she usually brought along for her bottled water, Elaine swore. Across from her mile marker was the gas station where she'd always purchase a bottle of water, whenever she reached this point, and take in a few sips before embarking on the second half of her journey.

Trying to quench the dryness of her throat with saliva, Elaine took a deep breath and started in the direction toward home. There was no sense in wallowing in self-pity. The quicker she got home, the sooner she could rectify the situation. With parched lips, the oncoming hill was going to be more demanding than normal, but she felt invincible.

One of the motivational tapes that she'd listened to the day before stressed the importance of staying positive. For Elaine, doing so was a daily struggle, but she was determined not to let Mason and his adolescent actions dictate her life. She'd run every day if she had to. If that's what it took to keep herself grounded, that was exactly what she would do. It was time for her to look out for herself. If Mason didn't want to spend time with her, fine! She refused to let her worth be defined by a man who didn't know how to appreciate her.

*I am woman, hear me roar!* Elaine thought, reliving the words chanted on the motivational tape.

"Hey, beautiful," the familiar voice called. "I have the water just like I promised."

Elaine was so caught up in her own thoughts that she didn't even notice that she had already reached the Goodyear establishment. Her eyes had been locked on the start of the hill that she'd have to conquer once more before being able to enjoy the ease of a downward run. She'd momentarily forgotten her dry discomfort, but just hearing the mention of water made her throat feel as though it had been crammed with cotton balls.

"I'm not a runner, but if that's what it'll take for you to talk to me, I'll run with you!"

Elaine almost laughed at his weak pick-up lines. As flattered as she couldn't help feeling, she still refused to look in his direction. By now, with the sweat that ran down her face and the body fluids that made her shirt stick to her skin, she had to look awful; but the mechanic was relentless. Elaine was certain that he pestered every woman who passed his way with the same compliments he'd given her, but to her starving ears, it made no difference whether he was being genuine.

Lack of hydration made the hill seem twice as high as it actually was, and Elaine grunted, clenching her teeth with unyielding fortitude. Defeat was unacceptable. That was another lesson she'd learned from the series of galvanizing lectures on CDs that she'd come to depend upon to get her through each week. If she didn't do what brought her happiness and fulfillment and made her feel good about herself, then she was accepting defeat. Mason was doing what pleased him, so Elaine was determined to take his negativism and turn it into something positive. She would do what pleased *her*. Conquering this hill would bring her joy, and it didn't matter how much her legs begged for mercy; she wouldn't stop pushing forward.

By the time she made it to the top and began her long-awaited descent, tears and perspiration trickled down her face. In a sense, they were tears of relief, as the heaviness she'd been carrying around in her heart began dissipating. She'd finally found the solution to all of her problems. On the recordings she'd been listening to, the woman said that when the messages ultimately sink in and when the listener finally gets her breakthrough, she will know it. The teacher was right. Elaine felt as though she'd gotten her resurgence when she put mind over matter and defeated the forces that wanted her to give up on mastering the hill.

"Yes!" she said aloud, basking in the pride of her accomplishment. "That one was for you, Mason Demps, and for all your stupid friends and your shallow-minded family members."

She made a mental note that from this point on, it would be all about her. If she didn't look after herself, no one else would.

Today's run had been beneficial in more ways than one. It didn't only give her extra exercise, but it also gave her victory over the onset of depression. Elaine didn't want to admit it, but her ongoing marital problems were causing her to sink deep into a depressed existence. In essence, Mason and his mindgames had been the root of everything that was going wrong in her life, and it took today's run and the remembrance of the words she'd heard spoken over the weeks through her stereo player to make her realize it.

As an added reward, her writer's block had been destroyed. As she took on the last quarter of a mile, Elaine became conscious of the fact that she'd been inspired. Everything in life happens for a reason. That was another point that her tapes stressed. Elaine reasoned that her failure to grab the fanny pack that housed her personal CD player and the money she would have used to purchase the water was all a part of the plan that her spiritual guardian had set in place for her.

The teacher on the tape said that every human being has a spiritual guardian known as their personal Guardian of Divinity. Each mystical GOD, as she referred to them, was set in place before the beginning of time, and if all people spoke to their assigned spiritual guardian on a daily basis and made their desires known, the GOD would line up the stars so that favors would be granted. For weeks, Elaine had been seeking her spiritual guardian and asking for direction. She was beginning to think that these mystical divine beings were nonexistent, but now she realized that she just needed to be patient. Her GOD had finally made itself known, and everything was clear to her now.

As Elaine figured it, had she brought the CD player along, she never would have heard the noises of the outside world, including the calls from the stranger at the auto shop. Had she brought along the money, she most likely would have lost focus when she shopped the convenience store for water. Staying on the sidewalk's path had kept her where her GOD wanted her to be. The man at Goodyear had been put in place to stimulate her imagination. She knew exactly what her next short story series would be about. She would chronicle her own experiences by creating a fictitious character that was facing a lot of the same issues she was enduring in her marriage to Mason. She'd put a face and a name to the mechanic and allow him to be her female character's knight in shining armor. It was perfect.

With a renewed spirit and drive, Elaine rounded

the corner that brought her back into Braxton Park. As she approached Braxton Way, she noticed that Essie had come down from her porch and was now using a water hose to irrigate the area where flowers were blooming around her tree.

As assured as Elaine felt for the larger portion of her jog back home, a feeling of uncertainty blindsided her when she passed the mailbox marked *216*. That urge to talk resurfaced, and when her eyes briefly met the kind eyes of the elderly woman, who took a moment to look up from her chore, Elaine felt the onset of new tears. This time they didn't feel so much like relief. She felt like a child who had done something ghastly and had just looked into the eyes of a mother who had trusted her to do the right thing. Elaine had a strong desire to throw herself at Essie's feet and bawl her eyes out. Instead, she returned the woman's wave and increased her pace so that she could outrun the urge to bare her soul.

Realistically, there was little or no chance that Essie could still see her in the distance that separated her house from the one on the corner lot. But even as Elaine fumbled for the key that had slid deep into her sock, she could feel Essie's eyes on her. Elaine's hands trembled, causing her to drop the single key twice before finally getting it to slip into the lock and turn. Her heart was pounding harder now than at any time during her two-mile run. It was as though someone were after her, and if she didn't get inside soon, she would be captured by some unknown force.

Stepping inside the door that led directly to her den, Elaine closed it behind her and immediately turned the handle to both locks, securing her inside.

She breathed a sigh of relief and stood for several moments, her back resting against the wooden entranceway, trying to gain control of her racing heart. It was the strangest feeling she'd ever experienced in her life.

Gathering herself and interpreting that she'd somehow allowed her imagination to get the best of her, Elaine stood upright and then laughed at her own foolishness. Then she glanced through her front curtain for assurance before picking up one of her motivational CDs and heading to the bathroom for a much-needed shower.

# Chapter 3

## *Saturday Evening 5:00 P.M.*

"How in the world did my life come to this?" Jennifer took a long look in the mirror through vision blurred by a combination of swollen lids and leftover tears.

She had done little else other than cry and question herself since her son left her standing on the porch, speaking words that meant nothing to him. The woman whose image was reflected in the glass in front of Jennifer looked ten years older than she. This particularly hard crying spell had left her eyes red and her light brown nose glowing like she had been suffering with allergies. But it was over now. She had no tears left.

Jennifer couldn't figure out where she'd gone wrong with Jerrod. She wanted to pacify herself by concluding that he'd turned out so poorly because she'd had no stable male figure beside her to reinforce her rules and regulations. But Jennifer knew of too many other boys who had been raised by single mothers and didn't turn out the way her son did. His "terrible twos" had lasted for more than twelve years, and she was at her wit's end. Jerrod's defiance had managed to rule both his existence and hers, and Jennifer felt that she couldn't live her own life because she constantly had to worry about his.

*Where is he? What is he doing? Who is he with?* These were only a few of the questions that haunted her every time Jerrod left the house, only giving the response, "Out," when asked where he was going. One of her greatest fears was that he was doing something illegal. Every evening when Jennifer listened to the news and heard about suspicious arsons or unsolved burglaries, she wondered if the culprit was Jerrod or maybe some of the crowd that he spent time with. Whenever the news reports showed distorted security camera footage of a young black male holding up a nearby bank or convenience store, she would approach the television screen and search the image to see if there was any possible way the armed gunman could be her son.

It was an awful state to be in to feel that her only child was capable of such heinous crimes, but he'd given her no reason to think otherwise. Late at night when her telephone rang and she knew he hadn't made it home yet, her heart would sink. Jennifer would brace herself before picking up the phone, preparing her ears to hear a policeman tell her that her son had been picked up, or even worse, that a lifeless body found somewhere had been identified as that of her fourteen-year-old.

When he wasn't home and she knew there was no threat of getting caught, Jennifer often searched his room for clues about who he was spending his time with, or what things he might be involved in. What she might possibly find kept her heart racing. The thought of uncovering a weapon, unexplained large amounts of cash, or stashed drugs would sometimes cause her to perspire as she ran her hands through his drawers and under his mattress. Jerrod's room was always in disarray, so Jennifer knew it would be almost impossible for him to determine whether she had been snooping.

She had just come out of the pigsty half an hour ago, and her investigation turned up nothing. Jerrod was too smart and too sneaky to leave a trail that she could follow up on.

When Jennifer found out, at the age of fifteen, that she was pregnant, it was the most frightening day of her life. Back then, South Carolina was her home. Jennifer remembered searching frantically for a way to tell her parents, who were in the process of getting a divorce at the time. She didn't expect them to condone what she'd done, but if she could have gotten the support of either one of them, Jennifer knew that it would have made a difference in how her life turned out. Her father was furious. For years he'd known and hated the family of the wayward sixteen-year-old that impregnated her. Her mother was even angrier. She theorized that Jennifer had gotten pregnant on purpose; either to get back at her parents for moving forward with divorce proceedings, or with the hope of keeping them together.

None of it was true. In essence, Jennifer had allowed herself to be fooled into thinking that somebody really loved her. And even after the boy made it clear that he didn't want to have anything more to do with her or the unborn child, Jennifer couldn't be persuaded by her parents to abort. In her mind, she finally had something to love, and this baby would love her back, unlike all of the other people that surrounded her.

Jennifer still remembered the day that she was put out of the house like a stray animal. Her father said that she couldn't move in with him because he was moving to another state and had no time to help raise an infant. Jennifer's mother gave her two choices: Terminate the pregnancy or get out. Jennifer had no place to go and no means of sustaining herself, but she chose to leave, not once thinking that it would be permanent. There was no doubt in her mind that the initial shock would wear off and, in a day or two, her mother would be combing the neighborhood in search of her one and only child.

The scared teenager found a temporary hideout to stay in and waited for her mom to begin looking for her. Sadly, she never did. For nearly two months, Jennifer lived off of her mother without her mother even being aware of it. There was a utility shelter in their backyard where her father had always stored the lawnmower and other spring and summer tools. It was untidy and reeked of gasoline, but it was enough to shield her from the winter air outdoors.

At that time, Jennifer still had a key to the house, and when her mother would leave for work each morning, she'd come out of the makeshift home that she hid in during the evening and night hours, and go inside to shower and find food and added warmth. She stocked the tool shed with non-perishable snacks and canned goods that she figured her mother wouldn't miss. Jennifer took extra blankets that had been stored in the attic and used them during the night to ward off the cold that she and the baby growing inside her were forced to endure.

As the winter turned to spring, Jennifer knew that her sheltered days were numbered. Soon, her mother would need the garden tools for the upkeep of her hedges and flowers.

Her stay ended sooner than she had planned. Apparently her mother sensed that she'd been coming inside and had all the locks changed, leaving her daughter completely helpless. For two days, Jennifer cried almost non-stop.

One of the harshest memories of the day that she had to confess her pregnancy to her parents was when her mother told her that if she kept the child, she would be throwing away everything that she ever dreamed of doing. At that time in her life, Jennifer had plans of becoming a lawyer. She did well in school despite the turmoil she endured at home. Her parents fought constantly and were so busy making one another's lives miserable that oftentimes it seemed as though they forgot that they even had a daughter. Everything that Jennifer did was in hopes of gaining her parents' attention, but nothing worked.

The unplanned pregnancy got their attention, but they threw her away so quickly and so easily that Jennifer was left to believe that all she'd done was give them the excuse they'd been hoping for to rid each of them of the burden of being the custodial parent in the divorce settlement.

It shouldn't have surprised her. Her childhood memories were far from loving. When her parents weren't abusing each other, they were abusing her, mostly verbally, but sometimes physically. She could remember being slapped to the floor numerous times by her father for reasons so insignificant she couldn't even remember them. And marks from several beatings administered by her mother with an extension cord that she kept in the kitchen drawer were still visible on her legs. So, her parents disposing of her at the first opportunity should have been expected, but it wasn't. Putting their daughter out of their lives was the first decision they'd agreed upon in years.

Jennifer was determined to make her parents' predictions nothing more than lies. She would not only finish high school, but however long it took, she'd also obtain a college degree. She would work hard and shower her child with so much love, he'd cherish her forever.

One breezy Saturday afternoon, she wandered into an unfamiliar park and watched the children play. She listened to their laughter and wondered if her child would ever know a day of happiness. After an hour of sitting and watching, a middle-aged woman approached and filled the space on the bench beside her. They began conversing, and it wasn't long before Jennifer was tearfully telling the woman her life story. Talking to strangers wasn't something that she often did, but it felt good to be able to unload the burden, something that no child her age should be carrying to begin with.

It turned out to be one of the best things she could have done. The lady became Jennifer's rescuer, driving her several miles away to a group home near Anderson, South Carolina, and introducing her to the people who provided her with a safe place to stay and the medical attention she needed.

After Jerrod was born, Jennifer enrolled in a local high school and succeeded in earning her diploma. While the other classmates had proud parents in the stands cheering them on, Jennifer had no one.

By that time, it had been three years since she'd

made the error in judgment that had changed her entire life as she'd known it. Not once did her parents try to contact her, even though she'd long before made her whereabouts known to both of them. Jennifer figured that time would eventually heal the scars that the blow of the unexpected news had delivered years earlier, but it became painfully apparent that she was wrong.

By the time Jerrod was beginning kindergarten, he was already too much for most teachers to handle. Even the daycare instructors at the facility that the State paid tuition for him to attend while Jennifer worked as a hotel maid had had their share of problems with controlling his behavior.

"It's just a phase," her co-workers assured her.

"He'll grow out of it," others would say.

Instead, Jerrod had grown into more trouble than she'd ever imagined. At least when he was small, she could spank him or lock him in his room until his tantrums ended. Now he was taller and probably stronger than she. Some days, Jennifer had to admit that she feared her own son. On those days, like today, when she tried to put her foot down and be the strict parent that he needed, she was sometimes afraid to close her eyes at night to go to sleep. Questions as to what state of mind her teenager would be in whenever he did decide to return home clouded her thoughts and robbed her of a peaceful sleep.

*Is he capable of harming me?* Jennifer didn't know the answer to that haunting thought that played over and over in her head. But there were times when he'd swear at her, and she would see rage in his eyes that made her wonder.

Jennifer had concluded two years ago, the first time Jerrod had cursed and balled his hand into a fist as though he wanted to strike her, that there was no way she'd put up with him becoming physically violent. She had no control over the fact that her parents had occasionally used her as their punching bag, but Jennifer would not accept such actions from the child to whom she'd given birth. She'd taken care of him his entire life, and she wouldn't tolerate abusive behavior from a boy who wouldn't have a place to lay his head if she hadn't worked like an Egyptian slave to prove wrong her parents and the rest of the world, who may have thought she had thrown her life away and sentenced herself to failure and poverty by deciding to keep her baby.

Jennifer walked to the corner of her living room and picked up the telephone. It was the third time in the past two hours that she'd dialed the same number and gotten the same voicemail message.

"What up, yo? You've reached Jerrod's crib. I'm busy and can't answer the phone right now. At the beep, say what ya gotta say. If you a honey, you get priority, so, holla. Peace."

No matter how many times she heard the message, Jennifer scowled. Her son was only fourteen, but he wanted so badly to be older. If she knew who his buddies were, she'd probably feel more comfortable with him being away from home so often and for such long periods at a time. She had never met any of the people Jerrod referred to as his friends. They never came to his house; he always went to meet them. Who he was with and what he was doing was a mystery to Jennifer, and not knowing was quite possibly the hardest part of all.

"Jerrod, this is your mother. I've left you two messages already. I find it hard to believe that you don't have your cell phone on. It's getting near dinnertime, and I want you home in time to eat. If you're not here by six, I'm calling the police."

When Jennifer forcefully hung up the telephone, it was more out of frustration with herself than her son. She'd handed out so many idle threats over the years that she knew none of her ultimatums had any merit. Before the words even left her mouth, Jennifer was fully aware that Jerrod wouldn't be home before six o'clock and probably not even before midnight. He'd get home when he was good and ready and not a moment sooner. The saddest acknowledgement of all was that there was absolutely nothing that she felt could be done about it. In the end, unlike how it was with Jennifer and her parents, Jerrod always won.

Somehow the vision she had for her son went awry. She thought she was giving Jerrod all that any little boy could ever want or need. There was a time that she worked two jobs to pay for toys and clothes that she really couldn't afford. Yet, he'd grown up to be a brute who didn't show any gratitude for anything that she did for him. Jennifer had counted on the surety that he would outgrow the stubborn and disrespectful behavior, but if he hadn't by this time, she feared that he never would.

She tried to keep their friction private, but Jerrod knew just how to push the right buttons to make her lose control. Jennifer had come to believe that he enjoyed taunting her and making her look like an incompetent fool while he dismissed every parental guideline that she attempted to set in place.

Today's exchange wasn't the worst between her and Jerrod, but it was still very heated. The fact that

Jennifer allowed it to get to the point where her next-door neighbor had a front-row view of the continuing drama in her household made her quite embarrassed.

Just before storming back into her house, Jennifer had caught a glimpse of the elderly woman watching Jerrod closely. She sensed that Essie wanted to say something but refrained from speaking, opting to just look on in silence. That moment in time, the moment that she saw the silent support in Essie's eyes, made Jennifer realize that there was someone who felt her pains. Unlike many before her, Essie didn't make an immediate conclusion that Jennifer was an unfit parent. Instead she had compassion for what Jennifer, as a single mother, had to endure. It was clearly written on Essie's face as she watched Jerrod speed away on his bicycle.

For the next hour after she had closed herself back in her house, Jennifer took breaks from her tears to steal an occasional peek though her side curtains, and saw the old woman still sitting on her porch, knitting. She wanted to walk next door, sit next to Essie, and pick her mind for any bit of wisdom she could share on what she could do to get a grip on her out-of-control teenager. Jennifer figured that she must have had children of her own or helped to raise somebody else's children during her lifetime. A woman Essie's age had to know more than she did. Jennifer had tried her best and thought she had all the answers, but Jerrod was hard-core proof that she knew nothing.

*"God's time is perfect time, and He makes things all right in His time. Lord, You know me in and out, and You know what I'm about. You will make me sing and shout in Your time."*

The sudden sounds of melody floated through the partially opened window in Jennifer's living room. Peeling back the curtain, she watched Essie gather her knitting and prepare to go inside her house. As if all was right with the world, her hymn was laced with cheer.

*"God's time is perfect time, and He makes things all right in His time. Lord, You're my everything, and for You this song I sing. You'll give me angel's wings in Your time."*

Essie didn't have the most polished voice in the world, but the words to the song rang delightfully in Jennifer's ears. She'd never heard it before, but something about the lyrics touched a tender spot in her heart, ducts that she thought had no more to give rendering new moisture that spilled down her cheeks. Thoughts formed in her mind of dressing up in her Sunday best and attending church with her grandmother when she was a little girl. It had been ages since she'd thought about her maternal grandmother, who'd died just before Jennifer turned ten years old. Nothing in her life seemed to go right from that day forward.

Grandma Pearl was the pillar that kept the family stable. Jennifer's parents had had disagreements before her grandmother passed away, but because she lived with them, Grandma Pearl would put a stop to it before it could spiral out of control. She was the only person Jennifer could talk to about anything, and the only one she could count on for the hugs and kisses that she never got from her parents.

If Grandma Pearl was alive when her fifteen-year-old granddaughter turned up pregnant, she would have been disappointed and hurt. But Jennifer was willing to bet any amount of money that her grandmother wouldn't have been in agreement with the decision to throw her out on the street. Grandma Pearl would never have allowed it to happen.

When Jennifer looked through the curtain again, Essie was gone. She found herself stepping closer to the window and straining to hear more of the song. The walls in the renovated homes had been built too thick for her to hear a sound coming from the house next door.

Turning away, she used her hands to wipe away the tears so that she could have a clear view of the clock on the wall. It was 5:45 and past time to get started with dinner. On the way to the kitchen, Jennifer reached for the telephone again. She knew Jerrod wasn't going to answer. Still, she dialed his number, cringed through the message one more time, and waited for the beep.

# Chapter 4

## Saturday Afternoon: 9:49 P.M.

Cooking dinner for one didn't leave many dishes to be washed. Essie finished the last of hers and used a paper towel to dry her hands before migrating to her living room, clutching a late-night hot cup of lemonade in her hands.

"Mmmm," she moaned as she took the first sip.

As far as Essie was concerned, there was nothing like fresh-squeezed lemonade. In the summertime, she drank it ice-cold, but in cooler temperatures, like tonight, she would pour a cup of her favorite drink and heat it in her kettle on the stove. The days had begun to warm up nicely, but the nighttime still held on to a chill that wouldn't allow Atlantans to pack away their sweaters just yet. Essie released a sigh and settled back on her sofa.

The television in front of her was on, but the volume was at such a low setting that she could barely hear the heated exchange between the two female characters. The television was one of two devices that got very little use in Essie's home. Most times when the Zenith brand floor model set was on, hardly anyone looked at it. Powering it up was just an old habit that Essie found hard to break. In her more youthful days, she would turn it on just to have some noise in the house. The sounds from the tube were a viable substitute for there being no other people in her home. Once she began caring for her employers, the television was used to keep them entertained while she did other household chores.

The only show that grabbed her attention was *The Price Is Right*. Essie remembered watching the first airing of the show in 1972. Somehow she had become addicted to it, like other folks were to soap operas. Every weekday morning at eleven o'clock, she set aside an hour to watch Bob Barker give away thousands of dollars in cash and prizes to those fortunate enough to beat the odds. When she sat in her chair and called out her bids, Essie celebrated as though she'd actually won something when her estimations were close. And she didn't mind calling contestants "big dummies" when their guesses were ridiculously far from being correct. For Essie, *The Price Is Right* was enough to appease her need for secular excitement.

The telephone was the other appliance in her home that was rarely used. Essie had never been much of a "telephone person." Even when the neighborhood was filled with people that she knew on a first-name basis, she wasn't one to do much calling. She and her other retired neighbors would walk to each others' houses and sit for hours, sharing recipes, garden tips, talking about family members, and just having good conversation.

"These young folks today don't know nothing about friendship," she mumbled while reflecting and taking another sip of her lemonade. "They spend so much time trying to make a living that they ain't got a minute left in the day to enjoy life."

The grandfather clock that stood in the corner behind her loveseat chimed. It was ten o'clock, an hour past her usual bedtime. Generally, by this time of night, Essie would be sound asleep, but today was disconcerting for her. The exchange between her next-door neighbor and her son, and the brewing trouble that she could sense from the couple down the street had been weighing on her heart for most of the day. The look and feel of her neighborhood sure had changed over the years.

For almost thirty-five years, she had lived in Braxton Park. When she first moved there as a live-in caretaker for Mr. and Mrs. Breckenridge, she had no idea she'd still be living in the same house this many years later. No one was more surprised than she at the reading of the last will and testament when she was named the sole owner of the Brecken-ridge fortune. Her award included the house where they'd lived and a combined half-million-dollar life insurance payout. For a woman who had never had more than five hundred dollars in the bank at any given time, five hundred thousand was almost too much to even calculate.

At sixty years old, Essie remembered sitting speech-less and looking at the lawyer who'd spoken the words as though he had lost his mind. Her jaw hung even lower than that of Mr. Breckenridge's only surviving sister. The woman, who had rarely come to visit her ailing brother, had only been awarded his tattered car and a pearl earring and necklace set that at one time belonged to their mother.

Growing up in the time of unwavering segregation, the Breckenridge family still believed that white people were superior. Essie knew early on that the reason she'd gotten the job as their caretaker was because in their eyes, she was a house slave caring for her masters. For Essie, it didn't matter how they viewed her, as long as they paid her every Friday as promised, which they did, without fail.

Over the years, Mrs. Breckenridge softened her stance and became very fond of Essie. She spoke to her with respect, and when she needed something, she had the good manners to ask nicely for it. Essie prayed constantly, as the couple's health began failing more rapidly, that Mr. Breckenridge would go first, but it wasn't God's will.

Mr. Breckenridge had outlived his wife by almost a year, and it was the worst eleven months of Essie's fifteen-year employment. Numerous times, she'd contemplated packing her belongings and leaving, but as cruel as Mr. Breckenridge was, she knew that if she left him, it would be like leaving an unattended baby with no one to care for him.

On the day that he died, the ninety-year-old was afraid to be alone. He'd asked Essie to sit with him and hold his hand. It was the first time he'd kindly requested anything of her. When Mr. Breckenridge took his last breath, it was Essie who brushed his thin, grey hair, changed his diaper, and cleaned his body so that he would be presentable when the director of the local funeral home arrived. As harsh as he'd been to her over the years, Essie couldn't help but shed a tear for him, just as she'd done for his wife, when she watched the hearse carrying his body pull from the driveway.

She'd always thought that the old man hated her, but somewhere inside of him there had been a heart of gratefulness that just didn't know how to show itself, at least not to the Negro woman who cared for him when he could do nothing for himself. Only after he was dead was he able to tell Essie how much she'd meant to him and his wife. It was a sad fact, but it just reiterated Essie's belief that timing was important to how things turned out. It was so crucial not to make a move until God said so. Essie was to inherit the fortune under the condition that she was still employed by the Breckenridges at the time of their demise. Had she let her emotions get the better of her, Essie would have walked out on the dying man, and in the end, lost the reward that God had for her. Sometimes Essie shuddered when she thought of how close she'd come to doing just that. Otherwise, she'd have been in a shelter somewhere. Not because she couldn't care for herself, but because she wouldn't have been able to afford to care for herself. With no family and few friends, Essie might easily have become a case for the government. Not only that, but now she felt good knowing that she could leave something behind for Angel and her family. The many times Essie had blessed them over the years would be nothing to compare to what they would receive once her time on earth was done.

Having her own home and being self-sufficient at this time in her life was a wonderful gift, and it had never been as clear to Essie as during those days when she watched her neighbors pack their belongings and move away, unable to remain in the new and improved Braxton Park houses. She often wondered where they'd all gone.

Making her way into the bathroom, Essie turned on her shower and undressed herself before stepping inside.

"Thank you, Jesus," she uttered as the warm water spewed over her body.

At her age, Essie didn't take anything for granted. Being able to stand, walk, and care for herself was a blessing and she knew it. Feeling the water beat against her flesh made her remember that Mr. and Mrs. Breckenridge were younger than she when they began needing help with simple things such as bathing themselves. They were both seventy-two years old when she first moved in to assist them in their daily living. For eighteen years, hers were the hands that kept them bathed and nourished. Essie's parents always did tell her and her two sisters that they were put on the earth to help others. It had come true for all of them, but since the death of her oldest sister two years ago, Essie was the only one left to recall the memories and tell the stories.

Stepping from the waters, she wrapped her body in a thick towel and stood in front of the mirror to brush her soft hair. Even at her age, Essie still saw signs of youth in her reflection. Though her face was defined with the deep lines that came with years, her skin was as soft as a baby's. Her once-thick hair had thinned over time, but she still had plenty of it, and mixed in with the thousands of silver strands were a few dozen black ones that mirrored her youthful heart. Standing at 5 feet 5 inches, Essie had legs that, back in the day, made her the focus of the young men and the envy of other young women when they saw her strut into church, wearing her high-heeled pumps. But as nicely sculpted as her legs were, it was her eyes that were most captivating. Essie's hazel eyes, a feature she inherited from her father's mother, had always been a trait that defined her. As the youngest of three, she had watched her sisters receive compliments for their singing talents, but it was Essie who was known for being the beautiful one.

"That baby of yours sho'ly do have some pretty eyes, Emma Jean," the neighbors would tell her mother.

"Buddy, if I was 'bout thirty years younger, you'd have to shoot me," her father's friends would tease.

By the time Essie was ten, she was capturing the attention of several of the older boys in the neighborhood, but by then, her heart had already been taken by an unsuspecting twelve-year-old named Benjamin Richardson. Ben and Essie had been playmates all her life, and until she was nine, she'd always seen him as a big brother. But that year, when Ben turned eleven, their families got together to throw him a birthday party. And when Ben was given the choice to share his first dance with any one of the girls in attendance, he chose Essie. Maybe he thought it was the safe choice. After all, none of his friends would pick at him for dancing with Essie Mae, the tomboy who liked catching grasshoppers and climbing trees. Everybody knew that he and Essie were pals and often played together. But that dance meant something to the little nine-year-old girl, and two years later, when Ben finally revealed his heart, she found out that it meant something to him too.

Her and Ben's love was what real love is all about. It was innocent, but meaningful. She knew that even the discussion of marriage before the age of fifteen was out of the question with her father, and by the time she had turned thirteen, Buddy was watching her every move. Essie thought that her growing affections for Ben were being kept secret, but her father let her know otherwise.

"I may not be the smartest man in the world," he warned her after she'd come in from an afternoon of playing with Ben and a few other friends, "but I ain't no dummy either. Benjamin Richardson is fifteen years old, Essie Mae, and you ain't no little girl no more neither. Y'all can't be playing together like you used to when you was kids. Now, from here on out, you need to find some girls to play with and leave that boy be, you hear me?"

"Yes, sir."

Essie tried to hide her hurt as she walked away from her father's lecture, but as soon as she was behind closed doors, she released the tears that she'd been holding back. It just didn't seem fair. She hadn't done anything wrong, but she'd been barred from spending time with the boy she loved. By the time her mother called her and her sisters to dinner, Essie had wiped all traces of the tears from her eyes. If her father knew she'd been crying over a boy, she would have gotten much more than a lecture.

Looking at herself in her bathroom mirror, Essie smiled at the remembrance of it all, even though the heartache she was put through (not spending any time with Ben) was no laughing matter. After she finished drying the water from her body, she slipped into her nightgown and knelt beside her bedside to say her prayers. Going to bed without praying was like walking outside naked, as far as Essie was concerned. Prayer was a central part of her life for as long as she could remember, and not a day went by that she didn't talk to God.

Finishing her prayers and removing her slippers, Essie heard the sound of a familiar truck coming to a pause at the stop sign near her house. It was the jogger's husband, getting home just before 10:30. His wife wouldn't be happy, but at least he was home.

Essie sat on the side of the bed and reached in the bottom drawer of her nightstand. Praying wasn't the only thing she did every night before she went to bed. She still had the original, stamped, yellowing envelope that held the very last letter she got from her husband before he died in the war. Praying kept her close to God; reading the letter kept her close to Ben.

In the early years following his death, she couldn't read it without crying and asking God why He'd taken the only man she'd ever loved away from her in such a cruel manner. But the years had brought her to a better understanding of God, and understanding Him taught her about His will and His perfect timing. Now, instead of feeling anger toward God, she thanked Him every day for allowing her to love, be made love to, and be loved by such a wonderful man. She'd reasoned that if God had decided that it was Ben's time to go, then so be it. But God didn't let him die before he was able to write her the letter that kept him forever in her spirit.

The pages were worn from years of being touched by her hands, and the ink that it had been written in now looked more grey than black, but every word of it, even those that had been smeared by tears she'd shed during those early years, was still legible. Every time Essie unfolded the pages, she could still feel the love that Ben had for her.

Placing her reading glasses on the tip of her nose, she looked at the words that she'd long ago memorized.

*Hello, my dearest Essie Mae,*

*I just wanted to write you once more before we go behind enemy lines to let you know just how much I love you. I don't know what will happen, but I do know whatever happens, God will be with me. I have your picture. I've pinned it under my uniform on the left side of my undershirt, closest to my heart, and it always seems to add this peace, this comfort, and this tranquility when things get rough. The other guys are writing their families, friends and sweethearts almost as if they don't think we will make it back home. But I know I will because I have so much to come home to. I have YOU.*

*Essie Mae, I have loved you since the first time your mama and my mama kept Mr. Charlie's house clean. I didn't know it was love then, but I know now that I fell in love with you the first day I looked in those beautiful brown eyes. I remember playing in the dirt with you when we were little more than babies, running through the clothes hanging from the clothesline when we were barely out of diapers, and walking to the coloreds' school together, kicking rocks along the dirt road that would get us there.*

*Essie Mae, do you remember our first kiss behind the ole Smith shed near the lake? If your daddy would have caught us, I probably wouldn't be here today. I know Mr. Buddy didn't like me very much back then, but that changed after we jumped the*

*broom and he saw that making you happy was all I
lived to do. Essie Mae, I love you. I love you more
than life itself. You have been my hope, my inspira-
tion, my oxygen, my everything. And for that I
can't wait to get home to you. We're going to dance
to new music by the King Cole Trio in the middle of
the floor and then make love 'til the break of dawn
so we can get started on that family we talked
about. I'm counting the days.*

*It's bad over here, Essie Mae. We have lost five
members of our squad already, and several others
have been injured. Some have lost arms and legs,
and sometimes the guys wake up in the middle of
the night crying in pain and screaming from the
nightmares. But I'm doing fine, because I know I
have you and I have God.*

*Until the next letter, I will be thinking about
you every second of every minute of every hour of
every day. I love you always.*

*Ben*

Essie's body trembled as she held the letter close
to her chest. Warm tears roll down her cheeks.
Nowadays, when she cried, it wasn't in sorrow, but
in appreciation.

Those who knew her questioned why she never
remarried, but in truth, Essie had no reason to.
There was no shortage of men who were enthralled
by the same eyes that captured Benjamin, so the
choice had definitely been hers to make. The opportunity to love again had presented itself to Essie
Mae Richardson on more than one occasion. Over
the years, she'd been wooed by many men. From
the time Ben died until she was well into her sixties,

men of caliber—doctors, attorneys, professors, preachers, and even a member of the U.S. Congress—vied for her affection.

The attention she received from them was appreciated and sometimes even flattering, but all of it was a waste of their time. There was no chance of her becoming the bride of any one of them. If she did, it would have been unfair to the man to try and live up to Benjamin's legacy. He'd never be able to. And how could Essie ever love another man with the same heart that her Ben still owned? Many people lived their entire lives not ever knowing how it felt to have someone love them totally and unconditionally. Perhaps her marriage was shortened by the evils of war, but the grenade that took away her husband's presence from her life couldn't touch his spirit or the memories and love that lived on.

"Timing sho' is everything," she said as she looked at the two-page love letter once more.

People often wondered why she'd adopted the saying and referred to it so much, but Essie's life had proven it to be true repeatedly. One of the reasons her father had been so undone with her and Ben was because they'd insisted on getting married the day she turned fifteen years old. Waiting until the age of fifteen was her father's own rule, but he didn't want to give his blessing when that time came. His other two daughters had already gotten married, and although Buddy never said the words, it was no secret that his baby was also his favorite. In his eyes, Essie wasn't ready, and the time couldn't be worse. He wanted to protect her from what could, and eventually did, happen.

The war was going on strong, and while getting his higher education at Tuskegee Institute, Ben also became a part of the first group of trained pilots there. The Tuskegee Airmen, they were called. Buddy knew that with African-Americans putting so much pressure on the government to make conditions equal for Blacks in the armed forces, it was only a matter of time before Ben would be sent to fight. He told both of them that they needed to wait until the end of the war before getting married. Ben disagreed, and so did Essie. Overriding Buddy's concerns, they moved forward to become man and wife.

Essie hated going against her father's wishes. But had they waited like her father had insisted, they never would have had the chance to marry, and she would have never known what it was like to be loved so deeply and with such intensity. She would have never experienced the ecstasy of becoming one with a God-given soul mate. Because of that, she couldn't regret a moment of her life with Benjamin, and in the end, even her father had to admit that he was wrong.

From her bedroom, Essie heard her grandfather clock chime again. It was eleven o'clock. Gingerly refolding the letter and tucking it back into the drawer, she removed her glasses, turned off her lamp, and lay back against the pillows on her bed. As she stared at the ceiling through the darkness, she heard more sounds outside her window. The clanking of chains was followed by footsteps ascending the porch next door. Essie smiled and pulled the covers close around her neck. She could go to sleep now. Jerrod was home.

# Chapter 5

## Sunday Morning: 4:18 A.M.

It was still dark outside when Colin's eyes opened and peered at the illuminating numbers on the digital clock on his dresser. It was a bit early for him to get up and prepare himself for the 7:30 service at Crossroads Christian Church, but he was too rested to go back to sleep.

Beside him, his wife snored softly, not even stirring at the sway of the mattress as Colin brought himself to a seated position and rested his back against the headboard. Rarely did he go to bed before eleven o'clock at night, but the incredible love-fest that he'd shared with his wife in the early evening had put him to sleep almost four hours earlier than normal. That, combined with the fact that he'd taken an hour-long nap the afternoon before resulted in him waking too early on this Sunday morning.

Feeling a familiar shifting beneath the covers, Colin quickly reached for his bedside lamp and turned the switch. Next, he pulled back the bedspread to see his baby's movement, but couldn't help but admire the beauty of Angel's whole transformed body before fixing his eyes on her stomach, which was pressed against his leg. He hoped that the lighting would help him see the activity that he'd just felt in the darkness. His son had a strong kick, and sometimes when Colin and Angel sat together in bed at night, they watched and could clearly see a foot or hand protrude from her belly as their child stretched and repositioned himself inside.

This was more than just another baby as far as Colin was concerned. This was a "miracle child." Battling with cancer since a teenager, he'd been told that he wouldn't be able to father children. Colin's doctors had informed his parents that the six-month treatment with chemotherapy had killed more than the cells that had caused his bout with leukemia. It had also all but destroyed his ability to have children.

At first, not having children had been of no great concern for Colin. He was just happy and thankful that God had helped him become cancer-free. But when he met Angel, everything changed. It was then that he began praying for just one chance to make a family with the woman he loved. Against medical odds, God answered his prayers.

"My son," Colin whispered, careful not to disturb Angel's sleep. He gently placed his hand against her swollen abdomen. "*My* son," he repeated, slower this time.

Colin wasn't gullible, and he didn't accept the word of just anybody. But when Angel returned home after her afternoon walk and told him what Essie Mae Richardson had said, Colin had no misgivings. In his heart he'd known from the moment the telltale line became visible on the home pregnancy test that the little one developing in his wife's stomach was a male child.

It was an overwhelming thought to know in just a few short weeks, he would be holding his own flesh and blood, his first-born, his son, in his arms. Sometimes he felt that no one in the world, including Angel, could be more eager for the day of their child's arrival. Colin had made it a point to go with her to her doctor's visits and Lamaze classes, and he'd read all the pamphlets so that he could absorb every bit of information he would need in order to know what to expect and how to be a good coach in the delivery room. Every time Colin thought of what his wife would go through to bring his child into the world, he loved her more.

"You are so beautiful," he whispered, moving strands of stray hair from Angel's face and tucking them behind her ear.

Over the months, as their son grew larger and forced her stomach to swell in order to make room for his development, their level of intimacy had not diminished, as one of the pamphlets had implied. Some of their positions had been modified to accommodate the changes in her body, and Colin had become increasingly gentle in consideration of both Angel and the baby. But the passion of their lovemaking only seemed to heighten as the day of delivery neared. From the glow of her skin to the increased fullness of her breasts, he loved the physical changes that impending motherhood brought on. There was hardly an hour that passed that he didn't catch himself staring mindlessly at the papers on his desk at the office, just longing for the workday to end so that he could get home to his wife.

There was something about Angel's presence that put her in a league of her own. Colin had dated women before her. He'd even been in love before her. But nothing he'd ever experienced could compare to the emotional and physical gratification he got from being Angel's husband.

He had always accredited her wonderful personality to the fact that she'd had nothing but love in her life from the time she was an infant. She had grandparents who adored her, parents who nurtured her, and siblings who supported her every dream. Angel's family was a rare find. Colin had grown up with both parents, but his family wasn't nearly as tight-knit or as spiritually rooted as Angel's.

He couldn't relate when the other men at the office complained of having nagging wives. Angel's name defined her spirit; and meddling in-laws was a foreign topic to Colin. From the day Angel brought him home to meet her parents, Mr. and Mrs. Patterson had embraced him as their own son. Their support of him had never been as obvious as when he lost his job two and a half years earlier. It was then that Angel's father signed the deeds to the home they now lived in over to the two of them, so that they would have one less bill to worry about paying. Since becoming gainfully employed as the senior audit manager at a local branch of Wachovia Bank, Colin had offered several times to pay for the house, but his father-in-law wouldn't hear of it.

When the time came for Angel to give birth, it would be a milestone for Mr. and Mrs. Patterson. They had two granddaughters already, but Colin couldn't help but feel privileged to be a part of giving them their first grandson.

The baby moved again. This time he seemed to

do an entire rotation, and the increased activity finally stirred Angel from her stillness. She released a lethargic whimper and then began the task of turning over onto her other side. At first, it seemed that she would just reposition herself and drift back to sleep; but as she turned, her eyes opened, and she froze at the sight of her husband looking down on her through the soft lighting that the bedside lamp provided.

"Colin?" Through narrowed eyes, she spoke the word in hesitance, as though not sure whether the image of him watching her was a dream or reality.

"Yes, sweetheart," Colin responded, erasing her uncertainty.

"What's wrong?"

"Nothing." He caressed the side of her face with his hand.

Using her arms for additional balance, Angel pulled herself up to a seated position and looked at her husband. Colin turned to face her and then stroked her cheek again. Her skin was as soft as butter.

She took a glance at the clock beside him. "Why are you awake?"

Colin grinned. "I'm awake because of you."

"I kept you awake?"

"No, baby." He leaned forward and planted a brief kiss on her lips. "You didn't wake me up; you put me to sleep. It's just that you did it so early that I couldn't sleep as late as normal."

It was Angel's turn to smile. "Should I apologize?"

"Please don't," Colin said as they both shared a laugh. "You go on back to sleep. I'll turn the lamp off."

"No. It'll be time to get up in about an hour anyway. If I go back to sleep, it might make us late for the early morning service. You know it takes me a minute to get dressed."

"It's okay, baby. Jesus ain't going nowhere. He'll still be there if we get there a few minutes late."

"I know. But I'm awake now."

He looked on in silence as she slid over to the other side and climbed off the mattress. Colin licked his lips like a famished tiger when she walked around the bed on her way to the restroom. She'd already given herself to him once, but as satisfied as she'd left him then, he felt a resurrected longing brewing inside.

The rumble in his stomach signified a different kind of hunger. Because of the timing of their intimate encounter, neither he nor Angel had eaten dinner. The Cheese Lover's pizza with jalapeños and mushrooms that Angel said she had a craving for hadn't been touched since Colin took it from the delivery man and set it on the dining room table twelve hours ago.

As though she'd been reading his thoughts, Angel called from the bathroom over the sound of the flushing toilet. "You think that pizza's still any good?"

Colin laughed as he wiggled from under the covers, walked across the floor, and grabbed his bathrobe from the chair that rested in the corner by the dresser. He had just slid his feet into his bedroom slippers when she emerged from behind the closed door, drying her hands on a paper towel.

"You think it's any good?" Angel repeated.

Colin scanned her body again. "Oh, yeah, it's *real* good,"

"Colin . . ." Angel's voice carried a twinge of scolding, but her expression showed a hint of approval.

"Oh, you mean the pizza." He began walking toward the door. "That's good too, I'm sure. Get back in bed; I'll bring you a slice."

"I love you."

Colin heard Angel call out the sentiment as the door closed behind him. It was almost said in a teasing manner, but all jokes aside, he knew she meant it.

The aroma of the planned dinner still lingered in the kitchen and the adjoining dining room. Colin opened the large box, placed two slices of the pizza on a plate, and slid it into the microwave for quick heating. While the seconds counted down on the timer, he sat at the table and looked at the baby book that Angel had been diligently recording information in throughout her pregnancy.

Colin smiled as he read the documentation that she'd made about how happy he was when the pregnancy test gave a positive reading, and how she'd cried the first time she felt their son kick inside of her stomach. On the next page, there was a list of potential names that they'd discussed. If the baby turned out to be a girl, the choices were Phylicia, Sanaa, and Olivia; if a boy, Michael, Austin, Joshua, Kyle, Emmanuel, Andrew, William, and, of course, Colin Jr. It was obvious from the difference in the lengths of the lists that they both were hoping for a son.

Turning the page, Colin stopped at the first photo he'd taken of Angel when she first began to show evidence of being pregnant. There she stood, leaning against the side of their car, pulling her blouse tightly against her skin so that the small bulge of her tummy could be seen. She was smiling with such delight that no one would ever have guessed that she'd spent the better part of that morning kneeling over a commode. Her battle with morning sickness had lasted a total of four months, but not once did she voice any regrets of her pregnancy.

Mixed among other photos that he and Angel had taken together was a picture of Essie on the bottom of the page. Under it, Angel had scribbled the words, "Your Great-Grandma Essie."

Angel had known the woman all of her life, but Colin had only been introduced to her shortly before he and Angel got married. He could never put his finger on it, but something about Essie Mae Richardson had made him fall in love with her upon their first meeting. She was warm and caring and had a way of making even the strangest of strangers feel accepted and at ease in her home. Prior to meeting Essie, he'd heard Angel speak highly of her on several occasions, and once he had the pleasure of making her acquaintance, he understood his fiancée's attachment. Colin knew that Essie's place in his wife's life was important. She had replaced the grandmother Angel lost to a massive stroke some years earlier.

With reality suddenly nudging at him, Colin jumped from his chair. He'd forgotten all about the pizza, the timer having gone off minutes ago. He opened the door of the microwave and removed the plate, the slices still steaming. He grabbed two forks and filled a large glass with water, splashing some onto the counter before heading back to the bedroom.

"I was wondering if you'd gone to sleep in there." Angel set aside the book that she'd been reading while she waited.

"I'm sorry. I got sidetracked."

"That smells so good." Angel reached up to relieve her husband of the plate in his hand.

Colin removed his robe and settled back in bed

beside her, watching as she said a quick, silent grace and used her fork to carve away a large piece of one of the slices.

When Angel placed it in her mouth, she grunted and then shuddered, as though she'd just sunk her teeth into a delicious slice of exotic dessert. No sooner did she begin chewing that piece when she cut out another chunk, this time, from the other slice.

Colin held up his unused fork in plain view. "Uh . . . baby, that was my piece."

"Oh," Angel said, her mouth full, "I thought these were for me. I'm sorry."

Colin could only laugh as she swallowed the pizza that was meant for him and then lowered the plate on her lap, looking like a child who had just been caught behaving badly.

"I'm sorry."

"It's okay," Colin assured her when his fit of laughter ended. "You go ahead and enjoy it. I'll get another slice."

He climbed back out of the bed, but her voice stopped him before he could reach for his robe. "Here," she said.

Colin turned to see her extending her fork toward him with a portion of the pizza slice attached to the end of it.

"I told you I'd get another."

"Please?"

Colin looked at her for a moment and then returned his sights to the morsel of food that she presented. Lowering himself back on the bed, he opened his mouth to receive her offering. He closed his eyes at the feel of her finger stroking across his bottom lip to remove any cheese that had failed to make it inside. All of a sudden, it didn't feel like any of what was transpiring was about eating pizza at all.

He said nothing as he sipped from the cup to quench the burning sensation that the peppers had left behind. Colin watched Angel feed herself again and then offer him another portion. As hungry as he had been just a few moments earlier, and as tasty as the meal was, Colin was no longer interested. When he removed the plate from Angel's hand without protest, he realized that she was just as unconcerned with the food as he. He set the plate on the nightstand and returned his attention to her.

A series of tender, almost playful kisses deepened as he pulled his wife closer to him and allowed his hands to explore her body. Without their lips ever separating, they lowered themselves against the covers. Colin made no attempt to hide the fact that he wanted more.

Angel was soft-spoken and generally quiet, especially when surrounded by people she didn't know well. But when it came to loving him, Colin knew that she had no reservations. At her silent command, he rolled onto his back and looked up into her eyes. She almost seemed to pause, just to give him a chance to admire her as she planned for the inevitable. When she lowered her lips to his chest, Colin moaned.

"Now, you know you're about to make us late for church," he whispered, anticipating her next move.

"It's okay, baby. Jesus ain't going nowhere."

# Chapter 6

## Monday Morning: 10:00 A.M.

In the distance, Essie could hear the pounding of footsteps to the pavement that led into Braxton Park. It was her cue to set up her table and roll out the welcome mat. Putting her knitting aside, she got up from her chair and buttoned the top few buttons of her sweater before disappearing into the house long enough to remove a pitcher of fresh-squeezed lemonade from her refrigerator and set it on the coffee table along with two of her best glasses. Returning to her porch, she sat and waited patiently while she hummed and knitted. Her handiwork was coming along nicely, but with slightly more than half of her task complete, the spool of yarn she'd been using was beginning to run thin.

"Looks like you gonna end up being more than just pink," she said to herself. Essie looked down into the box at the fibers to be weaved in with her design.

Knitting was a talent that Essie had learned from

the same woman who had showed her how to bake pies and braid hair. Her mother didn't actually sit down and teach the needlecraft to her, but as a child, Essie watched Emma Jean make all the blankets for their beds and doilies to decorate the tables, and it wasn't long before Essie, too, had mastered the art of knitting. Before Braxton Park went through such a metamorphosis, Essie used to knit special designs and wrap the finished products to give as Christmas gifts to her friends and neighbors each year. Now she didn't knit nearly as often, and when she did, it was mainly just to pass the time when she sat on the porch on days like today.

"Good mo'ning," Essie called out when she saw the familiar figure she'd been waiting for round the corner, headed toward the other end of the street.

"Morning, Ms. Essie," Elaine panted.

"Hold up just a minute, will you?"

Essie saw the look of surprise on Elaine's face. Until now, exchanging quick greetings was all the dialogue they'd ever shared. She stood from her chair and made slow steps to the edge of her porch and looked down on her neighbor, dressed in a pink jogging suit and carrying a bottle of water in her hand.

"You always in such a big hurry." Essie laughed. "I got some ice-cold lemonade in the house, and I wanted to offer you a glass to refresh you just a bit."

"Uh, thank you. But no thanks. I've been sipping on this water, so I'm good for now."

"Okay, then how 'bout we sit down and just talk like neighbors should. I know you busy and all . . ."

"Yes, ma'am. I have an article to write."

"So, you write for the newspaper?"

"Sometimes," Elaine said, "but mostly for magazines."

"See how little we know 'bout each other? I ain't asking you to spend the day with me. I just want to sit and talk for a few minutes if you got a few to spare for an old lady like me."

Essie watched as Elaine looked away, seeming to search for another excuse to turn down the offer. "Tell you what," Essie said, "I'll even throw in some peach cobbler I made yesterday evening. Now, if that ain't enough reason for you to come and join me on the settee, then I'm gonna be left to think you ain't human."

Elaine laughed as she turned to look back at her.

Essie could read from the expression on her neighbor's face that she'd made a breakthrough.

"Let me go home and get a shower. I'll be back in a little bit."

"I'll be waiting, sugar."

Essie watched Elaine break back into a trot and run the length of the sidewalk. Once she disappeared, Essie returned to her chair and started where she'd left off with her knitting.

"All that running," she mumbled with a shake of her head. "Sooner or later she gonna have to stop running away from them problems before she run right into trouble."


A million thoughts ran through Elaine's head as she allowed the shower waters to run over her body. To begin with, she could just kick herself for agreeing to waste away precious time sitting on some old sofa, sipping tasteless lemonade with Essie. Elaine had a deadline approaching and every minute of the day counted. The time she allotted for her morning jog was to help bring out the creative genius inside of her. But choosing today to get to know her neighbor was just stupid. It was a huge error in judgment that she knew she'd have to pay for once she returned home to begin playing catch-up with her article.

When Elaine stepped from the shower, she reached down to pick up the sweaty pair of jogging pants that she'd tossed to the floor. Just as she was about to drop the clothing in the laundry hamper, four quarters fell from the pocket and spun for a few seconds before coming to a stop on the ceramic-tiled floor. She gathered them and walked to the bathroom counter to stack them there. The half-full bottle of water that she'd placed beside the basin caught her eye, bringing back memories of why she'd had no use for the money.

Today, she had put a face to the voice she'd heard calling to her on Saturday. Like before, she had ignored his flattery as she charged toward her one-mile marker; but on her way back, the desire to know who he was and why he found her so intriguing finally got the better of her. Elaine tried to convince herself that it was a last-minute decision to stop and accept his offer of a cool drink, but the four quarters that she never even attempted to use once she was at the traffic light across from the gas station, were an indication that somewhere inside of her, there was always the intention of stopping at the Goodyear tire shop.

"I'm Dante Prescott," he said as he handed her the bottle of water that trickled of cold sweat.

"Elaine," she responded, careful not to disclose her last name. As captivating as he was, he was still a stranger.

Dante's eyes scaled her figure with hungry desire as he spoke. "You live nearby?"

Elaine took a step back. His gaze made her feel nervous and cautious, yet desirable. She broke the seal on the bottled water and took a sip, easing the growing dryness of her throat. "Not too far away," Elaine answered, licking her lips, wondering if she'd done it to remove excess water or to return his flirtation.

"So you're not going to tell me where?"

"You haven't told me anything about you, so why should I tell you anything about me?"

Dante smiled. He seemed to get more handsome with every passing moment.

"I'll tell you anything you want to know, baby. I have nothing to hide."

Elaine wished she could say the same. She consciously stood in such a manner that her wedding ring wasn't clearly visible.

"I live not ten miles from here," Dante continued, "but I was born and raised in Bermuda."

*That explains the sexy accent*, Elaine thought. Even in blue coveralls that were stained with oil and grime, he was far more handsome than she'd ever imagined. He had fair skin, full lips, heavy lashes and dark, sexy eyes. At 5 foot 7 she considered herself somewhat tall for a woman; and at the angle at which she had to hold her head to look up in his face, Elaine figured that Dante must have been at least 6 foot 2. He was taller, better-looking, and more muscular than Mason.

When she first turned to respond to his persistent call, Elaine was all set to let him down easy by lying about a happy home life. She was even planning to invent several small children to douse his interest.

But once she saw Dante, having no children became an advantage, and for a split second, she genuinely forgot that she even had a husband.

"I work here during the week and sometimes on Saturdays, as you can see," Dante added. "But I only work days. My nights are always clear." He reached in his pocket and pulled out a business card. "I would definitely like to see more of you."

"I-I don't know," Elaine stammered. "I work long hours. I don't have much time for leisure."

As she struggled to find more acceptable excuses, Dante reached for her left hand and Elaine couldn't move it away quickly enough. His eyes immediately fell to the diamond that glistened from her finger. Dante's countenance went from one of confusion to amusement.

Elaine couldn't mask her embarrassment. "I'm sorry," she whispered. "I should have just told you." Admitting she wasn't available was depressing, especially since she didn't *feel* like a married woman.

Dante gave her the card anyway and still flashed the same gorgeous smile when they parted ways, but Elaine was sure that her admirer would find a new object of affection after today's exchange. It proved to be just another disappointing chapter in her life. She'd need to listen to a few more motivational CDs to get beyond missing out on a catch like Dante.

Stepping into a pair of her favorite jeans and grabbing a simple button-down blouse, Elaine got fully dressed. Dealing with old people had never been her strongest point. She could still remember the time when she lived at home with her parents and they would all visit her grandfather at the nursing home at least three times a week. All of those wheelchair-bound people would scare her. Even at the age of twelve, Elaine would cling to her father's side, trying to avoid the outstretched hands of the patients as they smiled toothless smiles and tried to touch her as she passed. The home only had two odors. Either it had the stench of diapers and bedpans that hadn't been changed, or it carried a heavy smell of some type of chemical or cleaning agent that was almost just as offensive.

Speaking to the old lady down the street in passing was one thing, but having to sit down and hear her talk about the "olden days" just wasn't Elaine's cup of tea. After tying the strings on her spare pair of tennis shoes, she grabbed her keys and prepared to make the dreaded trek to 216 Braxton Way.

"I'm gonna gulp down this lemonade and get on back home," she told herself during the walk. "You get five minutes, Ms. Essie. Ten minutes tops and that's it."

Living in a neighborhood where most of the grownups worked in corporate America and most of the children were away at daycare or school during this time of day, the sidewalks and street that led Elaine to Essie's house were free of human activity. As she neared the house, Elaine saw Essie look up from her knitting and break into a broad smile before standing from her chair.

"Don't be shy," Essie said when Elaine paused at the bottom of the steps. "Come on up and come on in."

Elaine tried not to appear uneasy as she joined Essie on the porch and then stepped into the living room when she held the door open for her. The décor surprised her. She expected the sofas to be covered in plastic, the shelves to be filled with old whatnots covered in dust, and the air to stink with the odor of BENGAY or some other type of liniment. Instead, she found modern furnishings, nice African-American artwork on the walls, and air that smelled like it had been kissed by fresh, ripe peaches.

From the place she'd chosen to stop, just past the sofa, Elaine looked to her left into the bedroom that was exposed by the open door. The layout of Essie's house was almost exactly like to the one she shared with Mason; most of the houses in Braxton Place were similar. Essie's bedroom had a country-type theme. There was a straw hat mounted on the wall over the headboard, a sewing machine against the wall to the immediate right, a rocking chair in the corner by the head of the bed, and a queen-sized bed decorated with a patchwork quilt.

"Have a seat right here." Essie took a seat on the sofa and pointed to the space beside her.

Elaine turned at the sound of the elderly woman's voice behind her. She watched the woman's aged hands tremble slightly as she poured two glasses of the best-looking lemonade Elaine had ever seen. It was far from the bland mixture that she expected to see. There were actual slices of lemon mixed in that floated at the top of the glasses. If it tasted anything at all like it looked, it could possibly make Elaine's time at the house worthwhile.

"Are you always this quiet?" Essie lifted her glass to her lips.

"Not really." Elaine picked up her glass as well. "I guess I'm just not sure what to talk about."

"Well, you know my name and I don't know yours, so why don't we start right there?" Essie suggested.

"Oh, I'm sorry," Elaine said with a nervous laugh. "I'm Elaine Demps."

"Nice to meet you, Elaine." Essie patted her on the knee. "So, you planning to run in that July Fourth race on Peachtree Street or something? I notice you run near 'bout every day of the week. You must be training for something."

*Training myself not to kill my husband.* "No, ma'am. I run just to run."

Essie peered over her glasses. "In all my seventy-seven years I ain't never heard tell of nobody running just to be running. When folks run, they either running *for* something, *to* something, or *from* something. So which is it for you?"

Elaine squirmed in her seat. "Neither." Immediately, she turned her glass up to her lips, in hopes that Essie couldn't see her dishonesty. Deep inside, she had the feeling that she hadn't fooled Essie one bit.

"So, you say you write for magazines and such?"

Elaine breathed a sigh of relief, happy that the woman didn't try to press the issue. In her opinion, the only thing worse than an old person was a nosy old person.

"Yes, ma'am. I'm a freelance writer, which means I don't work for just one periodical. The articles and stories I write can be found in several different magazines."

"Well, I ain't never been much of a writer myself," Essie told her. "I used to love to read, though. I used to read a whole lot more than I do nowadays. Now, I just read my word. The Bible seems to be the only place I can read something that's good news. The newspapers and magazines always either telling stories about folks that's half-dead or half-naked, one of the two."

Elaine grinned and tried hard to hold back the

chuckle that was shaking the insides of her stomach. She was beginning to find Essie to be charming in her own way, and her bluntness amusing.

"It's the truth," Essie continued. "Either I got to read stories about men's brains being blown out their heads, or women's bosoms falling out their clothes. Them the kind of stories you write?"

Unable to hold it any longer, Elaine burst into a hearty laugh that sent her falling back onto the cushions of Essie's sofa. When she regained her composure, she found Essie sitting quietly, smiling and still awaiting an answer.

"No, Ms. Essie," Elaine said, feeling much more relaxed now. "Well, I do write some romance and sometimes it gets a little steamy, but that's just reality."

"Umph," Essie grunted. "I been married before and I *loved* that man, you hear me? But, sugar, some of that mess y'all be writing 'bout, I ain't never even thought about doing."

Elaine laughed again and then asked her next question with caution. "Your husband . . . did he die?"

"My Ben? Oh, no, baby, he didn't die. He took wings and flew up to Heaven to live with the Lord, that's all."

Looking into Essie's eyes, Elaine could still see love for the man she spoke of. A part of her almost felt guilty. There were days when she wished to God that Mason would take wings and fly. Heaven, hell, Puerto Rico, it didn't matter, as long as he just went somewhere and left her alone.

She drank more of her lemonade as Essie excused herself to check on the peach cobbler that she was heating in the oven. In the moments that Essie was away, Elaine took a closer look at her surroundings.

On top of the floor-model television sat a small, framed photograph of a group of uniformed black men. On one of the shelves near the wall stood a larger faded black-and-white picture of a very young, nicely dressed couple, the female clutching a bouquet of flowers in her hands. The girl's eyes were a dead giveaway. Elaine figured that it had to be a picture of Essie and the man she'd just referred to as "my Ben." They looked happy.

"Here we go," Essie said as she returned with two bowls of dessert in her hands.

"That smells wonderful," Elaine said, taking in the aroma from the steam.

"Wait 'til you taste it," Essie bragged. "I thought it would be warm enough before you got here, but you know things take a little longer to heat up in a regular oven. Y'all young folks like to use that ole microwave mess 'cause it's faster. But it ain't no telling what them electric waves be doing to the food y'all be heating up."

Elaine wanted to laugh, but one taste of the peach cobbler and all she could do was moan.

Essie was obviously pleased at Elaine's response. "Didn't I tell ya? You need to eat plenty, too, with your itty-bitty self. All that running up and down the street you been doing. Look at you. There ain't much left for you to lose, except your mind."

As comical as it sounded, what Essie had said was one of the best compliments Elaine had ever been given. The extra pounds she'd put on in the past three years had become an issue with her, lowering her self-esteem, especially since Mason began acting as though he'd lost all interest. To hear someone actually make reference to her with words that suggested that she was thin was music to Elaine's ears. If she knew her better, she'd hug Essie for that comment.

"Oh!" Essie suddenly said as her clock chimed. She jumped up from the sofa with vigor and grabbed the remote control. "I'm 'bout to miss my show."

Elaine laughed when she heard the music playing and saw the curtains open on the screen to reveal Bob Barker. She hadn't laughed this much in quite some time. This action by Essie truly brought back memories of the nursing home where her grandfather spent the last two years of his life. The patients there loved *The Price Is Right* and never missed an episode.

While she ate every bite of her dessert, Elaine watched with her neighbor and was amazed at how spellbound Essie had become and how excited she sounded when she tossed out bids as though they mattered. Elaine even found herself becoming absorbed in the game show that she hadn't watched in years. The last time she watched, Bob Barker's hair showed no signs of grey, but now, although he still had a full head of it, his hair was completely white.

Half an hour into the show, Elaine glanced at her watch. Oddly enough, she hated that she needed to leave so soon. The visit she had once dreaded turned out to be surprisingly pleasant.

"Ms. Essie, I have to leave now," Elaine announced.

"Already?"

"Yes, ma'am. If I don't get to my computer soon, I'll miss my deadline."

"Well, I don't want to be the cause of that." Essie stood with Elaine and walked with her to the door.

"Thank you for inviting me over. The cobbler was delicious."

Essie extended her arms for a hug, and Elaine reached back without hesitation. Embracing her aging neighbor felt natural.

"You're welcome, sugar. You're welcome to come back anytime you want. I ain't the best talker, but I'm a good listener."

"Yes, ma'am."

"And you be careful when you out running, hear? Sometimes these old dogs get loose and they be out there on the prowl. It be the ones that look the nicest that make you want to pet 'em, but them be the same ones that end up biting your hand off. So keep your eyes open."

"Yes, ma'am," Elaine repeated.

On the walk back to her house, Elaine was plagued by Essie's last words, but she brushed away the thoughts. She had been running the same path now for months and not once did she see any unleashed dogs that she had to watch out for.

# Chapter 7

## *Monday Afternoon: 3:28 P.M.*

A folded slip of paper passed from the back of the classroom up to the desk situated directly by the window on the second row. Jerrod was careful to be discreet as he tucked his hand behind his back long enough to accept the note and then slowly opened it while his sixth period teacher's face was turned toward the chalkboard. With less than fifteen hundred registered students, Alpharetta High had one of the smaller enrollments of any of the high schools in the city. Even so, it still had its problems, and lately, one of them was named Jerrod Mays.

*Dogs are barking at WBP.*

It was a short note, but Jerrod knew what it meant. The Dobermans, the group of troublemakers that he was hoping to become a full-fledged member of, were having a meeting at Webb Bridge Park, which was within long-range walking distance of the school. That meant that, once again, Jerrod wouldn't be catching the bus and his mother would just have to wonder and worry about his whereabouts until the meeting was adjourned and he had clearance to head home.

Alpharetta High School, like all the schools in Atlanta, had a zero-tolerance policy when it came to gangs or gang activities, but that didn't stop the students from forming their rowdy cliques. Without turning around to make eye contact with the boy in the rear who had sent the note, Jerrod nodded his head twice, a code that promised his presence at the meeting.

"Would you like to solve this problem, Jerrod?"

Ms. Shepherd's question snapped his attention back to the pages of the textbook in front of him. Math was by far Jerrod's least favorite subject; he wasn't a fan of any of his classes other than gym, but Algebra was the worst.

"Jerrod." Ms. Shepherd stepped aside so that he could see the figures on the board.

Jerrod stared ahead without responding. To his eyes, they looked like Greek scribbling.

"Would you like to at least take a guess at it?"

Jerrod snickered and then shrugged. "Naaah, that's a'ight. You can go 'head and have it."

His response drew laughter from his classmates, but his teacher failed to see the humor. Ms. Shepherd shook her head slowly, her eyes showing more sadness than anger. Jerrod almost felt regretful enough to apologize to the young, first-year educator, but if he did, he would lose all credibility with the other two Doberman pledges who took the class with him.

Before Ms. Shepherd could respond, the bell that signified the end of the school day resonated throughout the building. Immediately the classroom came alive with chatter and other noises as the children rushed to gather their belongings.

"Jerrod," the teacher called just as he was headed toward the exit door.

"Dang!" Jerrod whispered, disappointed that he wasn't able to escape.

"We'll wait for you at the lockers, man," one of his friends said as he watched Jerrod approach his teacher's desk.

Ms. Shepherd waited until all the others had left before she began speaking. "Jerrod, are you trying to fail my class?"

"No."

"I was looking over your scores from last August until now, and although I've always had to talk to you about your behavior and had to separate you from a few of the others, you started out making moderately good grades in my class. Now, it's like you're not even trying. Is there anything that you want to talk to me about?"

She didn't know it, but Ms. Shepherd was one of Jerrod's favorite teachers. Although he hated the subject that she taught, he really did like her. Not only was she pleasant to look at, but she had been nothing but nice to him. Even on those occasions when she reprimanded him for talking in class or not paying attention, she had never done it in a way to demoralize or belittle him. Other teachers had openly chastised him for his plunging grades and blasé attitude, but Ms. Shepherd respected him even when he didn't always return the favor.

"I just don't get this stuff, that's all."

"You were getting it a few months ago, Jerrod. What we're doing now is just a step-up from what we were doing then. If you want to stay after school for extra tutoring, I'll be happy to do what I can to help."

"Naah, I can't be staying after school. I got too much stuff to do."

"You couldn't sacrifice a half-hour every day?"

Jerrod shook his head.

Ms. Shepherd sighed and tried again. "Can't you meet me halfway, Jerrod? I want to help."

"And that's cool, yo, but I just ain't got the time. My moms be needing me at the crib. As a matter of fact, she's waiting for me right now, so I really need to bounce."

"Jerrod," Ms. Shepherd said through a heavy sigh as he turned to leave.

"Yeah?"

"Can you at least promise me that you'll try a little harder?"

"A'ight," he said as he threw his backpack over his shoulder and walked out the door. Deep inside, he meant it.

Once in the hall, he began running to make up for lost time. He couldn't be late for the meeting. The "big dogs," the fully inducted members of the group, were unforgiving when the new boys, or the "puppies," were late.

Apparently, Jerrod's meeting with Ms. Shepherd had lasted longer than the other boys anticipated. By the time he made it to his locker, they had already left. He had homework that needed to be completed, but if he carried the heavy backpack with him, it would slow him down from making the two-and-a-half-mile journey in time. Shoving all of his belongings in the locker, Jerrod secured the lock and immediately shifted into a sprint.

Pushing aside schoolmates blocking his path, Jerrod darted down the hallway and out the front exit, totally ignoring the calls from one of the instructors for him to stop running. Once he reached the edge of the school's property, he looked both ways for oncoming traffic and then took long strides on Webb Bridge Road toward the park.

So far, he had no strikes against him. Most freshmen who wanted to be a part of the popular group never made it before becoming sophomores because they weren't able to master the challenges that the big dogs issued. At the rate at which he was progressing, Jerrod had the potential to become a full member sooner than any of the other puppies, and he didn't want to start messing up now.

Accustomed to being challenged by others to race around the track during gym, Jerrod's running skills were as good as any of the boys on the school's track team. As he ran along the side of the road, he pumped his arms like he'd seen his favorite track star, Maurice Greene, do during the 2004 Olympic Games. He learned that if he held his head a certain way, it gave him leverage to run against the wind that pressed against him.

Webb Bridge Park was a Saturday-afternoon favorite for children and grownups alike. In the late afternoons, it would sometimes get a bit crowded during the week, as children who lived in nearby homes finished their homework and met at the park to play competitive sports. The park had three soccer fields, four tennis courts, four baseball fields, a walking trail, and even a Webb Zone playground for the little ones.

Dipping under the Webb Zone arch that marked the entrance to that area of the park, Jerrod was tempted to stop and catch his breath. With only minutes to spare before he'd be considered late, he kept pushing, even hurdling across two seesaws along the way. Just before entering the clearance where he knew the other boys were gathered, he stopped to rest. He'd made it with four minutes to spare.

"Puppy J!" one of the big dogs exclaimed as Jerrod walked calmly into the assigned space.

Instantly the sounds of barking boys rang out as the members and pledges pumped their fists and greeted Jerrod in their usual way. The reception made him feel important. His perseverance had won the respect of the big dogs and that was a huge point in his favor. He could hardly wait for the day he'd be able to call himself a Doberman.

Looking around, Jerrod saw that he had somehow arrived even before the friends who had left the school before him. He didn't notice them along the way and wondered where they could be. Time was running out.

"I was beginning to worry about you, Puppy J," Freddie said.

Freddie Townsend was an upperclassman and this year's leader of the group. He had been a member of the group since he was a sophomore. Although it had taken him six years to do it, at the age of nineteen Freddie had finally earned his way into the senior class of Alpharetta High and into the position of ringleader for the Dobermans. Each year, a senior was chosen to be the top dog and lead the pack. It was the accomplishment that Jerrod hoped for one day.

"Naw, man." Jerrod lightly pounded his right fist into his left hand. "This is me we talkin' 'bout. You know I wasn't gonna be late. I would've been here earlier, but Ms. Shepherd kept a nigga after class for not knowing the answer to a question, and then I had to outrun one of them other teachers who was trying to slow me down."

"So you had problems with Ms. Shepherd, huh?" Freddie asked.

"Yeah, but it's all good, yo. I'm here."

Freddie looked at his watch. "Wish I could say the same for your buddies, but it's time to get started. Puppies over here, big dogs over here." He pointed in the respective directions as he spoke.

Like the other two pledges who had arrived before him, Jerrod took his place in line by the bench. He listened while Freddie complimented them on being serious about their assignments and arriving on time.

As soon as they all sat down to see what their orders for the week would be, sounds of approaching footsteps caused all the boys to turn and look. The two missing boys had just arrived. Nobody barked or pumped their fists to greet them, and their solemn faces and downcast eyes told the story—They knew Freddie and the other big dogs weren't happy.

Swearing in anger, Freddie slapped both boys across the face.

Jerrod winced as if it had been his own cheek that had been hit. He could only remember one time in his life that he'd been slapped. He was very young, only three years old at the time, but he could still recall the moment clearly. He had been playing in the parking lot of the housing project where he and his mother lived at the time, while she and her new beau stood hugged together beside the boyfriend's car. Jerrod had asked more than once to go inside, but Jennifer made him wait because the man wasn't ready to leave yet. As he continued riding his tricycle to keep himself occupied, Jerrod's tire hit a rock on the pavement, and he somehow lost control. The tricycle came to a stop when it crashed into their visitor's car, throwing him onto the ground.

Jerrod wasn't injured, but he remembered the fear he felt inside when the man he barely knew saw the scuff mark on his vehicle. His face covered with anger, the man approached Jerrod, called him a "stupid punk," and slapped him across the face without warning.

Jennifer ran to his rescue and screamed at her boyfriend for hitting him, but the next day, the boyfriend was right back at their house again. For many weeks after that, Jennifer allowed him in their living room and their kitchen and even in her bedroom. His mother had protected him that day, but she still kept the man in her life. Jerrod had never forgiven her for that.

"Where have you mutts been?" Freddie demanded.

"Mr. Felton saw us running down the hall and called us in to his room," one of the boys answered.

"That's all you got?" Freddie asked, showing no sympathy. "Puppy J had to stay after class 'cause Ms. Shepherd had a problem with him today, but he's here." Freddie pointed toward Jerrod. "And you know what else? One of the teachers was trying to make him stop running too, but he kept running anyway. You think Mr. Felton could have caught you? No! It's all about how bad you want to be here, and it seems to us that you don't want it bad enough. Now, get in the doghouse where you belong!"

In obedience, the boys sank onto their hands and

knees, crawled under the park bench, and sat there while the others got down to business.

So far, Jerrod had successfully completed several challenges, which included stealing two phones from a neighboring cellular store, swiping the answer sheet to a test, rolling and smoking a marijuana joint, calling in a bomb threat to the school without being caught, and last week he'd learned quicker than any of the others how to hotwire a car. This week, his homework was to find a way to come up with two floor-seating tickets to Friday night's home game, when the Hawks would play the Philadelphia 76ers.

"Now," Freddie said as he prepared to end the meeting, "I hope everybody knows what you gotta do and how you gonna do it. Anybody got a problem with their assignments?"

Jerrod's mind raced. Those tickets would cost him at least one hundred dollars apiece. He looked at Freddie, but swallowed the words that he wanted to speak. He had no idea where he'd come up with that kind of money, but he knew he had to do it somehow. Jerrod shook his head along with the others.

"Good," Freddie said, sporting a grin that showed a gold tooth in the front of his mouth. "Now, just for being late, you two babies can go on home to your mommies. But, remember, we're meeting here every day this week at the same time. See if you can get it right tomorrow."

With their clothing soiled from the hour that they'd been made to sit in the dirt beneath the bench, the boys turned slowly and walked away.

Freddie watched them for a minute and then turned to face Jerrod and the others who had made it in time. "Yours truly, Big Dog Freddie, is having a party at my crib," Freddie told them. "I got some snacks, some smokes, and some sistahs that's gonna be coming over to spice things up. For being here and doing ya thang, you puppies get to hang out with me and the other Dobermans. How 'bout that?"

"Cool," Jerrod said, matching the grins of the others.

"Let's do this then," Freddie said, leading the way to the parking area toward his car.

# Chapter 8

## *Monday Evening: 7:00 P.M.*

Elaine feverishly typed another installment of the soap opera-style story that she'd been writing for a national magazine that highlighted the latest Hollywood gossip and featured articles geared toward women. Every week, the steamy tale of Diana and Paul continued, and according to the publisher, the readers were praising her storyline and begging for more in the letters that the magazine's editor had been receiving. That was good to hear. Elaine knew that as long as the consumer was sending in positive feedback, her paid position as a staff writer to the popular magazine was secure.

The chirping of her home's security system was a signal that someone had opened the front door and entered the house. She looked at the clock and felt a boiling in her stomach. Mason had arrived home more than an hour ago but didn't even bother to come inside. She'd heard him outside, getting out of the BMW that he'd driven to the trucking company today and getting into his Mazda Miata. Every fiber of her being wanted to get up and run outside to ask him where he was going, but Elaine was tired. She was fed up with all of the fussing and heated discussions. All of her energies were spent, and after their argument that morning, she had been left feeling like a boxer who didn't even have enough strength to hold up his gloves to guard his face. Elaine could hear Mason's footsteps approaching her office door.

"Hey," Mason said as he ducked his head inside the room.

Pretending that she was so engrossed in her project that she didn't hear him, Elaine continued to type. The music that streamed from the computer's speakers helped to make the illusion that his greeting went unheard more believable. She hoped he'd just go away, but instead he stepped closer.

"Hey," Mason repeated.

Elaine took a deep breath, turned away from her screen, and gave him an uninterested glance. "Hey," she responded.

"What's for dinner?"

Even though a mere three words, it was a statement that was strong enough to push her over the edge. Not long ago, Elaine had listened to a thirty-minute motivational talk from her collected series.

*"Stay in tune with your Guardian of Divinity,"* the woman said in a soothing voice, almost sounding as if she were a hypnotist. *"Remember that it's all up to you. You and your GOD working together have the power to conquer all fears, doubts, and any outside forces that come to make you lose control. Many people don't know how to get in touch with their own inner savior and divine power; therefore they run to churches, chapels, and synagogues in search of help from some unseen, unproven,*

*unknown being that they call Lord, Jesus and God. **You** are that power. **You** are that being. **You** are that savior. **You** are GOD! Believe in yourself!"*

Immediately after the speech ended, Elaine felt indestructible and omnipotent. But with one single question, Mason managed to dismantle all of the inner strength she thought her Guardian of Divinity had empowered her with.

"What's for dinner?" Elaine said, obviously insulted.

"What's wrong with you?"

"What's wrong with *me*?"

"What? You some kind of parakeet now?"

Elaine stood from her computer chair and faced her husband. "You've got some nerves coming up in here and asking me, 'What's for dinner?' You think I didn't hear you drive up earlier and switch cars? Where did you go? What's the matter—your *boys* didn't feed you? You spend all your time with them, so let *them* cook your meals for you. I ate my dinner already. I don't know what *you're* gonna eat."

"What's that supposed to mean? Oh, you're not cooking for your husband anymore?"

"*Now* you remember you're a husband? Is that all I am to you, a cook? I ain't your maid, Mason. I'm your wife, and I'm tired of being home by myself while you spend all your time with your friends."

"I wasn't with them, for your information, Elaine. I went to get the car detailed."

"For what? You got it detailed two weeks ago."

"And? Most people get their cars detailed every week."

"When they drive them every day, maybe. You've only driven that car twice in the last two weeks. Why would it need detailing again?"

"I don't need this." Mason began walking away.

"Yeah, that's right. Jump into one of your other cars and run off like you always do. You think I care?"

Mason walked out of her view, but Elaine heard him utter an oath. Then she heard the sound of jingling keys.

"And you wonder why I don't want to be here with you! See ya when I see ya!" He slammed the door behind him, sending shockwaves through the concrete walls and causing the window in Elaine's office to vibrate.

"Nigga, you ain't said nothing but a word." Elaine reached for the card she'd tucked inside of one of her magazines. Flipping it over, she picked up the telephone and began dialing. "Two can play at this game."

For the third time in as many hours, Jennifer pulled back the corners of her curtain and looked outside for signs of her son. In the distance thunder rolled and early darkness blanketed the area, not that the lateness of the hour meant anything to Jerrod. He'd gotten home as late as two o'clock in the morning, but that was on a weekend. During the week, he made it home before midnight most nights. Right now, it was just nearing eight o'clock, but as a mother, she couldn't help worrying.

As though the view that the porch provided would make her see what she couldn't see through the gap in the curtain, Jennifer opened her front door and stepped out onto the porch. The night air was a bit chilly and she folded her arms to provide a shield of warmth.

"Hey, there."

Jennifer's heart seemed to jump from its cavity at the sound coming from the dark porch of the house next door. She saw a moving figure, heard a scuffle of feet, and then the bulb that was attached to the front of the house lit up. Standing in the doorway was her next-door neighbor.

"It's just me," Essie said. "I didn't mean to scare you, sugar. How you doing this evening?"

Jennifer watched as the porch returned to its dark state. "I'm fine. How are you?"

"I'm doing fine too, thank the Lord."

Jennifer strained her eyes to see the shadowy figure of Essie through the moonlight. "Why are you sitting out here in the dark?"

"Well, now, that's one question with two different answers," Essie said. "I'm in the dark 'cause when the light is on, them bugs just have a field day around my porch. But I'm sitting out here for the same reason that you standing out here."

Jennifer was confused, and she assumed that her neighbor was too. "No, I just came out to see if I could see—"

"Jerrod?" Essie chuckled. "I told you we was out here for the same reason. I'm looking for him too."

"You are? Why? What did he do?" Jennifer's heart pounded at the thought that Jerrod had possibly burglarized the old woman's house, or scratched her car, or broken a window.

"Calm yourself down, honey. He ain't done nothing wrong. I just know I didn't hear him running across the yard this afternoon, and I just been looking, trying to make sure he got home okay. You want some lemonade?"

"Lemonade?"

"Uh-huh. Made some fresh-squeezed this morning and still got plenty left. Come on over. It'll give us a chance to talk."

Jennifer had never even been on the woman's property, let alone inside her home. She expected to feel apprehensive, but walking down her steps and walking up Essie's almost felt ordinary, like she'd done it several times before. As Essie held the door open, Jennifer walked in and looked at the sofa that the woman pointed toward.

Once her guest had been seated, Essie quietly walked to her kitchen. First, there was the sound of running water, then the sounds of clinking glasses. All the while, Jennifer sat and looked around the impressively decorated room. She saw the paintings on the wall and the photos on the shelf. Tossed over the arm of the chair across from her was a colorful pink-and-blue unfinished blanket. She'd seen Essie sitting on the porch working on it several times.

The eight o'clock chime brought Jennifer's eyes to the grandfather clock. Instinctively, she turned and looked at the closed front door.

"Don't worry yourself none, sugar," Essie said as she joined her in the living room. "If he come riding up, I'll hear him."

Jennifer looked at the aging woman in doubt. As far as she could tell, Essie wasn't wearing a hearing aid. From inside the thick walls of her home, there was no way she'd be able to hear the sounds of a boy walking across the paved sidewalk or on the grassy area in front of the house next door.

"I promise you, I will," Essie said it as though her ears were keen enough to hear the pondering of her guest.

"Yes, ma'am." Jennifer was almost afraid to say anything more than that.

"Well, I know your son's name is Jerrod 'cause I done heard it said so much." Essie poured two glasses of lemonade. "What's yours?"

"Jennifer. Jennifer Mays."

"Do you know mine?"

"Yes, ma'am. I hear the kids who play across the street speak to you every Saturday."

Essie broke into a wide grin and removed her reading glasses from her face. "Bless their hearts. Children are so precious, ain't they?"

Jennifer nearly had to bite her tongue in order to prevent a profane word from escaping her lips. She hadn't had a "precious child" since hers had been potty-trained.

"Even Jerrod," Essie said, almost frightening Jennifer with her uncanny words. "He's precious too. He's a handful though. We been living next to each other for two years now, and I see how you have your problems here and there."

"Here and there?" Before Jennifer could stop them, words began pouring from her mouth, and tears streamed from her eyes like a dam had broken inside of her. "I don't know what's wrong with that boy. I can't recall a day in his life, since he was about three years old, when he hasn't been a problem. I know I've done everything that a mother can possibly do. I've always worked hard and made sure that he had a decent place to live and food to eat. He's always had good Christmases and birthdays, too. I've given him everything, and all he's ever given me is trouble."

"Here, now." Essie moved to the sofa where Jennifer sat and took the glass from her hand. "My lemonade ain't gonna taste too good if you get all that salt water that's running from your face in it. Come here, sugar. It's gonna be all right."

The woman pulled her into her chest and rocked her like a little girl.

Jennifer didn't resist Essie's comforting. She hadn't been cuddled with such love and tenderness since her grandmother was alive. For the first time in years, Jennifer felt like there was someone she could count on.

Essie never said a word until the fountains of her eyes had run dry. She reached into the pocket of her dress and pulled out a knotted handkerchief that housed several coins. Jennifer watched as she untied the knot, dumped out the quarters, and handed the cloth to her. "I know I got a box of tissue 'round here somewhere, but for now use this to wipe your face and blow your nose."

"I'm sorry," Jennifer said, suddenly feeling childlike and vulnerable.

"You ain't got nothing to be sorry for, honey. Them right there was tears that needed to be set free. Everybody needs to cry 'bout something sometimes. Even Jesus cried when the time called for it."

Jennifer nodded. "I know, but it seems like I just don't ever stop crying, Ms. Essie. Do you know what it's like to cry all the time? Even when I'm not crying, I *want* to. I just don't know what to do."

"I been there."

Essie got up from the sofa and picked up the frame that stood on the television. She returned to the sofa and handed the picture to Jennifer. "You see that man right there in the front? That's my Ben."

"Your husband?"

"My *everything*. Baby, you ain't never cried 'til you done had to bury the only somebody you ever loved." Essie smiled.

Jennifer's heart went out to the old lady.

There were several men in the photograph, but Ben's was the only image that Essie's thumb caressed with fondness. The photo was a bit faded, but his handsome, dark features were still visible.

"Good-looking man, ain't he?" Essie said with a proud smile.

"Yes, ma'am. He was in the war?"

Essie nodded. "He stepped on a grenade on August twenty-third, nineteen forty-five. The war ended on September second. Just a few more days and he would have been home with me, but instead, the good Lord saw fit to take him home with Him."

Jennifer placed her hands on top of Essie's and squeezed. "I'm sorry."

"No need," Essie said as she got back up to replace the picture. "That was a long time ago, and I ain't got nothing but good memories of him. I know he's in a place where he ain't regretful, so I had to learn not to be regretful either. I'm gonna see him again one day."

Not wanting to seem selfish, Jennifer sat quietly beside her. She wanted badly to ask for advice where Jerrod was concerned, but somehow the conversation had taken a different turn. She reached forward and picked up the glass that Essie had taken from her hand earlier and took in a few gulps of the beautiful yellow liquid. It was the best lemonade she'd ever tasted.

"Now, let's talk about you and Jerrod."

Jennifer flashed a brief smile. It was just what she needed to hear. "I'm scared for him, Ms. Essie. He's never at home, and I know he's doing something he has no business doing. He's grown into this mean and hateful boy that I know is headed to somebody's prison."

"Hush up!" Essie whispered. "Don't you dare speak words like that! Don't never give up on your child, baby."

"I'm just being realistic. I love Jerrod with my whole heart, but there are some days when I come real close to hating him too. I know that's bad, but it's the truth. Sometimes, I just don't know."

"Children nowadays got so much more to be faced with than when I was a girl. They got more to face than you had too."

"I've been on my own since my parents put me out of the house when I was barely older than Jerrod is. I made one mistake, Ms. Essie, and they threw me away. I know about problems. I dealt with a whole lot when I was a little girl."

"I'm sho' you did, sugar, but believe me when I say that the world is a different place now than it was twenty years ago. You said he been acting like this since he was three years old. Honey, you best believe that ain't normal. Somehow you need to get to the root of what's going on inside your child. That boy is hurting, and all this foolishness that he's been doing is just the part that you see. It's what you don't see, that part that he's hiding in his heart, that you need to find out."

Jennifer drank the rest of her lemonade and stood from her seat. "I appreciate what you're saying, Ms. Essie, but I've been trying for years to talk to Jerrod. I'm tired now. All of his life I've been setting rules just so he can break them and then dare me to do anything about it. Tonight I'm putting my foot down. If Jerrod isn't home by eleven o'clock, I'm going to bed and putting the deadbolt on the door. That gives him less than three hours. If he's not here by then, he can go right on back to whoever's house it was that he stayed at that late, 'cause they're the ones who are going to have to give him a bed to sleep in."

# Chapter 9

## *Monday Night: 11:30 P.M.*

Angel lay with her head on her husband's chest and listened to the racing of his heart as it drummed against her ear. Several moments had passed since she brought him to ecstasy (for the second time in as many hours), but Colin lay still, occasionally quivering from the aftermath of their latest passionate encounter. Angel knew, as soon as the rain began to pour from the heavens on the outside, they were in for a romantic evening. From the very beginning, rainfall had always had that effect on them.

"Doesn't the rain sound like an orchestra on our roof?" Colin had said three years ago in a breathtaking suite at the Shakaland Zulu Village and Hotel in Cape Town after they'd consummated their love for the very first time.

Their honeymoon in South Africa was the most overwhelming experience of Angel's life. Colin had totally surprised her with the heavenly ten-day experience, which included overnight stays in Johannesburg and in the Kruger National Park area. She'd never traveled to Africa before, so sharing her first experience in the beautiful Motherland with the man she loved was awe-inspiring, to say the least.

Since the day they'd promised their love and lives to one another, Colin had made her life an enjoyable adventure. No day with him was mundane, and no night was lonely. Even if they were apart for whatever reason, he'd call and sometimes they'd talk until they fell asleep. It was almost as though they were still sleeping in each other's arms. Passionate nights like tonight were not a rarity in the Stephens' household.

"I love you," Angel whispered.

Still speechless, Colin's only reply was a moan and the tightening of his arm around her body. If history was any indication, Angel knew that he would be asleep in just a few minutes. He was an awesome lover, but a talker afterwards, he wasn't.

Smoothing her hand over his smooth, dark chest, Angel felt beads of perspiration being wiped away. "Colin?"

"Hummm?"

Angel lifted herself so that she could look into his face. Candles had been lit to add to the room's ambiance, and with the glow they provided, she was able to see him struggling to keep his eyes open.

"Colin," she called again, nudging him in the process.

"I'm awake, sweetie."

"What do you think about Colin Austin?"

Her husband opened his eyes fully and looked up at her. "For our son?"

"Yes."

"I told you before that I'm really not big on having my name being a part of his. All my life, I've been faced with the task of correcting people about the pronunciation. Everybody always assumes the *o* has a long sound, like Colin Powell's name does. It's a minor thing, but it can get frustrating and I don't want to put my son through that. I think we both want to name him Austin, but let's give him something different to go with it."

"Okay." Angel nodded. "We still have a little time to give it some thought."

Placing her head back on his chest, she relaxed to the feel of Colin's hand stroking her back. As she lay there, Angel stared at the flickering of the candle on the nightstand beside the bed. The flame, in an odd way, seemed to sway to the rhythm of the soft music coming from their portable studio. Like rainy nights, Maxwell was also a favorite for both of them, especially in moments like this. The uniquely soothing sounds of the talented singer's voice, combined with the relaxing motion of the rise and fall of Colin's chest, made Angel's eyelids heavy.

"What about Austin Benjamin?"

Angel's eyes snapped open. At first she thought it was part of an oncoming dream, but when she pulled herself up and looked in her husband's eyes, she realized that he was the one talking. "What?"

"Besides your mother, Ms. Essie has probably been the most important woman in your life. Her husband died before they could have any children of their own, so there's no one to carry on the legacy of his memory. Our son will have my name automatically. His last name will be Stephens and that's me. Let's pay tribute to Ms. Essie and that man that she's loved all these years by giving the baby a portion of his name."

Tears rushed into Angel's eyes. She probably never would have thought of the idea on her own, but she loved it. Benjamin Richardson had died long before she was born, so she'd never been fortunate enough to meet him. But over the years, as she listened to the sweetheart stories his wife told, Angel had, in a way, always loved him.

"You like that?" Colin asked.

She nodded and then placed her head back in its resting place, wrapping her arms as far as they could go around her husband's waist.

*Austin Benjamin Stephens.* She ran the name over and over again through her mind, and every time she thought of it, she liked it more. Keeping it a secret from the woman who had been her grandmother's best friend was going to be hard, but she had to try. It would be a wonderful surprise.

"I love you," Colin suddenly whispered, breaking the silence that had blanketed the room.

It was Angel's turn to be speechless. Too overcome with emotions to form words for what she felt for him, she kissed Colin's chest, tightened her grip, and held on until they both drifted off to sleep.


It had been a restless night for Essie. She had gotten into bed at her usual time, but no matter how hard she tried, sleep kept escaping her. After thirty minutes of tossing and turning, she got up, prepared a cup of heated lemonade, and began with her knitting.

The blanket was beautiful, if she had to say so herself. On the day she ran out of the original yarn she'd been working with, Essie went to her stash and found a sky-blue color that meshed well with the soft pink. For the last three hours, all she'd been doing was using the knitting needles to twist, turn, pull, and tighten the yarn unraveling from the spool. Just a few more inches to go and she would be done.

For two months she'd been working on the blanket, at first working on it sporadically. When she began weaving the yarn, Essie had planned to make something small to throw across her couch. The pink would have looked good against her grey sofa. Somewhere in the process of knitting, she changed her mind, not really knowing why. Before long, the size of her project was becoming larger than she'd first anticipated, and for some reason, she wasn't satisfied with it until now. Once the blue spool was empty, she would have finished her task in her two favorite colors.

Every now and again, especially on nights like tonight when there was rainfall outside, she could feel in her aged hands the aches that time had a tendency to bring. But tonight was a good night, and her hands moved in rapid motions.

The chiming of her grandfather clock reminded her of how late it was. Essie couldn't remember the last time she'd been so fully awake and active at midnight.

The next sound that she heard brought her hands to a stop. Somebody was coming, running through the rainwater that had pooled on the pavement outside. She heard the feet round the corner and come closer until they bounded up the steps next door. Essie continued to sit in silence, wondering if Jennifer had kept her word. She heard persistent knocking, and then the calls began.

"Ma!"

The sound of his voice was muffled by the rainfall and the concrete walls that separated the houses, but Essie knew it was Jerrod.

"Ma, open the door! You got the other lock on, and I can't get it open. Ma!"

Essie shook her head. This wasn't the night to decide to buckle down and mean business. The rain had caused temperatures to drop, and although the day had been beautiful, the night air was chilly from the moisture.

"Ma! Wake up and open the door!" Jerrod yelled.

Essie put her knitting down and walked to her front door. She slid the lock aside and turned the knob. The rain was pouring heavier now. Stepping out under the light on her front porch, she pulled her robe close around her body. The roofing over the porches of the houses in the area provided a shield from the waterfall, but the winds pushed the rains. Essie could see the boy getting wet even standing near his door.

"Jerrod!"

When he turned to look in her direction, she beckoned for him to come to her house. Jerrod stood for a moment and just looked at her, as though he'd never seen her before.

"Come on, baby," Essie urged, trying not to raise her voice level too high at that time of night. "Your mama could be too deep in a sleep to hear you. Come on over here and get out that rain."

Jerrod looked back at the door in front of him for a moment and then ran down the porch steps and raced to meet his neighbor. Essie stepped inside the house and then allowed him to follow. He was drenched in water, and a large amount of it pooled onto the welcome mat that covered the hardwood floor beneath him.

"You stand right there," Essie told him. Then she walked into her bedroom and then into her closet.

When she returned, Jerrod stared at her in disbelief. "What's that?" he asked without making an attempt to accept the garment she held out for him.

"It's a nightshirt," Essie told him. "You need something to sleep in. You can't go to bed in them wet clothes you got on."

Jerrod began shaking his head vigorously. "I don't need a nightshirt. I just need to use the phone to call my mom and wake her up. My cell phone battery went dead on me, so I couldn't call her just now when I was outside. Can I use your phone?"

"Boy, do you know what time it is?" Essie put one hand on her hip. "You ain't 'bout to call nobody this time of night. Your mama got to get up early in the morning for work, and she needs her sleep. Now, take this here shirt and go right in there and get a bath. I got fresh towels right in there by the tub."

"I can just use the phone," Jerrod tried again.

Essie looked up into the ceiling as though she could see God's face. "Lord, I know I'm talking English 'cause I don't know no other language." She looked back at Jerrod. "It's after midnight, sugar. Now unless them friends of yours are still out there and gonna let you go back home with one of them, then you ain't got but one choice."

She could see his jaws tighten, but Essie would not be intimidated. Jerrod was used to having his way, but not tonight. She knew that if he had to choose between sleeping outside in the unfavorable elements or inside the warmth and comfort of her home, he would make the right decision.

Slowly, he reached out his hand and took the shirt.

"Bathroom is right there on the right." Essie pointed in the direction of her hallway.

Shortly after he disappeared, she could hear the water running in the shower. While he bathed, Essie turned on the oven and then used her mop to dry the water that trailed from the front door to the bathroom.

By the time Jerrod returned, she had brought a pillow out and fluffed it before placing it in the corner of the sofa. (Her spare bedroom had been turned into a sewing room years earlier.)

"Now don't that feel much better?" Essie stood at the front door once again.

Jerrod looked down at his borrowed attire. "Feels like I got on a dress."

Essie laughed at his grimace and then pointed to the sofa. "Let me tell you something," she said, assuming her knitting post, "you the first man in sixty-some-odd years to put on that shirt. That's the shirt my Ben used to wear to bed just about every night. I made it for him myself."

"Who's Ben?"

"He's my husband. He went to be with the Lord a long time ago, but that was his favorite nightshirt. And my Ben was a good man too." Essie continued to work on her weaving. "He was a good husband and a good soldier. You know, he's a part of the reason that you live in a country with as much peace as we got."

"Oh."

"What you doing out this time of night?"

"Just hanging," Jerrod said with a carefree shrug.

"Let me tell you something about that. Used to be a time when black men were just hanging—It was because they were being lynched. That means they were being led to the slaughter. You don't ever want to be just hanging, son. Hanging ain't a good thing for nobody."

"I didn't mean it like that."

"Maybe not, but that's still what it means. When men were hung, it left the women in their lives to do nothing but cry. Wives, sisters, mothers, they all was left to cry. Your mama was worried 'bout you when you didn't come home from school."

Jerrod smacked his lips. "She'll be a'ight."

Essie looked up from her work and directly into Jerrod's eyes. "Don't you care that your mama was hurting?"

"What for? She ain't never cared when *I* was hurting. Not enough to stop doing what she was doing, anyway."

Essie's mind traveled back to when Angel was a girl around the age of twelve. She'd been bullied in school but would clam up in fear and not talk to her mother about it. Even her grandmother couldn't get it out of her. Essie had told them to give her just ten minutes alone with Angel and she guaranteed them that she could get whatever the child was withholding out in the open. Little children had a tendency to tell other people what they wouldn't tell their parents, and Essie knew it. In less than five minutes she coaxed Angel into not only telling her what had been going on, but she'd gotten her to give her the names of all the children involved. Now, looking at Jerrod, she knew it was only a matter of time before she would know what Jennifer hadn't been able to figure out for years.

"So that's what you call yourself doing? Getting your mama back for something she did?"

Jerrod turned his face away.

Instead of pushing him for information he wasn't ready to give, Essie got up and went into the kitchen. When she rejoined him, she had a bowl of hot peach cobbler in one hand and a glass of milk in the other.

Jerrod's face lit up when she placed both items on the coffee table in front of him.

"Eat up," she said while walking away again. "I'm gonna get these wet clothes out of the bathroom and put them in the washer so they will be clean and dried by the time you wake up in the morning. Make sure you say your grace now, hear?"

Essie was almost sure that Jerrod didn't obey her last order, and when she came back from her chore, she didn't ask whether he said his grace.

Spooning up chunks at a time, Jerrod stuffed the dessert in his mouth as if he hadn't eaten all day.

Essie smiled as she sat back down to carry on with her project. She loved to see children eat heartily. "So what's your favorite subject in school?"

Swallowing down gulps of milk, Jerrod said, "I like my gym class. We run the track a lot, and I like doing that."

"Good exercise," Essie said, without looking up from her knitting. "What else you like to do?"

"Hang—" Jerrod stopped briefly. "Be with my friends."

"Having friends is a good thing too." Essie pretended to not notice that she'd already taught him something positive. "Most of my friends are gone on now, but I'm making new ones. I met the lady down at the end of the street a couple of days ago, and I met your mama today, and both of them are nice ladies. Your mama don't seem to have many friends."

"That's 'cause she works a lot," Jerrod said, seemingly more comfortable now. "She used to have a lot of friends, though, when we lived in the projects."

Essie looked down in the box beside her chair. She could see the end of the string of yarn. Just a few more minutes and she'd be finished. "I guess her working, plus making sure you're taken care of, takes up a lot of her time. She was really down when you weren't home for dinner."

"She just wants me around 'cause she ain't got no man right now." Jerrod's voice was filled with anguish. "If she had a man, it wouldn't matter whether I was home or not."

Setting her needles in her lap, Essie leaned forward and looked at the teenager whose heart had obviously been carrying around bruises that he hadn't given a chance to heal. "Jerrod, sometimes when parents are young, like your mama was when she had you, they just don't know how to handle everything that comes their way. She made a lot of mistakes, I'm sure. But I promise you that don't nobody love you like your mama do."

"She don't love me."

"Yes, she does, baby. She sat right here on my sofa with her eyes filled with the same tears that's in yours right now. She told me that she loved you with all her heart and that she's trying to figure you out so she can help."

Using the back of his hand, Jerrod swiftly wiped away a tear that had dropped from his eye.

"Let me tell you a little something about hurt, Jerrod. Almost one hundred percent of the time, it turns to anger and eats away at you little by little. Then before you know anything, you ain't even yourself no more 'cause anger done destroyed all the good in you. You start doing things that God ain't never meant for you to do, and hurting the people that love you the most. You even start looking for love in all the wrong places, and Lord knows, that don't lead to nothing but trouble."

"I don't care if nobody don't love me," Jerrod said, wiping another tear.

"Yes, you do, baby. Don't make no never mind what nobody say; everybody wants to be loved, and there is somebody who loves each and every one of us. You know who that is?"

Jerrod shook his head in silence and kept his eyes fixed on her as he placed his head on the pillow.

"The good Lord, that's who. We all His children, but evil is always out there trying to make us do the wrong thing. You a good boy, Jerrod. I see good all in you. I know you like being with your friends, but sometimes the people you think are your friends ain't your friends at all. If they got you doing bad things and making your mama cry, then they ain't your friends. You ain't got but one mama, sugar, and I know you love her just like she loves you. Time is too short not to love."

Essie got up from her seat and took the empty bowl and glass from the table and placed it in the kitchen sink. Coming back into the living room, she sat quietly in her seat and began knitting. There was so much more that she could say to Jerrod, but for now, she felt she'd said enough.

As soon as the last of the yarn had been hooked into her creation, Essie heard a deep snoring sound come from the couch.

"Good Lord, boy," she said with a chuckle. She gathered the finished product and placed it across the sleeping teen. "You sound like a freight train. I sho' hope I can get to sleep tonight."

# Chapter 10

## *Wednesday Morning: 10:45 A.M.*

*W*ith one gentle, but powerful sweep of his strong
     arms, Paul lifted Diana from her feet and carried
her into his bedroom. No time was wasted on needless
words or senseless teasing. Like a ravaging animal, Diana
tore at the terrycloth that hid the sculpted body beneath.
Paul was beautiful, and tonight, in his arms, she felt
beautiful too.

Elaine stopped typing. She was almost done with
the short story that she was working on when it became clear to her that she was no longer writing fiction. The tale of Diana and the unhappy home that
had now led her into the arms of another man read
almost like a journal of her own actions. Diana lived
in a different town, had different friends, worked a
different job and drove a different car; but it was
clear to Elaine that she'd just written all the details
of what her life had become in the last two days.

On Monday night, while the rain was falling,
Elaine was soaring. In Dante's arms she felt attrac-

tive and desirable. He told her things that she hadn't heard from Mason in years and ignited passions in her that she'd thought were all but dead. Dante was Paul, the man in her story; and almost every description, every detail, and every quoted dialogue was a direct copy of what had gone on behind his bedroom door.

When Elaine called Dante after the fight with her husband that evening, she was surprised when Dante so quickly invited her over. She was sure that the sight of her wedding ring earlier that morning had extinguished his infatuation; but by no means was she right. When he answered her knock at his door, Elaine hardly recognized him. There was no sign of the oil and grease that she was used to seeing him wear on his face and clothing. Instead, Dante looked and smelled like he'd just stepped out of the shower and he greeted her wearing nothing but a partially closed bathrobe.

In her brief telephone conversation with him, all she'd asked for was a few moments of his time. Elaine told him that she'd had a bad day and just needed someone to talk to. She mentioned nothing more, but somehow Dante knew. Maybe he'd heard it in her tone or read between the lines of her words. Whatever the case, he seemed to be fully aware of what Elaine had been lacking, and he was prepared to fulfill every desire that she'd been craving and even some she hadn't. During the hours that she had spent in his arms, in his bed and in his grasp, the world was a lovely place.

At first, when it all ended, she had a feeling of intense guilt. But when she pulled into her driveway after midnight and Mason still hadn't made it home, Elaine felt vindicated. *He's probably out doing the same thing*. In some small way, holding to the possibility that Mason was involved in an extramarital affair of his own made her feel better. So much so, she found herself in Dante's arms again last night. Her Bermudan lover was like Mason used to be in those earlier years of their marriage. His touches were thorough, his kisses tender, and his words sweet. Dante was like a fantasy come true.

Elaine jerked from her thoughts and from her seat. The terrifying barks of an angry dog seemed to come from the direction of her office window. Hardly anyone in their neighborhood had outside pets, and those who did kept them in fences, as Georgia's leash law demanded. Elaine followed the sound, but by the time she looked outside, there was nothing to be seen. The barking ceased as suddenly as it began.

"Good thing all the kids are in school. That dog would have scared them half to death," she said aloud as she made her way back to the computer to resume her story.

Just as she began typing, her eyes fell on the photograph at the corner of her desk. She and Mason had taken it a little over three years ago when they cruised to Nassau, Bahamas. The trip was magical. It was on the Carnival Conquest in cabin number M544 that she'd gotten pregnant for the third time. Once she made it past her first trimester, Mason had promised that they'd make cruising in the summer an annual family event, and two weeks later, he made it official by going online and booking their next cruise nearly ten months in advance. By then, the baby would be born, Elaine would have recuperated, and the trip would be a celebration of him finally having the family he wanted. But like the baby she was carrying,

Mason's excitement was short-lived. After the miscarriage, not only were the travel plans canceled, but the subject of cruising was never mentioned again.

Their marriage had been rocky for some time now, but deep inside, Elaine knew that it was no excuse for the level to which she'd taken her dejection. When Mason walked out two days ago and basically told her he didn't want to be with her; that had been the final straw. His words had cut to the core and she wanted to lash out and hurt him in return. As detached and absent as Mason had been over the past couple of years, Elaine knew that he would be torn if he had the slightest clue of how she'd spent the last two nights.

"I can't go on like this," she whispered as she ran her hands through her hair and placed the picture back on her desk.

There was a heated battle going on inside of her. A fraction of her wanted freedom. She wanted to be away from the man who had made her marriage lonely. The motivational CDs had told her that she had the power to make herself happy. In Elaine's mind, she interpreted that as advice to leave the dying situation she was in and find life somewhere else. She could walk out on Mason and start a new life with Dante, a man who would treat her like the priceless gem that she was. *Nubian queen* was what Dante called her as he made love to her last night.

His words sounded good to her ears that had been starving for expressions of admiration. But leaving Mason wouldn't be an easy decision to make, not just because she had been with him a total of twelve years, but because she loved him. Even after all the angry discussions, silent treatments and lonely nights, Elaine still loved him. She just wished there was some way she could make him understand how much she needed him to love her back.

\* \* \*

*What's up, Austin-Boston!*

*This is your daddy. I should be asleep right now, but it seems like I haven't slept since we found out you were on the way. Everyone thinks you're a girl, but I know you're a boy. I can feel it. You are my son, my miracle. Some might question how I can love someone I've never seen, someone I've never touched, but I love you. God knows I do.*

*Austin, I never thought I would be blessed to have a family, let alone a baby boy, but God is, in spite of all my wrongs, giving me a son. I can't wait to hold you. I can't wait to play with you, to bounce you on my knee. I can't wait to play catch, go to ball games, and take you fishing. I can't wait to read bedtime stories and go to museums with you and do all those things fathers and sons enjoy.*

*God is giving me a miracle and my miracle is coming through a blessing—your mother. Austin, you are so lucky to be blessed with a mother like Angel. I can't think of another woman in this world (other than Sanaa Lathan—smile) that I would have chosen to be your mother. Angel is as precious and as rare as a flawless diamond. It is my desire to be the best father I can be to you and for you. My greatest prayer is that I can always take care of you and make sure you have all you need to be an asset to this world and not a liability. God has given you to me, and for that, I give you back to Him. You are going to be somebody special. You already are. And, Austin, although you will be your own person, you will always be a part of me. I am*

*always here for you. Please don't ever doubt that. I'll*
*see you in seven months, son. Until your arrival,*
                                        *I love you.*
                                        *Your Daddy*

The tears that rushed from Angel's eyes almost blinded her as she read the letter for the fourth time. She'd had absolutely no idea that the love letter that Colin had written to their child even existed. Noting the date at the top, Angel realized that he'd written the letter only two weeks after she'd taken the home pregnancy test.

She'd had an appointment with their doctor yesterday and Colin was with her, just like he was at every appointment she had throughout the pregnancy. Essie's words and the belief that Colin had voiced all along were finally confirmed. The image on the screen in the doctor's office clearly was that of a baby boy.

"There it is," Colin exclaimed when they saw the full frontal view of the thumb-sucking infant. "That proves it. That's my Austin-Boston!"

Until reading the letter, it was the only time she'd heard him call their son by that name.

The doctor had given Angel some advice that he suggested she follow over the next few weeks. One was to pack the suitcase that she'd be taking to the hospital. "Once you start to get near that one-month mark, anything can happen," he told Angel. "Babies can be born as early as two weeks before the due date and it would still be considered a normal pregnancy cycle. It's always better to be ready ahead of time than to wait until the labor pains are coming before you get your bag together."

Packing her suitcase was what Angel had been

doing when she found the letter. She'd been looking for a novel to take along that would be a good hospital read for the day or two that she would spend there after the baby's birth. When she pulled one of the books from their overcrowded bookshelf, the letter was tucked between the front cover and the first page. Colin was going to be a wonderful father, just like he'd been a model husband, despite his infatuation with the beautiful actress who seemed to have made a lasting impact on him since he saw her star in *Love & Basketball* some years ago.

When she read the words on the paper, Angel imagined seeing her husband and son together as Austin grew from infancy to adolescence. Not only could she envision them tossing a football back and forth to each other in the backyard, but Angel could see them with prime tickets, season passes to every Atlanta Falcons game. She laughed aloud as a picture formed in her mind of Colin and Austin wearing matching Mike Vick jerseys and screaming in the stands as the star quarterback rushed to make the winning touchdown.

Angel walked into the bathroom and returned with Kleenex to wipe away the evidence of her earlier emotions. From the time she met Colin during a simple visit to the bank, she knew that he was the man she wanted to spend the rest of her life with. That was almost five years ago, and to this day, she still believed that everything that happened on that Friday was in divine order.

At that time, Angel was a beauty consultant with her own brand-new cosmetician business and had gone to the bank to cash a large check from a client. To her dismay, she was told that the funds in the account were insufficient and the check could not be cashed. With a vital out-of-town trip scheduled for the following morning, Angel was devastated. She was counting on the check to get her there. At the time, Colin held the position of one of the bank's assistant managers and had overheard the exchange between Angel and the teller.

"Ma'am, could you step into my office, please?" he'd said to her. "I'll see what we can do to assist you."

That day, behind closed doors, Angel told Colin her desperate story in hopes that there was some way that he would approve an advancement of the money on their customer's account and then allow the woman who had given her the check to deposit money later, to pay it back. Bank policy would not allow him to create such a transaction, but Colin went into his own pocket and gave her the money she needed for the trip. As much as she wanted the money, Angel was apprehensive. She didn't feel comfortable accepting such a large loan from a man she'd never met before, and she expressed that to him.

"I understand," Colin said, "but this is not a loan. See it as my investment in the future of your business. Every business accepts investors and sponsors, right? I'm not asking you to pay it back. Take it and receive it as a blessing."

His hand touched hers when he handed her the cash, and from that very moment, Angel knew that it wouldn't be the last time she saw him. She thanked him repeatedly and then gave him her business card.

"If you know of anyone who wants to buy or sell a great line of cosmetics, please have them call me," she said, hoping, in her heart, he'd find a reason to use the card himself.

One week to the day that she met him, Angel got her phone call. She and Colin had been virtually inseparable ever since. As soon as their relationship became serious, he told her about his childhood battle with cancer and that he had little or no chance of having children. All of her life, Angel wanted to one day become a mother, but she knew that with or without a child, she needed to be with Colin. She'd hoped for a man who would be strong for her, like her grandfather was for her grandmother; a man who would pray with her, like her father did with her mother; and a man who would love her, like Benjamin did Ms. Essie. In Colin, God had given her all three. And now, almost like an unexpected dessert after a delicious meal, He had now given them a son.

"A very active son," Angel said with a laugh as the baby moved inside of her. "Austin Benjamin Stephens. Austin B. Stephens. Sounds like the name of somebody important. Are you going to be the first black president of the United States?" She looked at her stomach when she spoke, as if the infant could hear her and would answer back.

"Maybe you'll be a football player. Your daddy would love that," she added. "Just like your daddy said on this letter, God gave you to us and we're giving you back to Him. Whatever you become, we know that you'll be successful and you're going to make us proud."

Angel folded the letter and tucked it back in the book where she'd found it. She then placed the book in her suitcase so she could have it with her at the hospital. She decided to wait until then to let her husband know that she had seen the thoughts that he'd placed on paper so many months ago. The weeks ahead were going to be a time of excitement and new beginnings for her family, and the day couldn't come soon enough.

All of the packing, crying, and talking to her unborn baby had made Angel hungry, that and the fact that she'd overslept and had not yet eaten breakfast. Her pregnancy had brought on strange cravings for foods that she never ate on a normal basis, the cheese pizza with mushrooms and jalapeños being the main one. She had also frequently eaten peanut butter and banana sandwiches, and tuna salad and pretzels, her craving right now.

For the past three months, Colin had grimaced every time he saw her take a pretzel stick, scoop up the tuna, and place it in her mouth. Angel made a fresh batch of tuna salad the night before and, after several failed attempts, finally persuaded Colin to give it a try. After all those weeks of turning up his nose, he had to admit that it wasn't half bad. They sat together on the bed for over an hour and snacked on the awkward combination while watching back-to-back reruns of *The Andy Griffith Show*.

The unclosed cabinet doors in the kitchen served as visible evidence that Colin was running late for work this morning. Often, he would grab a piece of fruit or a cereal bar and a large cup of water on his way out the door to prepare him for the rush-hour traffic that awaited him. When he was pressed for time, he had a bad habit of not taking the time to close the doors after fishing out whatever it was that he took on any given day.

Angel closed all of the doors and then took a dishtowel and wiped away water on the counter that her husband had apparently spilled in his rush.

Clumsy spills were a habit for him as well. After drying the water, she went to the refrigerator and pulled out the tuna. When she opened the top, she had to laugh. There were clear signs, from the amount in the bowl, that Colin had spoon-dipped some out for himself this morning.

Taking a plate from the dish rack, Angel raked some of the salad onto it and then put the leftovers away. The pretzel bag was already sitting on the counter, and she poured some next to the tuna salad. Her mouth watered at the thought of combining the two, and before she even took the time to put the bag away, Angel picked up two sticks and swirled them in the mixture before putting them in her mouth and savoring the flavor. She slid the pretzels back in the corner on the countertop and headed to her room to enjoy her meal.

"Ughhhhhhh!"

An invisible puddle of water on the floor had caused Angel's bedroom slippers to slide from under her. She tried frantically to grab the counter for balance but couldn't move quickly enough. The plate that held her meal flew from her hand, and Angel heard it crash to the floor just before she did the same. The landing was hard and painful, and for a moment she couldn't move. She'd done her best to shield her stomach from the impact, but landing on her left side, her swollen belly still took some of the blow. "Oh, my God!" she whispered in terror.

# Chapter 11

## *Wednesday Afternoon: 5:10 P.M.*

Jerrod stood in line along with the rest of the puppies while Freddie marched back and forth in the sandy area around the picnic benches where they had gathered. The head dog had ranted and raged for more than twenty minutes before he'd finally taken a break and chosen the silent pacing. The quiet huffing didn't last long.

"How y'all gonna roll with the big dogs when you ain't nothing but a bunch of punks?" Freddie spewed. "Y'all niggas think we a bunch of sissies or something? We the Dobermans, yo. Ain't no room for no poodles up in this pound!"

Jerrod's heart hammered. He wanted to speak, but he knew better. When one of the other boys tried to defend himself he'd been delivered a jab to the stomach that brought him to his knees. Ever since then, all five of them had stood silently and allowed Freddie to unload his frustrations.

"All you had to do was find a way to make sure

the back door to the school didn't get locked yesterday!" he yelled in the first boy's face. "And *you*," he said to the next, "you were supposed to sneak away in your uncle's car and be at one of the big dogs' crib last night to pick him up so he could take care of some important business. Did you show up? No!"

Now Freddie was standing in the face of the boy directly to Jerrod's right. "And what was the problem that you couldn't put a key to the paint on Paul Patterson's pickup truck and pull a scratch down the side?"

For every word that began with the letter *p*, Jerrod could feel particles of spit land against his arm. He could only imagine the saturation his classmate's face was taking. But wisdom told both of them that it wouldn't be in their best interest to wipe away the disgusting moisture.

"Puppy J!" Freddie shouted.

Jerrod's body stiffened as the boy came to a stop in front of him and gazed in his face. Tall for his age, Jerrod almost stood eye-to-eye with the nineteen-year-old senior. Freddie had been nice to him over the past few weeks, but they'd never had a day like today. He'd started on one end of the line for a report on how well the puppies had fared with their assignments, and so far, no one had delivered good news.

"You know what?"—Freddie took a step away from Jerrod—"I ain't gonna sweat you, Puppy J. Up until today, you ain't never let yo' top dog down, and I got to give you your props for that. All these other mutts been screwing up every other week, but you been straight, nigga. And as bad as I want to be in the stands watching our boys take it to the net this week, I'm gonna let you slide."

Jerrod felt a wave of relief run through his body. In his mind, he thought of ways to right the wrong he'd done. Maybe he could correct the horrible, desperate deed that he'd carried out the night before, before anyone discovered. A smile tugged at his lips, but he held it.

Freddie moved on. "What y'all got?" he asked the two boys on the other side of Jerrod. "Did y'all punk out too, or what?"

The unresponsiveness was all the answer that Freddie needed. His language turned foul as he expressed in no uncertain terms how disappointed he was. Although he'd said that he would let Jerrod slide, his angry speech was directed at all of them, and suddenly the reprieve that Jerrod had gotten earlier didn't seem to have much meaning.

"All of you have let all of us down," Freddie said.

The other big dogs nodded in agreement.

"Being Dobermans ain't just about a bunch of niggas getting together to climb trees. If you want that, you can join the Boy Scouts! In this gang, we do what we gotta do to survive, and if y'all don't do no better than this, then y'all ain't gonna make it up in this pack. And if you ain't tough enough to be a Doberman, then you always gonna be a scared puppy with your tail between your legs while some other kind of dog scares you half to death. Is that what y'all want to be? Some punked-out puppy dog whimpering for your mama to rescue you?"

While Freddie was talking, Jerrod's mind traveled back ten years. He could remember the fear he experienced while his mother's boyfriend stood over him after he had damaged his car. The angry boy called him a punk, and back then that's just what he was, a punk needing his mother's protection; and even then, she failed him.

*No more!* he thought to himself. Never again did he want to have to depend on his mother to rescue him from danger. Never again.

"Big Dog Freddie?"

Freddie's turned to face him.

Jerrod saw the look. He broke the rule, and the look on Freddie's face mirrored his disapproval. All of the puppies knew the rules. When the top dog was talking, all they were supposed to do was listen.

Freddie walked with slow, intimidating steps and came to a stop with his face only inches away from Jerrod's. "Did you just say something, Puppy J?"

Reaching his hand in his pants pocket, Jerrod grabbed the paper inside and slid it out. He held his hand up.

Freddie looked down at the passes he presented. Without speaking, the top dog took the tickets from Jerrod's hand and looked them over closely. A broad grin stretched across his face, and he pulled Jerrod in for a quick embrace before holding the tickets up in the air for the other big dogs to see. The immediate sounds of loud barking followed.

Now the swear words Freddie uttered weren't laced with anger. He pulled Jerrod out of the lineup and turned him to face the other boys pledging for a chance to become a Doberman. "That's what I'm talkin' 'bout!" Freddie yelled as the barking of his peers calmed. Looking directly at the failed youngsters he said, "Y'all take a good look at Jerrod, 'cause this the last time any of us gonna see him as a puppy or call him a puppy. Listen to me and listen to me good. From this day on, this right here is Big Dog Jerrod."

Jerrod grinned at the sound of the words and the sounds of the other big dogs, whose celebratory barks rang out like a crowded kennel. He'd made it! The trial period still had two weeks to go and he had already done what the others couldn't. Never again would he be intimidated by anyone, because he had friends who would always watch his back.

"We'll make it official in two weeks," Freddie announced. "But if any of the rest of y'all even have a chance of making the cut, y'all gonna have to work hard and don't make no more mistakes—starting with tonight. We gonna do it up around midnight tonight, just for our newest dog. Everything that happens tonight is for you, J."

Jerrod's elation began to melt. He hoped that his next words wouldn't bring the celebration to a screeching halt, but he knew that if he didn't get home before eleven, he'd have to sleep at his neighbor's house again. Not that he had a problem with Essie. Jerrod actually enjoyed the time he'd spent at her home a couple of nights ago, and oddly enough, her couch was more comfortable than his bed.

Spending time with her wasn't the problem. The problem was that Essie had struck a cord with him during their talk. When the old woman told him that his mother had cried and told her how much she loved him, something inside of Jerrod clicked. He had never seen his mother cry because of his actions, and he couldn't remember the last time Jennifer told him that she loved him. All he'd ever seen was her anger and disapproval, and all he'd heard was her yelling on a daily basis about his misbehavior. But knowing that he'd made her cry had hurt him inside. Her crying was a sign that she cared, and that meant something to him. Knowing how much she cared almost made him hold on to the tickets he'd just given Freddie.

"I 'ppreciate what y'all want to do and all, but I can't hang. I mean, I can't stay out late tonight. I can go and chill at your crib a while and all, but I'm gonna have to bounce around eight. I-uh-I got a late date with a honey. You know how that is."

"I heard that, nigga!" Freddie laughed. "Go'n and get your doggy style on. You a big dog now, and we *got* you. Me and the boys still gonna roll out and celebrate in your honor tonight. We doin' this for you, nigga. We gonna make you proud to be a Doberman, and after tonight, everybody gonna know that the Dobermans ain't nobody to mess wit'. You feel me?"

"Yeah, man, I feel you," Jerrod said, glad that his lie was enough to exempt him.

"That'll be one hundred twenty-eight dollars and fourteen cents," the cashier announced.

Jennifer usually did her grocery shopping every two weeks on Sundays, but it seemed that her refrigerator was running out of everything; plus, yesterday, she'd promised Essie that she would go to church with her this Sunday. It was the least she could do to pay her back for giving Jerrod a warm, dry place to sleep on Monday night.

Jennifer heard him knocking, but she was determined to teach her defiant son a lesson that he wouldn't forget. She had barely slept a wink that night after the knocking stopped. Tossing and turning, she wondered where he'd gone, worrying about his safety. When she saw Jerrod walk out of the house next door the following morning, she wanted to run to him and hug him tightly, but she didn't.

"Hold on a minute," she told the clerk as she opened up another section of her wallet and felt for the money that she was sure she'd placed in the main compartment. Still, there was nothing. Jennifer was beginning to feel embarrassed. The line behind her was long, and the people closest to the end of it were beginning to stretch their necks and murmur among themselves. Even the gum-chewing cashier looked as if she worked on commission and was losing money while Jennifer looked for hers.

There was a zipped pocket in her purse where she'd tucked away the money she would need to pay her overdue telephone bill. Jennifer pulled it out, already knowing that it wouldn't be enough to cover the cost of the grocery bill. She unfolded four twenty-dollar bills and then looked back at the annoyed cashier.

"I'm sorry," she said in mounting shame. "I've misplaced some money. I need to take some of these items off.

Rolling her eyes and releasing a heavy, aggravated sigh, the girl began pulling items from the bags that she'd just packed with groceries.

The hour was growing late and it would be time for them to go inside soon, but for the last two hours, Essie had enjoyed looking at the children play together in the clearing across the street.

Generally, Angel would stop by to see her twice a week on Saturdays and Wednesdays. Today she hadn't come by, but Essie knew that pregnancy had a way of changing schedules. She'd never had a baby herself, but she'd known plenty of women who did, and those last few weeks weren't always easy ones. Essie decided she'd give her telephone some use and call Angel the following day.

While Essie watched the children chase one another around in circles, her mind raced at the same pace as their feet. Something was different about this week than any other time in her life. With the late hours that she was getting to bed, she had gotten little sleep over the past few days. Oddly enough, Essie felt as rested as if she'd been getting a full ten hours every night. Maybe she'd heard the message her pastor had preached on last Sunday and was putting it into action.

"God commands us to love our neighbors just like we love ourselves," Reverend Owens said as he paced the floor in front of the churchgoers at Temple of God's Word. Reverend Owens was relatively short in stature, but a giant in his knowledge of the Bible. "That's what He told us to do," the preacher continued, "but some of us got neighbors that we *know* are in trouble and we won't even show God's love by lending a helping hand or a word of comfort. How can we say we love God, who we have never seen, and can't show love to the people that we see every day? Y'all don't hear me!"

Essie heard him loud and clear. In her lifetime, she had heard the sermon preached at least a hundred times. But it had never moved her like it did on last Sunday. In years past, she'd helped less fortunate people and had even volunteered at homeless shelters and helped with feeding the hungry during holidays when Hosea Williams was still alive and running his charity program. But it had been a while since she'd ventured out and helped those who lived around her. It was as though Rev. Owens's words were directed right toward her and had somehow given her a sense of urgency. For months, years even, she'd known that trouble loomed in her neighborhood, but Essie refrained from addressing any of the issues. Instead, she sat quietly on her porch and watched the problem escalate until it was almost out of control.

Taking the sermon as a personal charge and deciding to do something about her surroundings made Essie feel more than rested; it made her feel useful again. For years, especially after Mr. and Mrs. Breckenridge passed away, she had been left to wonder what it was that God wanted her to do. She didn't have the education or the ability to speak grammatically correct like her Ben. In her eyes, Ben could have become anything and anybody that he wanted to be. Unlike her, he had finished high school and had gone on to further his learning at Tuskegee Institute. All she'd ever known was cleaning houses and caring for the elderly. Now, *she* was the elderly. But God had shown Essie that even in this cycle of her life, she wasn't useless.

"Lord, I don't know why you waited 'til I was this old to teach me this lesson, but I sho' do thank you." Essie's eyes searched the darkening skies above. "Just goes to show that Your word was right when it said our timing just ain't the same as Yours."

As if putting an exclamation point at the end of her sentence, Essie's grandfather clock chimed on the other side of her wall. It was seven o'clock and the children were finally starting to disperse.

"Bye, Ms. Essie!" several of them called.

"Bye, honey. Y'all watch out for them cars now."

Essie waved as they scattered toward their own homes on different streets within the subdivision. Rarely did cars travel through these roads during this time of night, but there was one that almost always did, and Essie could hear it coming now.

When the BMW rounded the corner, it came to a stop directly in front of her home. Seconds later, Mason Demps stepped out and rounded his car, stopping every few feet to look underneath.

Getting up from her seat, Essie walked to the edge of her porch. "Is everything all right?" she asked.

Mason turned and looked at her.

It was the first time she'd gotten a relatively close view of what Elaine's husband looked like. Generally, his features were hidden by the tinted windows of one of his vehicles, or he would be driving too fast for her to see. Essie slipped her glasses on her face for an even better look. Mason was handsome and had a medium brown complexion. He appeared to be in his late thirties, was clean-cut, and wore a pair of denim jeans and a pullover shirt.

"I don't know," he answered. "Right when I turned into the subdivision, I started hearing a rattling under my car, like something had gotten caught underneath and was pulling it to a stop. I think it's okay, though."

Essie watched as he walked around the car for a second time, doing the same examination that he'd done before. When he failed to see anything unusual, he climbed back in the driver's seat and started to drive.

From where she stood, Essie could hear the odd-sounding racket too.

The car came to a stop again, backed up to the place where it had been parked before, and once again, Mason got out.

"I heard it myself," Essie told him. "Looks like it might need some work."

She heard him curse before he got down on his hands and knees and ultimately on his back and disappeared under the front of the car.

"Ugly words ain't gonna help none," Essie mumbled as she found her way back to her chair. "For what it's gonna cost to fix that kind of car, you better be calling Jesus."

Several minutes passed before she saw Mason reappear. He stood and used his hands to attempt to remove from his clothes the loose dirt picked up from the road.

Another familiar car appeared from the other end of the street and slowed down as it neared the place where Mason stood.

"Hey," Mason called out. "Where are you going?"

Essie knew right away that it was Elaine sitting behind the closed windows, and she knew that Elaine had seen Mason standing there. But without stopping, she drove around his car and turned the corner to leave the neighborhood.

That action brought another oath from Mason as he stood with his hands perched on his hips in aggravation and watched the car disappear.

Essie stood from her chair. She knew she'd made that fresh pitcher of lemonade for some reason. "Come on in here and get yourself cleaned up before driving off," she called when she saw Mason reach for the door handle of his car. "That's a nice car you got there. You don't want to mess it up with them nasty hands of yours."

"I hate to be a bother," Mason said as he approached and began climbing her steps.

"Ain't no bother, honey. You ain't asked me for nothing. I'm the one who offered." Essie saw the trickle of blood that ran from his finger. "And let me get a bandage for that cut."

"Thank you."

"You're welcome, sugar. The bathroom is right down there." Essie pointed. "Got some clean towels on the counter."

By the time Mason returned, she had poured two glasses of lemonade and was already handing one in his direction. He took the glass with his left hand and allowed Essie to place a bandage on the index finger of his right hand.

"Thank you." Mason extended his repaired hand to shake hers. "I'm Mason Demps."

"You Elaine's husband, ain't you?" Essie shook his hand and then led the way back onto her porch and pointed toward the empty chair on the other side. She didn't want him sitting on her furniture with remnants of dirt and leaves still stuck to the back of his shirt and pants.

"You know my wife?" Mason asked in a stunned voice.

"Uh-huh." Essie nodded. "Sweet woman."

Mason laughed. "No, I don't think you know *my* wife."

"Oh, she sweet, all right. She going through some stuff right now, that's all."

Mason turned to look at her. "What did she tell you? Maybe you know something that I don't know. She's just acting real stupid these days, you know. I can't figure her out, so if you know something—"

"I don't know nothing, but it don't take no genius to see that she's going through something."

"Well, I'm going through something too, and she's the one who's putting me through it."

"Let me tell you a little something." Essie looked directly at him. "See that cut you got on your finger? If it hadn't been tended to, it would have just kept on bleeding. The bandage is the only thing that stopped the blood from running. Elaine is just like the blood from that cut. As long as she ain't being tended to, she gonna keep right on running. And a sore that's ignored ain't gonna go away. It's gonna get worse and worse until infection sets in. Then when infection sets in, that's when you risk having to have the whole thing cut off. If you had let that finger get infected and have to be cut off, you still would have been able to use your hand, sugar; but it wouldn't have been easy and you would wish every day that you had just tended to it so that it would still be around."

Mason stared at Essie. His expression was one of bewilderment, and he didn't say a word.

"Elaine done already been cut. She done already been bleeding. She done already been left unattended and infection done already set in. Don't let her be cut away, baby. As hard as life might be right now, it's gonna get a whole lot harder if you have to live your life without her. You know why? 'Cause you love her, that's why. If you didn't love her, it wouldn't make a hill-of-beans worth a difference. But you do. Don't let her get cut away."

The next few moments passed in utter silence. The clinking of ice cubes against the bottom of Mason's glass was the sound that finally ended the quietness.

"That was delicious. Thank you," he said, handing the glass back to Essie. "I'd better be going now."

"Wait a minute," she said, quickly disappearing

into the house and returning with the blanket she'd finished just two days ago. "Put this up under you when you drive so you don't get your car all dirty."

Mason looked down at the beautifully woven design and then turned his attention back at Essie. "But this is so nice," he said. "I don't want to mess it up."

Essie shrugged. "It's machine washable. Just clean it when you're done, and either you or Elaine can bring it back by tomorrow."

"Thanks," Mason said, still confused by the remarkable woman he'd just spent the last several minutes with. "Thanks for . . . everything."

"You're welcome."

Essie watched as he took slow, thoughtful steps toward his car. When Mason started the engine and drove away, the earlier disturbing sounds that caused him to stop in the first place were no longer heard.

# Chapter 12

## *Wednesday Night: 10:06 P.M.*

"Are you sure you're okay?" Colin asked as he sat beside the place where Angel lay on the bed.

Angel's partial smile didn't appear genuine, and the hesitation before her nod did little to make Colin feel more at ease. Inside, he felt that there was more to her awkward behavior than what his wife had revealed. She stared at the shading that covered the window near the bed. Feeling closed out and helpless, all Colin could do was smooth his fingers through her hair and wonder if she was being completely truthful with him. At least a dozen times now, Angel had told him that she was feeling all right, but every now and again, Colin would see tears in her eyes and couldn't help but ask again.

A few hours earlier, when he got in from work, he found Angel lying in bed asleep and when he touched her arm as he leaned down to kiss her forehead, she winced before opening her eyes. Colin thought he'd just startled her, but a closer look revealed a swollen bruise on her left arm.

"I fell," was all the explanation she'd given him, but for Colin it wasn't enough. He'd walked into the kitchen and seen the broken plate and the scattered food. He wanted to take her to the doctor for reassurance, but Angel protested.

"I'm fine, Colin. I just need to lie down for a few minutes."

The sternness in her voice concerned him.

A few minutes stretched into four hours, with her only getting up once to use the bathroom. Even then, her movements seemed painfully slow. As Angel lay in the bed, she kept her arms cradled around her stomach, as if she were protecting their child from something that couldn't be seen with the natural eye. Colin wanted to touch her abdomen to feel the baby's movement, but Angel wouldn't even allow his hands through the protective barrier her arms formed.

"Let me get you some more ice." He removed the cold compress that was resting on her bruised arm and left the room.

In reality, Colin used the ice pack as an excuse to break away from the tension, the silence in the room. He walked into the living room and sank onto the cushions of their white leather sofa. The thought that water may have been left on the floor during his quick exit for work this morning was almost too much to handle, but Colin knew his habits, and when he realized that Angel's fall had taken place in the kitchen, it was all he could think about. In his mind, he played back everything that he'd done that morning as he was scampering about, grabbing last-minute items.

During the rush, Colin filled a small Tupperware

bowl with tuna salad and poured some of the pretzel sticks into a sandwich bag and zipped it shut. He had a can of soda, so there was no need for him to take water, as he normally did. The only reason he'd turned the faucet on was to rinse the plastic bowl that he used.

*Could I have splashed the water on the floor in the process or could it have dripped from the bowl on the way out? Is she blaming me for this? Is that why she's shutting me out?*

"Oh, God," he said, burying his face in his hands.

Colin couldn't even count the number of times Angel had asked him to take time to close the cabinet doors and wipe up after himself when he wasted juice and water. It was a hard-to-break lazy habit that had followed him from childhood.

Colin's mother was always cleaning up after her husband and her three sons. "Don't worry about it; Mama's got it," she'd say when any of her boys spilled food or drinks.

Colin tried to do better when he realized that his wife didn't live by the same rules as his mother, and over the years he'd made a conscious attempt to be more mindful. But this morning, he'd slept later than normal and was in a bigger rush than on most days. Colin had an early-morning meeting he couldn't be late for, and he knew that he wasn't too alert while he prepared his lunch. Maybe he *did* unconsciously become forgetful. Maybe it *was* his fault.

Gathering himself and walking into the kitchen, Colin dropped one ice cube at a time in the vintage ice pack that he'd had since going camping with his father as a teenager. He badly wanted to ask Angel if everything felt right with the baby, but Colin didn't want to cause undo worry by bringing up the possibility that their child could have been harmed.

"If I've done anything to cause damage to my son . . ." Colin shook his head vigorously to try to rid himself of the thoughts that were beginning to flood in. Just considering the likelihood that something could be wrong was tearing him apart inside. For the sake of his own sanity, he had to find a way to think more positively. *God gave me this child. There was no way He would allow anything to destroy my blessing so close to the date of delivery.* "Please, God," he prayed softly, fighting the threat of tears.

When he walked back into the room nearly thirty minutes after leaving to refill the pack, Colin found Angel in the same position and with the same stare that she had when he left. A lump the size of his fist seemed to rise in his throat as he eased onto the mattress beside her and replaced the cold pack on her arm.

"Sweetheart, talk to me," he coaxed, hoping that he wouldn't regret his decision not to let the subject rest. "I need to know what you're feeling."

"I'm fine," she whispered.

Although he was positioned behind her, Colin was perched on his elbow and could see the side profile of her face. He noted the water that had begun to seep from the corners of her eyes and trickled onto her nose. Whether it was due to worry, fear, pain, or anger, he hated to see Angel cry. She was such a marvelous woman with superb character traits that it seemed unfair for her to have to shed tears caused by anything other than joy.

Colin took a deep breath and then asked the question that was plaguing him most.

"Are you angry with me?"

Her elongated silence made his heart sink to a new level. Colin's earlier question of whether or not he'd been the one to create the spill that had caused her fall was answered without his wife saying a word. Removing the pack from her arm and setting it aside, Colin gently placed his lips on the reddened area and kissed it. Her flesh was cold from hours of the ice treatment. The earlier swelling had decreased, but the fresh bruise was a harsh reminder of what his carelessness had caused. "I'm sorry, Angel."

"I know," she responded.

Lying so closely beside her that their heads shared the same pillow, Colin caressed her arm. He found comfort in the fact that Angel allowed him to touch her without pulling away because he knew how disappointed she was in him. There had been very few times in their marriage that they argued, but even when they did, they always honored the commitment that they made to one another the day before their wedding. Both of them had promised to never go to bed leaving loose ends of a disagreement dangling. All disputes had to be settled before the lights went out for the night. It was a vow that they'd kept, and possibly more than at any other time before, Colin needed Angel to honor it tonight.

"Tell me what you're feeling," he implored.

Her only immediate reaction was a quiet sniffle, but Colin waited patiently, sensing that there was a more detailed response on the way. In the time of silence that lapsed, he continued the tender massage of her wound and prayed inwardly that she didn't burst into hysterical tears. The quiet ones were hard enough to deal with.

"I was scared," she finally whispered.

Colin kept silent in hopes that she would continue speaking, but in his mind he visualized her fall and imagined her fear as she came crashing to the floor. What if she had hit her head on the corner of the counter? What if she had not been able to pull herself up and had cried for help? There would have been no one nearby to hear her calls. Even worse, what if she'd been knocked unconscious in the process? It would have been hours before she would have been discovered. Angel's speaking pulled Colin's mind from the visual terror that had set in.

"All I could think about was the baby," she said through new sniffles. "I tried to hold my stomach so that if I fell the wrong way . . ."

Her voice drifted as though finishing the sentence was too difficult, her arms still wrapped in a protective manner around her stomach.

Colin's third attempt to feel for the movements of his child failed.

"It was painful," she added. "Really, really painful."

"I'm sorry, sweetie." Colin felt helpless and riddled with blame. Voicing his apology didn't seem like enough, but it was all he could think to do. "Are you hurting now?"

He hoped she'd ease his guilt by saying there was no lingering discomfort, but when she nodded, Colin closed his eyes and squeezed his lids as tight as he could. But he couldn't block out the realism of what had transpired due to his negligence. From this point on, no answer was necessarily good, but some could definitely be better than others.

"Where is it hurting?" Colin braced himself, almost afraid of the response that she might give.

"Everywhere," she replied.

Colin took another deep breath. "When you say everywhere, do you mean—"

"I fell hard, Colin. My arm and shoulder hurts. My neck is sore, like I've been in a car wreck or something. I have a headache. That's what I mean when I say I'm hurting everywhere."

Her tone wasn't exactly harsh, but Colin could still hear her disappointment in him. He searched himself for something he could say to alleviate the physical pain. "Did you take a Tylenol?"

"No."

"I'll get you some water." Colin began bringing himself to a seated position. "The Tylenol will help, I'm sure."

"It won't help everything."

Her words stopped Colin's motion like a freeze-frame on a motion picture. For the immediate seconds that followed, he felt like a sudden-stroke victim who was unable to move from the neck down. Without turning around, he could determine from the heavy breathing behind him that Angel's tears had increased.

Colin's movements came in increments. First, he wiggled his fingers, and then bit by bit, gained full mobility of his joints and muscles. Repositioning himself on the mattress, he turned so that he faced his wife's back, and swallowed. "Angel." His words were barely more than a whisper. "Is the baby okay?"

When she didn't respond, Colin jumped from the bed and walked around to the other side, so that he could look her in the face. Her eyes were closed and her arms remained securely locked around her inflated mid-section.

"Angel," Colin said, this time at a more audible volume. "Is Austin okay?"

"I don't know." She choked.

"What do you mean, you don't know?"

"I don't know! I don't know!" Angel screamed.

In frantic motions, Colin pulled the covers off of her. "Are you bleeding?" He searched the underlying sheets for signs of trauma.

"No," she answered.

"What then?" Colin asked with his face close to hers, using his fingers to wipe away her accumulating tears. "Why do you think something might be wrong?"

"A portion of the side of my stomach hit the floor when I fell."

Colin felt a slight wave of relief. If that was her only reason, he could calm himself a little. Surely a bump to the side of her stomach wouldn't be enough to do any damage to their son. "It's okay, baby," he said. "I'm sure everything is okay. I'm going to get you some water and you're going to take a couple of caplets for the soreness. If it doesn't go away by the weekend, I'll take you to that same spa that I took you to a couple of months ago and let them give you a good massage to relax your muscles. Okay? Everything will be fine. I'll take care of you and I promise that this won't ever happen again. If I have to carpet the kitchen floor, I will. But this will never happen again."

Colin kissed her forehead, brushed away more tears and then stood. He covered her with the spread that he'd snatched away earlier and then headed toward the door to get her the water he'd promised.

"He's not moving, Colin."

This time the paralysis seemed almost permanent. Not only had Colin's movements stopped in mid-stride, but it felt as though his heart had stopped as well. He struggled just to release the breath he'd just inhaled when he heard Angel's words. Using the edge of the cherry oak dresser near the door to help him balance himself, Colin turned and faced the bed.

"What?" he asked, although he'd heard her clearly the first time.

"He's not moving." The words were accompanied by the onset of another flood.

Colin rushed to Angel and knelt by the side of the bed. She winced when he pulled her arms away from her belly and replaced them with his hands. Generally, when he massaged her stomach a certain way, their son would react by repositioning himself. It was a nightly ritual that Colin looked forward to. Tonight, his touches got no reaction and he was beginning to panic, despite his attempt to stay calm for his wife's sake.

"Get up, baby," he said. "I'm taking you to the emergency room."

"No, Colin."

"Yes, Angel. Get up!"

"No!" she yelled back at him.

Colin's patience was wearing thin. He slid his arms beneath her body and attempted to lift her, but Angel fought back through the soreness in her joints.

"What's wrong with you?" Colin asked in a raised voice. "We need to have a doctor check you out. Angel, please!"

"No!"

"Why?"

" 'Cause I don't want to know!" she wailed. "Please don't make me go, Colin. If they told me my baby was dead, I couldn't handle it. I don't want to know!"

*If they told me my baby was dead.* Those were the words that drove the dagger in Colin's heart. As much as he wanted to insist that she go, or call the ambulance if she continued to refuse, Colin realized that he wasn't prepared to hear that kind of news either. He couldn't bear to hear those words from their doctor, knowing that he was the cause of the fall, the fall that had killed the only child he might ever have.

Reaching for his distraught wife, Colin pulled her into his chest and held her there. As he comforted her, he lost his own battle with the tears fighting to be released for the past few hours.

During his lifetime, Colin had overcome a lot of challenges. As a sixth grader, he'd taken on a bully and won. As a teenager, he'd taken on cancer and won. As a young adult, he'd taken on the challenges of the Alpha Phi Alpha fraternity and won. But, even with all the victories of his past, if he lost his son, Colin didn't know how he'd go on living.

# Chapter 13

## *Thursday Morning: 9:15 A.M.*

"*Ask of the Lord, dear kingdom child; in time, the answer will come. Pray without ceasing and know all the while, in time, the answer will come. In time, the answer will come. In time, the answer will come. May not come today, but as sure as I say it, in time, the answer will come. Ask of the Lord, dear kingdom child; in time, the answer will come . . .*"

Essie stopped singing as she heard footsteps approaching outside of her house. On most days she was on the porch sitting in her rocking chair and watching at this time of the morning, but when she woke up as the sun was just beginning to break through the darkness, she had an urge for more domestic duties.

She got up early this morning when she heard the neighborhood children heading to the bus stop. That was two hours ago; and since that time, she'd given her already neat house an extra boost by dusting the shelves in her living room and folding laundry that she'd washed and dried before going to bed the night before.

Once she'd finished that, Essie headed into the kitchen and began cooking a meal of smothered fried chicken, collard greens, and macaroni and cheese. She had already set out the ingredients needed to bake a cream cheese pound cake, and as soon as the oven was free, she would get started on that too. But the knock on her front door had put her plans on pause. Essie washed her hands under the water that flowed from the kitchen faucet and then dried them on her apron before walking to the front of her house.

"Well, hey, sugar," she said as she opened the door and saw Jennifer standing on the other side. "Ain't you supposed to be at work? You feeling okay?"

Jennifer folded her arms.

Essie detected tears that were either about to be released, or were left over from an earlier crying spell.

"I took the day off," Jennifer said in a voice that mirrored her expression. "Can I come in?"

"Sho' you can." Essie stepped aside and allowed her neighbor to pass.

As if she remembered the spot where she'd sat the last time she came to Essie's house, Jennifer took her place on the same sofa and leaned back against the pillows behind her. "It sure does smell good in here. Are you expecting company?"

"Well, you say that like cooking ain't normal," Essie said with a brief laugh. "Honey, I been cooking near 'bout every day of the week since I was a teenager. I admit that I usually don't do it this early in the morning, but my schedule got switched around today, I guess. No, no company. I just felt like cooking, that's all."

"Oh." Jennifer stared up at the ceiling.

"Is that why you came over?" Essie asked, knowing full well that there was far more on her neighbor's mind. "You smelled the food and came for a plate? I got plenty, but it ain't quite done yet. It's enough in there for both you and Jerrod."

Jennifer's eyes shifted down to her hands as she began to wring them together.

Essie watched and waited for her to speak, but when she didn't, Essie spoke for her. "Jerrod in some kind of trouble?"

"I don't know, Ms. Essie." Jennifer got up from her seat, walked over to the window and looked out as though she expected to see someone.

"I been hearing him get home before his curfew," Essie said. "I thought he was doing better."

"He gets home before eleven, but I don't know if he's doing better or not," Jennifer said as she turned to look back at Essie. "I'm missing two hundred and fifty dollars."

Essie's eyebrows rose in surprise. "How in the world did you misplace that kind of money?"

"I don't think I misplaced it, Ms. Essie." Jennifer walked back to the couch and sat again. "At first, I thought I did, but now I don't think so. I didn't know it was missing until I got to the checkout counter at the grocery store yesterday and ended up having to put thirty dollars' worth of my shopping back. I've never been so embarrassed in my entire life.

"After I left the store, I went back to my job and

retraced my footsteps, but couldn't find it anywhere. Now, Jerrod has done a lot of things, but as far as I know, he's never stolen, at least not from me. I hate to think he did it, but I do."

"You sho' you checked everywhere?" Essie didn't want to believe that the boy that she'd had the talk with just a few nights ago had done such a thing, but she had a sinking feeling that Jennifer was right.

"Yes, ma'am. I even checked in my car, thinking maybe my purse could have turned over on the drive from work and the money could have fallen out. It's nowhere to be found."

"Well, have you seen Jerrod with anything new that he could have used the money to buy?"

Jennifer shook her head. "I wish I did, though. At least, then I would know that he spent it on something legal."

Essie stood from her chair. "Chile, what you thinking? You can't be thinking what I think you thinking."

"Yes, ma'am. I think Jerrod is on drugs. How else can the missing money be explained? He doesn't have new clothes or shoes. I even looked through his room for any new CDs or jewelry. There's nothing new. So, if he's not wearing it or listening to it, all I'm left to believe is that either he smoked it, snorted it, or shot it up his arm. Now all the behavior problems make sense."

"Now, you hush up," Essie scolded softly. "You hush up right now. The devil is a lie. I just ain't gonna believe that boy using no drugs. I ain't saying he didn't take the money, but I pray for that boy every single night, and I just ain't gonna believe my prayers ain't doing no better than that."

Jennifer looked at her in surprise. "You pray for Jerrod?"

"I most certainly do," Essie said. "Every single night and I just ain't gonna believe . . ."

"Ms. Essie—"

"I just ain't gonna believe it, I say. Now, me and you together gonna pray for Jerrod and we getting ready to do it right now. We ain't gonna just turn him loose like that. Now, I was planning to ask Reverend Owens to pray special for y'all come Sunday, but this here can't wait 'til Sunday. God ain't promised none of us that we'll be here Sunday, so we need to pray right now."

"Yes, ma'am. But all I'm saying is—"

"Shhhhhh." Essie held her finger to her lips and tilted her ear in the direction of her door. She knew that Jennifer couldn't hear the same footsteps that she could.

Jennifer stared at her with inquisitiveness for a moment. "Is something wrong?"

"No. Just somebody coming, that's all."

Jennifer still looked baffled momentarily, but within seconds, the sound of someone climbing the front steps could be heard by both women.

Essie began walking to the door even before the knock could be delivered. "Well, good morning to you," she greeted.

"Good morning, Ms. Essie," Elaine said as she stood there dressed in a pair of shorts and a cropped tank top. She was holding the blanket that her husband had borrowed the day before in her hand.

"Come on in."

"No, thanks," Elaine said. "I'm headed for my morning jog. I just wanted to bring this back to you."

Essie took a step back and took a closer look at Elaine's outfit. "That's all the clothes you wear when you jog nowadays? You ain't scared something's gonna fall out?"

The same bluntness that Elaine found amusing and endearing on her first visit to Essie's house seemed to offend her this time around. "Well, the weather is warming up now. It's too warm for the jogging suit."

Essie saw a blindsided look in Elaine's eyes just as she attempted to explain her choice of garments. Not convinced, she said, "Chile, people in hell wear more clothes than that; and it don't get no hotter than hell. That right there is what my mama used to call a shall-I-go-naked outfit."

"A what?" Elaine continued to look insulted. She placed one hand on her hip and gave Ms. Essie the identical defiant stare she'd given Mason just a few days earlier. The *I-dare-you-to-try-and-explain-your-self* glare that she used to intimidate Mason didn't work at 216 Braxton Way.

"That's right," Essie said, not the least bit threatened. "It looks like you went to your closet, narrowed it down to three outfits and said, 'Shall I wear this, shall I wear this, or shall I just go naked?' And from the looks of things, the third choice won out."

"Well, I'll see you later," Elaine responded, clearly not in the mood to be lectured.

"Them streets ain't gonna get moved before you can get there." Essie pulled Elaine into her living room. "Come on in and join us."

"Ms. Essie, I can't—" Elaine's protest was ignored.

"Sure you can. This here is Jennifer," Essie said, pointing to the woman who still sat on her sofa. "She lives right here in our neighborhood. Have you met her?"

"Uh, no," Elaine said as Jennifer reached for her hand. "Nice to meet you."

"Same here." Jennifer smiled.

"Now, ain't that a shame? Two fine women like you living right 'round the corner from each other and ain't never met. Have a seat, sugar." Essie paid no attention to the look on Elaine's face. Instead, she made her way back to her chair and sat down, facing the two women. "Jennifer is having some problems with her teenager. We just over here discussing it; and you know what they say, the more the merrier."

"Well, since I don't have any children, I don't see how I can help," Elaine said, still obviously trying to get out so that she could get to her morning run.

"I ain't got none either," Essie reminded her. "So, maybe today is just a good day for you to stop running so much and talk a while. While we helping her, you might find some help for your own problem."

Elaine's body stiffened. "What problem?" she asked in a defensive tone. "I don't have a problem."

"All who believe that can stand on their eyelids," Essie said. "Now, God sent you by here this morning for a reason; just like he sent Jennifer. She got problems with Jerrod and you got problems in your marriage and ain't none of us here to point fingers. We gonna pray 'bout *all* of it."

Standing in defiance, Elaine shook her head. "Ms. Essie, I don't need to talk to some unknown, unproven being to get answers for anything. I have the power to determine my destiny. Besides, who told you that I was having problems in my marriage? I should have known something was going on when I saw Mason's car parked out front. Was he over here talking about me? I know he wasn't talking, with his no-staying-at-home, paying-more-attention-to-his-cars-than-his-wife, can't-pay-his-bills self. What did he say about me? I'm about tired of his—"

Essie snapped. "Hush your mouth, child!" She rarely raised her voice, even when she was scolding; but this time she did. "Now, you gonna watch your mouth up in this here house, you hear me? And you got the nerves to sit there and say you ain't got no problem! Oh, you got a problem whether you want to admit it or not. You a married woman and look at you . . . showing all your business in that half-naked outfit you got on. That boy ain't come over here to tell on you. He was parked out there 'cause that's where his car gave out on him. You just told on yourself, sugar."

With a clear look of embarrassment, both in her outburst and her outfit, Elaine eased back on the sofa and used the blanket that she still had in her hand to cover her partially exposed cleavage.

Jennifer looked on in silence and she remained quiet, almost seeming afraid to talk.

Essie was the only one standing now, and she wore a no-nonsense expression on her face. "Now, you listen and you listen good," Essie said, still looking at Elaine. "There are a lot of things in life that you might have to wonder about, but the good Lord ain't one of 'em. You gonna shape your mouth to say He's unknown? *I* know Him. Ain't I somebody?"

Elaine took on a child-like appearance as she sat with her head bowed. All of the open defiance that she'd displayed earlier had disappeared as she sat and took her reprimand from the woman she barely knew, but couldn't help but respect.

"And how you gonna say He's unproven? Ain't you breathing? You think you keeping yourself alive or something? Chile, 'til you know you ain't nothing without the Lord, you gonna always be in trouble. All this running up and down the street every morning ain't the answer. You gonna run yourself right into a mess that you can't get out of."

Elaine swallowed, but didn't move from her position.

"If you think you can do anything without God's help, sugar, you'd better think again. Ain't nothing gonna get straight 'til He straighten it, and that goes for both of you. It's all about timing, y'all." Essie paced the carpet in front of the two women like a preacher addressing her congregation. "If you want God to make time for you, you got to make time for Him. Now, I done lived a lot of years, and I done forgot more than y'all will ever know, but the one thing I ain't never forgot is how good God been to me every single day of my life."

"Well, He hasn't been all that good to me, Ms. Essie," Elaine blurted. "I'm in a loveless marriage with a man who don't give a—" She stopped and respectfully regrouped her thoughts. "A man who doesn't care anything about me at all. You had a man who you loved and he loved you back. I don't have that."

"What makes you think you ain't got that? I talked to your husband and I know he wants your marriage to work."

"He said that?" Elaine looked at Essie with hope in her eyes.

"He ain't had to say it. I saw it in his face and I heard it in his voice. Just like I can see and hear it in yours that you want the same thing. Marriage is both give and take, honey. And you got to treat each other like you want to be treated."

"But, I do treat—"

"You think about that before you say it," Essie said. "I ain't saying he no angel; but you reckon whatever it is you doing to him, you'd be all right with him doing it to you?"

Elaine's eyes returned to her lap.

"I just want both of y'all to think about what this old lady is saying, 'cause you ain't got but one husband, and Jennifer, you ain't got but one son. I done talked to both of them, and I know they love y'all. Sometimes people get off-track, and God knows ain't none of us perfect, but love ain't nothing to give up on."

"I'm not giving up on my son, Ms. Essie. I'm just not gonna put up with his foolishness. This is different than a husband-and-wife situation. I'm his mama and I make the calls. If he's stealing from me to pay for a drug habit, I'm putting him out for good."

"Ain't that the same *call* your parents made on you?" Essie said, silencing the room once more.

Jennifer stared at her as though it was a concept to which she'd never given consideration.

Essie could see the tears pooling in her eyes. "Don't you see that what you 'bout to do to that child is the same thing your mama and daddy did to you? You giving up on him and shutting him out. He ain't but fourteen, sugar. You remember how scared and lonely you was when you didn't have no place to go? You remember how bad you felt when you made a mistake and because of it, you was left all by yourself? You a grown woman now, and it still hurts, don't it? Is that what you want for Jerrod?"

With silent tears streaming down her face, Jennifer shook her head.

"It's gonna be all right 'cause we 'bout to take this to 'the man upstairs.' " Essie handed Jennifer a tissue from the box on the coffee table. "You got something against praying?" she asked, looking toward Elaine.

Elaine's response was slow. "I guess not. I'm just confused. I can't remember the last time I prayed for something."

Essie laid a hand on Elaine's shoulder. "What do you do in times like these, baby? Don't you know where your help come from?"

"Well, I've been listening to this motivational speaker who says that our Guardian Of Divinity is who we should seek when we need help."

"Our guardian of *what*?" Essie asked with a disturbed expression on her face.

"Guardian Of Divinity—*G-O-D*." Elaine spelled out the acronym. "She said we are our own GOD. We don't need to—"

"Honey, that ain't no *G-O-D*. That's the *D-E-V-I-L*," Essie injected. "You need to gather all them tapes and throw that mess out the door. That's why you running up and down the street like somebody who ain't got no sense. God is God and there ain't no substitute for Him. He's good even when times are bad, and all you got to be is humble enough to go to Him. All this turmoil that's going on in your home and inside of you is because you looking in all the wrong places for help. You understand what I'm saying?"

"I think so," Elaine said. "Maybe I—"

"Shhhhh."

Both women looked up at Essie as she held her finger to her lips and tilted her ear toward the door.

Jennifer had seen the pose before, and although she didn't hear anything, she knew that there must have been someone approaching.

Sure enough, the sounds of a slow pace climbing the front steps could be heard and Essie was already en route to the door. "Hey, baby. I was gonna call you today. How you?" Essie greeted.

Angel's only reply was a burst of tears as she fell into Essie's arms and wept.

Holding her close, Essie repeatedly smoothed her hands over the back of Angel's hair and whispered comforting words in her ear. "It's okay, baby," she said as she led her into the house. "Ms. Essie's here, now. It's okay."

The women on the sofa moved closer together to make room for the newest guest.

Essie helped lower Angel on to the sofa and Jennifer pulled out two of the Kleenex tissues and placed them in Angel's hand.

They waited for several minutes, none of them speaking another word until Angel had calmed, and the heavy flow of tears had slowed.

"I don't know what's wrong," Essie said, "but it don't matter none right now. Whatever it is, we gonna just lump it right on in with everything else we praying about. You came at just the right time. Me and these other nice ladies was just getting ready to go before the Lord, and I know that you know 'bout praying, right?"

Angel nodded and grabbed another tissue in the process.

"Now, all y'all stand with me, and we gonna hold hands. Y'all ain't got to say a word. Just let Ms. Essie do the talking. Me and Jesus been knowing each other for a long time."

# Chapter 14

## *Thursday Morning: 11:22 A.M.*

An eerie hush blanketed the generally noisy assembly of students who, in the middle of second period, had been directed to report to the gymnasium of Alpharetta High School. It was as if someone had hit the mute button and the entire room had been silenced.

There had been whispers, mostly among the girls, at the lockers and in the hallways throughout the early morning, but Jerrod was not able to figure out what was going on. It was clear that somebody had gotten word of something, but everybody seemed too afraid to discuss it out loud. Jerrod shrugged it off.

One thing about secrets between the girls of his school, he knew that somewhere between the first and last periods of the day, whatever it was always became common knowledge. Gossip wasn't abnormal, so there seemed to be no real reason for concern.

The day started out progressing as usual. On the way to his second-period class Jerrod high-fived and barked at one of the big dogs in passing. He got the notion that the celebration in his honor had gone well last night and couldn't wait to hear the details today when he gathered in the park with them. It would be his first meeting as the newest big dog, and he was excited.

But the words that their principal had just spoken had drained him of all his enthusiasm. For several moments, it seemed that not one of the fourteen hundred students made a sound. There was no coughing, no laughter, no whispers, no shifting of feet; nothing.

Jerrod clasped his hands together and locked them between his knees to try to stop the trembling that had become obvious. Just a few feet down on the bleacher where he sat was one of the puppies who had caroused with the big dogs last night. Jerrod was tempted to look at him for some sign of whether his thinking was accurate, but he didn't, for fear of what he might find out.

"As of an hour ago, the doctors still were not releasing any detailed information on Ms. Shepherd's condition," Mr. Wright, the principal announced over the microphone, breaking the silence. His expression was somber, as that of all the administrators who stood around him. "All we know right now as far as her medical condition is concerned is that she's comatose. According to her fiancé, as Ms. Shepherd slept, her house was broken into and ransacked. At some point during the horror, she was beaten, raped multiple times, and then beaten some more and sustained some serious head injuries in the process.

"We ask for your prayers, and that as her students,

you will be attentive and mindful to the substitute that will have to replace Ms. Shepherd until we can find out if . . . until we can find out *when* she will be able to return. Notes will be sent home with each of you to give to your parents concerning this tragedy. Please return to your classes in an orderly manner."

Even as the teenagers climbed from the highest point of the bleachers and descended to the gymnasium floor, noise was held to a minimum.

Jerrod joined in with the stream of children that headed for the exit door. He looked across the gymnasium at the senior class, and for a brief moment, he caught Freddie's eyes. In an instant, Jerrod's stomach seemed to curl up into a knot that tightened with every step that he made. Just the thought that Freddie and the other dogs might have done this to Ms. Shepherd as a part of celebrating his induction into the group was sickening. Jerrod wasn't sure what it was that he was expecting them to do, but he knew that this wasn't it.

Breaking away from the crowd and entering the nearest bathroom, Jerrod closed himself in one of the stalls and tried to take deep breaths to slow the rapid pounding in his chest. He turned and faced the commode, feeling ill to the point of nausea.

*Rape? Assault? It can't be. The Dobermans wouldn't do anything this big. They wouldn't put a teacher in a coma.*

Although the school didn't recognize the Dobermans or any other non-school affiliated group, almost everybody, the teachers included, knew that the gang existed. As long as no gang-related activity took place on school property, there was really nothing that the educators could do about it. No one had mentioned or even implied that what had happened to Ms. Shepherd had been caused by the troublemaking boys, but the unwavering ailing in Jerrod's belly made him wonder about the possibilities.

If he could just vomit, the sick feeling would ease, but as badly as he felt, there was no relief. Finally, he came out of the stall, avoiding the eyes of other students who had entered. He walked over to the sink and splashed his face with cold water to rinse away the perspiration that had gathered. The paper towels that he snatched from the roll soaked up the moisture, momentarily hiding his guilt from anyone who might be able to decipher it in his eyes.

The sounding of the bell meant that he was already late for his next class. Jerrod brushed past the other lagging students and walked out into the halls that were now almost empty. A hundred excuses to give Freddie so as not to make today's meeting flashed in his mind, but Jerrod knew that none of them was good enough. After today's assembly, it would be too obvious if he tried to duck out of the meeting, since he'd never missed one since the day he began pledging. Freddie would know something wasn't right.

Jerrod pushed the door open to his English class and walked toward his seat, trying hard not to look anyone in the face in the process. Being tardy for class was nothing new for Jerrod, but today it felt as if everyone's eyes were fixed on him. He slipped into his desk, opened his book and stared mindlessly into the pages. The churning in his stomach continued.

All while his teacher was talking, Jerrod was repeatedly playing the three-day-old conversation in his head. He remembered the moment of special interest that Freddie took in his mention that Ms. Shepherd had kept him after class that day, almost making him late for the meeting with the Dobermans. It seemed irrelevant then, but now . . .

"Mr. Mays, would you like to expand on what we've already said about complex-compound sentences?"

Jerrod heard his name called, but he never took his eyes off the open book in front of him. Mr. McNeil, a bearded man who looked like an oversized leprechaun, was his least favorite teacher of all. And unlike Ms. Shepherd, he seemed to bask in the thrill of singling him out for the purpose of making him the example. Ignoring Mr. McNeil had become Jerrod's new way of dealing with him. He'd learned early on that his English teacher was good with words, and it was hard to outtalk him or say anything that would draw a laugh from the class. Mr. McNeil was too smart for that. He always had a comeback, and most times, his vast knowledge of the English language gave him the upper hand in a word war.

"We're waiting, Mr. Mays," the teacher said.

The last time Mr. McNeil called him out like this Jerrod sat in silence, not as a way to ruffle his teacher's feathers, but because he genuinely couldn't think of anything to say to combat the big words that the teacher had thrown at him. What Jerrod came to realize that day was that Mr. McNeil despised being ignored, and today's disregard of him was done specifically for that reason.

"I'm talking to you, Mr. Mays!" Mr. McNeil snapped. "You walk in my class after the tardy bell, causing a break in the flow of my tutorial, and then you have the audacity to just sit and be noncompliant? If you think being condescending makes you look ingenious, you couldn't be more erroneous."

Perhaps as a high-school freshman, Jerrod should have known what all of those four-syllable words meant, but he didn't. Nonetheless, he was not going to open his mouth to speak and give Mr. McNeil the satisfaction of knowing of his ignorance. Instead, Jerrod brought his eyes up from his book and stared at the man, hoping that he was making Mr. McNeil just as uncomfortable as the teacher was making him.

His strategy worked. The overbearing teacher turned away and return to the lesson, leaving Jerrod free to sink back into a state of depression.

What Jerrod had hoped for was a free ticket to the principal's office. Last time he'd ignored Mr. McNeil, he had been sent to the office to "think about whether or not education was important" to him. Just sitting there in the chair across from the receptionist made the class period pass slowly, but it was better than having to listen to the fat ogre that he hated so much.

"I wish you were the one who had kept me after class that day." Jerrod whispered the words too softly for anyone to hear.

Closing his eyes, he let out a miserable sigh. He thought about what Essie told him the night he'd stayed with her. She'd warned him about false friends, but he didn't listen. He wanted to believe that the Dobermans were different. His father had never been a part of his life, and his mother couldn't understand him. The big dogs were the first people to give him a real chance, and they were the first to praise him when he did well.

Jerrod tried to convince himself that his thoughts

were wrong. Maybe what had happened to Ms. Shepherd had nothing to do with the Dobermans. Maybe it was just coincidental that the teacher that had been the one to keep him after class was the same one who'd been brutally attacked. Maybe it was all a mistake. But the only way Jerrod would be able to find out for certain was to stick it out and be at the meeting this afternoon.

For the last hour, Mason had been searching for anything that might give him a clue to how Elaine was really spending her days while he was at work. The day before, just ninety minutes after he'd left to head to work, he had to return home because he had forgotten his wallet and couldn't make his haul without it.

As he headed toward Braxton Park, he caught a glimpse of his wife talking to a man at the Goodyear shop. They were in the parking lot, standing far too close for Mason's comfort. He turned his car around and pulled into the lot across the street, hiding his cars among the others parked there. For twenty minutes, he watched the two of them chatting and laughing together as Elaine sipped on a bottle of water. She looked good, and the lavender jogging suit she wore hugged curves that, until that moment, Mason didn't even notice she had.

His focus on his wife's figure was interrupted when he saw the stranger take his finger and whisk a strand of Elaine's short hair from her face. The gesture was too intimate. At one point, they even embraced, and the hug lasted too long, sending the temperature rising on Mason's insides. It took every ounce of restraint he had not to pull from the lot and drive full speed ahead, running over the man who dared to put his arms around his wife.

When Elaine passed by Mason on her way out of the subdivision while he was pulling into it yesterday evening, he couldn't help but wonder where she was headed. It was nearly midnight by the time she returned home, and although he was wide-awake and inwardly fuming, he clenched his jaws and pretended to be asleep when she eased into the bed beside him. He could smell evidence of a fresh shower. Wherever Elaine had spent the past several hours, she had cleansed herself before coming home. It was another disturbing piece of the puzzle that was now beginning to make sense.

This morning, Mason had taken the day off, but he left the house as usual so that Elaine would think that he was working his normal schedule. He'd driven to the same parking lot and waited for his wife to come jogging down the street. But before he drove to his hideout, Mason had packed a loaded pistol in his glove compartment; and having served four years as a Marine and earning his pin for being a sharpshooter, he had no plans of missing his target.

Several times, the Goodyear employee had emerged from the garage and walked to the edge of the street. Mason stewed in anger, knowing that the man was looking for Elaine. That let Mason know that this wasn't a relationship that just began yesterday.

*"Elaine is just like the blood from that cut. As long as she ain't being tended to, she gonna keep right on running."* Essie's words rang in Mason's ears as he sat and waited for his wife to run up the street and into the arms of another man.

At one point he got fed up with seeing the man constantly stroll into the lot, anxiously looking for Elaine's arrival. He pulled the gun out and had a clear shot that would've placed a bullet right in the middle of the man's forehead, but more of Essie's words stopped him from pulling the trigger. *"As hard as life might be right now, it's gonna get a whole lot harder if you have to live your life without her. You know why? 'Cause you love her, that's why."*

Those were the words that held his finger in place. The old lady was right. He did love his wife, and he knew that if he carried out the premeditated assassination, he'd probably never see her again.

Mason knew that lately he hadn't been showing Elaine much affection. As much as he hated to admit it to himself, he was partially to blame for whatever was going on between Elaine and the greasy mechanic. He threw the gun back into the glove compartment, slammed his fist against his dashboard, and sped toward home.

He was surprised when he didn't find his wife still there, but he seized the opportunity to investigate. He went through the papers on her desk and the folders in her file drawers. Now, he was searching the files on her computer for any answers he could find. He didn't want to confront her until he had unmitigated proof. Somehow he had to find out for sure. Clicking on a file that had been minimized at the bottom of the screen, Mason's eyes scanned the contents of the page:

*Diana felt Paul's lips caressing her shoulder. She knew that what she was doing was wrong, but it felt so right. Paul had a way of making her forget all the sadness, loneliness, and anger that marriage had become. Steven* used to know how to touch her in all of those special places and ignite fires from every crevice of her body, but not anymore. He'd lost interest.

Now, Diana's husband had found other loves and other passions that didn't involve her. Now, the leather he caressed wasn't the fabric of her pants, but the fabric that covered the seats in his cars. Instead of bathing her body like he used to, he found smoothing a soapy cloth over the curves of his Miata more enticing.

"You are so beautiful, my Nubian queen." Paul's native tongue only accentuated his sex appeal.

It was hard to say no to a man who knew how to love her in ways she'd never been loved before. Her body ached to be loved, and Paul was the antidote that she needed. He was just about everything a girl could hope for. He was sexy, handsome, 6 foot 2, and 200 pounds of solid muscle, but when she looked into his eyes, Diana couldn't see a future, no matter how hard she tried.

She hated that she still loved Steven, a man who didn't love her in return. Why couldn't she love Paul? Why?

"I want you."

At his sensual words, Diana turned to face him, allowing his lips to cover hers. So what if she didn't love him? What good was love if it had to hurt anyway? Losing herself in Dante's passion, she pulled him closer.

"*Dante?*" Mason scowled as he saw the sudden name change in the story. He sank into her desk chair and stared at the page that he'd just read. There was more, but he'd read enough. *Could the name change be a simple error on her part? Am I reading more into this than there is?* "No," Mason whispered. He shook his head at the questions that had risen in his mind. "I ain't crazy. This isn't just a story. This is Elaine's story. This is *their* story."

A wave of mixed emotions engulfed him. His

breaths began to come quicker. He felt betrayed, angry, hurt, and guilty. How could she do this to him? After all they'd been through together, how could she?

"Okay, Mason," he told himself when he began to feel his body trembling, "you've got to get it together."

The pep talk failed.

As soon as the words left his lips, Mason stood up, picked up the computer, and slammed it onto the hardwood floor, sending glass and electrical sparks flying everywhere. The thick concrete walls of the house muted his distraught scream, and if they didn't, Mason wouldn't have cared.

"Nigga, you betta hope your name ain't Dante," he said as he headed toward the front door with his keys in his hand, " 'cause if it is, solid muscle or not, I'm 'bout to whip yo'—"

The slamming of the door saved the angel fish that swam in the large glass tank in the living room from hearing the less-than-angelic words that followed.

# Chapter 15

## *Thursday Afternoon: 2:20 P.M.*

Standing with his back resting against one of the pillars that upheld the roofing over his porch, Colin looked out at the beauty of spring. The outside temperature was almost perfect. Flowers and trees that decorated his yard and the yards of neighbors were covered with blossoms, buds, and brand-new greenery. His unbuttoned shirt gaped open at the sudden blast of wind that blew, exposing the firm definition genetically passed along to him by the men on his mother's side of the family.

Colin couldn't remember the last time he'd taken a day off from work. When he notified his secretary that he wouldn't be in the office today, she immediately became concerned. There were days that fifty-year-old Edna acted more like his mother than his administrative assistant, but she meant well, and Colin embraced the fact that she always had his best interest in mind.

"Are you sick, Mr. Stephens?" Edna asked. "Is there something I can do?"

"No, Edna, I'm not ill," Colin replied. "I just had some things come up and need a day to take care of them,"

"Is it the baby?" Edna's voice took on an excited tone. "Mrs. Stephens isn't going into labor, is she? If she is, you're gonna need more than a day. I told you before, I've been through what she's got to go through a half-dozen times, and those early days are something else! So, if your wife is about to give birth, you make sure you give her all the time she needs. I can handle things around here for a couple of days."

Colin struggled to maintain his composure as he assured Edna that Angel wasn't experiencing the onset of childbirth. He wished she was, though. Right now, he would settle for Angel feeling any signs of life, even if they came in the form of painful labor.

The knowledge that he'd indirectly caused the accident that may have fatally injured his unborn son haunted Colin again and again since he'd learned of Angel's fall. He'd gotten very little sleep the night before, and the small amount he did get was restless. Throughout the night, he kept having fleeting dreams that he couldn't clearly remember once he'd awaken, but Colin was sure that they had something to do with his baby. There seemed to be sadness in his dreams, but simultaneously, there was also some indication of joy. The images that appeared so vivid at the time were now just shadowy pictures held hostage in the back of his mind.

The neighborhood was quiet. He'd come out on the porch because the silence in his house was unbearable; now, the outdoors had greeted him the same way.

When Colin woke up this morning, the place on the bed where his wife generally lay was empty. The sun had barely come up. He got up and looked out the window of their living room and saw Angel sitting in the rocking chair on the porch, tearfully cradling her stomach. He wanted to say something, anything to make it better and to ease her fears, but he closed the blinds and crawled back into bed alone.

What would he say? Angel had barely spoken to him since admitting her adamant unwillingness to go to the doctor. She was scared, and although he would have loved to say just the right words to calm her fears, Colin was just as frightened as she.

For nearly two hours, he lay in the bed, staring at the ceiling, waiting for her to come back in the house. When she didn't return, he got up and again peered back through the blinds, but this time he saw no signs of his wife. The rocking chair that she'd been sitting in earlier was empty.

At first, Colin panicked. Angel was in a fragile state of mind, and he wasn't sure what she would do or where she would go. He got dressed and looked for her, even walking into the yards of neighboring houses, calling her name. A calming engulfed him when he walked to the end of the street and spotted Essie's house sitting on the corner of Braxton Way. The door was closed. He saw no signs of Angel, but somehow Colin knew that his wife was inside and was safe.

He could have approached and knocked on the door just to be certain, but he needed no assurance.

He knew she was with Essie and realized that what Angel needed more than anything from him was space. Although he wanted to walk up the stairs of the house and apologize to his wife one more time for his carelessness, Colin backed away and returned to his own home. That was more than four hours ago. He hoped Angel would have come back by now.

As nice as the afternoon breeze felt, Colin walked back in the house and stopped as he passed the door that led to the nursery that he'd just finished setting up two days ago. His hand moved in slow motion as it grabbed the knob and twisted. It was his first time going into the room since Austin stopped moving.

Nothing had changed, but for some strange reason, the room looked and felt different. The wooden crib was positioned against the back wall as it had always been. The walls had been painted in bold colors with images of alphabet blocks throughout. A varnished rocking chair sat near the cradle for those nights when they might need to rock their son back to sleep. The people at the church and on Colin's job had been just as generous as members of their families. The corner beside the baby's dresser was filled with gifts that had been presented to Angel during separate baby showers a month ago, and Austin's closet was already filled with clothing in different sizes, enough to dress him for a year.

Everything was set, and all that was left to do was to bring the baby home from the hospital. Just a few hours ago, all was perfect. Now, there were no certainties; just questions that both he and Angel were afraid to have answered.

With accumulated water clouding his vision, Colin

slowly lowered himself into the empty chair. He had prayed so much that he felt he was troubling God, but as he buried his face into his hands, he prayed again. Maybe it was too late. Maybe his son's fate was already sealed. In any case, Colin knew that the situation was far too big for both him and his wife. God was his only hope, and prayer was his only answer.

"Don't be scared to squeeze plenty of juice in that pitcher, now," Essie told Jennifer. "That's what makes my lemonade so good. It's got plenty of fresh lemon juice in it. That's right, squeeze it on in there."

Covered with the colorful knitted blanket spread over her, Angel lay across the sofa and listened to Essie give away all of her cooking and baking secrets to the women who accompanied her in the kitchen, as if they were her daughters. The whole house smelled delicious enough to dine on, but although Angel hadn't eaten anything that day, she was too concerned with other matters to feel her own hunger.

Earlier when they were standing and holding hands, Essie had prayed a prayer like none Angel had ever heard. She didn't get loud or overemotional like many of the church mothers sometimes did, but her words were heartfelt and genuine. Individually, Essie had called the names of the three women who stood with her and asked God to forgive their sins, heal their hearts, renew their faiths, and strengthen their minds. By the time she was done, there wasn't a dry eye in the living room. Even Essie was shedding tears when they all embraced afterward. God had indeed stopped by the house that sat on the corner of Braxton Way.

The prayer was just what Angel needed, but now her fears were resurfacing. She couldn't help being concerned about what she felt, or more specifically, what she didn't feel. Not since her third month of pregnancy had she gone a full day without feeling her child move inside of her. Angel wanted to tell Essie about her situation, but everyone else felt so much better and had been in such good spirits after the prayer that she didn't want to risk bringing them down. Angel thought she'd just wait until Jennifer and Elaine left to talk to Essie, but they never did.

Chatting like old friends who had known each other for years, the women were excited when Essie asked them if they'd like to help her finish dinner and bake her cake. Angel already had the recipe. Essie had showed her how to master the art of the cream cheese pound cake when Angel was still a teenager. It was one of Colin's favorites. She knew most of Essie's other special recipes too. Essie had taught her more about the kitchen than her own mother.

"You want to taste a little of this macaroni?" Jennifer asked, interrupting Angel's thoughts, as she walked from the kitchen into the living room.

It was the first time that Angel gave attention to the fact that she was hungry, and the fork in Jennifer's hand with the cheesy mixture attached to the end looked mouthwatering.

"You know you're eating for two," Jennifer reminded her. "You've got to feed that baby."

Just that quickly, Angel's hunger was pushed aside and forgotten again. She swallowed back the tears that seemed to well up in her throat. *Eating for two*. She hoped that Jennifer was right, but with the passing of each motionless minute, Angel's faith was fading. "No thanks," she replied. "Not right now." She quickly wiped away the onset of a teardrop when Jennifer turned and walked back into the kitchen.

Earlier, when Essie had walked in, Angel knew that she could see the sadness that lingered in her eyes. She could fool Jennifer and Elaine, but she was well aware that she couldn't so easily fool her grandmother's best friend. When Essie asked her what was the matter, she responded by saying that she was just tired because she was unable to sleep all night.

It wasn't a total lie. Angel had, in fact, been awake most of the night. Although there was no dialogue between them, she knew that Colin was awake much of the time as well. When he did doze off, he tossed and groaned constantly. She knew that guilt over the entire situation was torturing him, and last night she wanted *him* to suffer. Angel had been so outdone with the avoidable accident and the possible results that she wanted Colin to be in torment. She kept telling herself that she shouldn't have to bear the physical or the mental pain alone. His carelessness had left her bruised and sore and possibly killed their child. Last night, she was hurt and angry, and it brought her a misplaced sense of satisfaction to know that he was hurting too.

Today, even though she still felt miserable about what happened, she was no longer angry. Her heart went out to Colin. It was an accident. Just an unfortunate mishap. She understood that her husband would never do anything intentionally to harm her or their unborn son. Angel knew that they meant everything to Colin, and the last thing he needed from her was to be blamed.

"I ain't had this much life in my house in a long time," Essie exclaimed as she entered the living room, stirring something in a bowl that she held in her hand.

Angel smiled. She could tell that having the women in her home made Essie feel good.

Instead of taking her seat in her chair as normal, Essie made her way to Angel, smoothed out the blanket she'd thrown over her earlier, and then sat on the edge of the sofa where Angel lay. "I brought you some grits." She handed Angel the bowl. "You need to put something on that empty stomach of yours."

How Essie knew her stomach was empty, Angel didn't know. She'd stopped asking most questions a long time ago. Essie always had what almost appeared to be a sixth sense. Angel's grandmother used to tell her that Essie had a private line that connected her to Heaven and that God told her things He didn't tell anyone else. As farfetched as it sounded, Angel believed it. She took the bowl and thanked Essie for bringing it to her.

"Oh, you welcome, honey. Now, you ready to tell me what brought you to my house today?"

"Ms. Essie, you act like I don't ever come over," Angel said, still trying to hide her true feelings. "I was supposed to come by yesterday. Did you notice that I missed my Wednesday visit with you?"

"Chile, when you get as old as I am and you don't get much company as it is, believe me, you know when somebody skips a visit. I had already planned to give you a call to see where you were."

"Well, here I am." Angel blew on the spoonful of grits she had scooped up and forced a smile that she hoped looked genuine.

Essie shifted her position on the sofa, straightening out her smock in the process.

For a moment, Angel thought that she'd successfully avoided having to go into detail about the goings on in her life. But when Essie stopped bouncing on the edge of the couch, she looked back at Angel again. No words were spoken, but Angel knew that she wasn't going to win this battle.

When silent tears began draining from Angel's eyes, Essie took the bowl from her hands and replaced it with several sheets of tissue that she retrieved out of the box beside her.

On several occasions, Angel tried to speak, but the tears choked back her words.

Essie never rushed her. Instead, she sat quietly and rubbed her aging hand over Angel's knee in comfort.

"We were going to name him after Mr. Ben," Angel whispered, wiping away fresh tears.

Her words brought an end to the motions of Essie's hand. "What you say?"

"Austin Benjamin Stephens," Angel said. "That was the name that Colin and I agreed on for the baby."

Essie seemed pleasantly surprised by the tribute to her deceased husband. "Why you talking in the past tense? Did you change your mind 'bout what you gonna name him?"

With the threat of another spill of tears, all Angel could do was shake her head in a negative response.

Removing the blanket that covered Angel's stomach, Essie placed both of her hands on the roundest point of Angel's belly and slowly moved them around.

Angel knew she didn't have to say anything further. Essie had already figured out where the conversation was headed.

"How long it been since you felt him move?"

By the time Essie asked the question, they had captured the attention of both Jennifer and Elaine. The concerned women walked out of the kitchen and stood back in the distance, watching while Essie's hands explored for signs of life. Her movements were slow; almost like that of a blind woman reading braille.

"I fell yesterday morning," Angel answered through tearful gasps. "I felt him move before the fall, and I think I felt him move shortly after the fall; but that was it. Ms. Essie, I'm so scared."

"Of course, you are, baby. Who wouldn't be? Did you tell Colin?"

Angel nodded. "He knows. I think he may have taken the day off from work today. He was still at the house when I left this morning."

"What you mean, you *think* he took the day off?"

It pained Angel to admit that she hadn't spoken to her husband. She knew Essie didn't believe in the silent treatment or any other action that put distance between married couples. Before Essie could scold her for her behavior, Angel told her about the circumstances that led to her slip and fall. She hoped that knowing about Colin's failure to clean behind himself would help Essie understand why she'd been angry with him, but it didn't.

"You don't think what might have happened to the baby was punishment enough?" Essie asked. "It must feel like he's walking around with a knife stuck in his chest to know that he was the reason you fell. And you being mad at him is like you pulled out the knife just so you could pour salt or alcohol in the open wound."

Angel nodded. She knew that Essie was right. "I was just so upset," she whispered.

"I ain't never seen that boy treat you like nothing less than a queen, Angel. The way he loves you reminds me of the way my Ben loved me. It's that kind of love that wakes you up at odd times of the night just so you can make sure you ain't been dreaming that you got somebody so wonderful laying beside you. Yeah, he should have cleaned up the water, but everybody got the right to make a mistake now and then. Colin can't be perfect all the time, baby."

Elaine approached cautiously and knelt beside the sofa. "Angel, I don't know much about you and your husband, but from what I'm hearing, he sounds like a great guy."

"He is," Angel said.

"Well, believe me when I tell you that there are women who wish their husbands treated them like queens. I'd even settle for being treated like a princess." Elaine paused for a moment, realizing that she'd just totally exposed the unspoken troubles of her marriage. "All I'm saying is, I hope to God that you're wrong about the baby. I hope he's okay. But if he's not, at least you're not alone. You'll still have a man who loves you, and his love isn't based on whether or not you can give him a baby." Elaine's voice broke at the end of her sentence.

Angel could see that childbearing was a tender subject for her.

Essie reached over and gave Elaine a supportive pat on the back. "Neither is yours, sugar. Some men know how to talk about what's going on inside of them, and some don't. Angel happens to have one of them husbands who can express his feelings most of the time. Mason might not be like that, so he shows his some other kind of way. What y'all need to do is to go back and find what it was that drew you to each other in the first place.

"Me and Ben wasn't together that long, so our love never had a chance to grow old. I'd like to think that our love wouldn't have ever changed, but only the good Lord knows that for sure. But the thing that keeps me loving him so much all these years later is the memories. He wrote me letters that I still read to remind me of who he was and how much he loved me. I got one that I read every single night before I go to bed.

"If I don't remember, then I'll forget, and that goes for all of us. Time has a way of doing that to people, but there's a way to make time work in your favor. Go back and remind yourselves of what Mason and Jerrod, and even Colin, were like before their hearts got hurt. If you can come out of your present, go back to your past and define the moment that things went wrong, with the help of the man upstairs, you can change your whole future."

The three women looked at Essie in thoughtful silence. Angel didn't know if the others got the same message, but she knew that each of them learned a lesson from the shared wisdom.

"Now, here's what we're gonna do." Essie stood from the sofa and picked up the bowl of half-eaten grits that had now gotten stiff. "We gonna shut down all this cooking and take care of more important business. Let's go pick up Colin and get you to the doctor so y'all can hear it from a professional that li'l Austin Benjamin is all right."

Just hearing the words come from Essie's mouth made Angel feel better. A kick, a squirm, a shift, any type of movement in her stomach would give her the extra assurance that she needed, but for now, Essie's confident words, and the prayer that she'd prayed with her new friends earlier, were all Angel had to hold on to.

# Chapter 16

## *Thursday Evening: 7:00 P.M.*

It was the same couch that had made him feel superior over the past few weeks. Being invited to Freddie's bachelor's pad and given permission to lounge on his sofa with him had meant something to Jerrod ever since he began pledging to be a part of the gang that would give him the confidence that he'd been lacking all of his life. This was the fourth time he'd been allowed in the top dog's house, but it was the first time Jerrod was there out of obligation and not desire.

Jerrod had told Freddie that he didn't feel well when they'd first convened in the park for their after-school meeting. So, when the official celebratory announcement was made that the big dogs, along with three of the puppies, had beaten and gang-raped Ms. Shepherd, nobody made the connection when the vomit boiling in Jerrod's stomach suddenly released itself in the dirt beneath his feet. He had reached the coveted big dog status now, so Jerrod could do no wrong in the eyes of his gang brothers. They didn't even cringe when the food he'd nibbled on during lunch reappeared, and as a punishment to the puppies who reacted unfavorably to Jerrod's illness, Freddie made them use their hands to scoop mounds of sand and cover the mess until no signs of it could be seen.

Being recognized as a big dog had its advantages. Jerrod no longer had to run the two-mile distance between the school and the park to avoid being late. Now, he could ride in the car with Freddie and the others, and wait for those that were still in puppy status to arrive on foot.

For a nineteen-year-old without a job, Freddie seemed to have quite a bit. His car was an early-model Honda, but it ran well, had a brand-new paint job, and sported wheels with rims that continued to spin long after the car stopped. Even his apartment, though small, was well furnished. The flat-screen television alone must have cost a fortune. With the new decreased respect that he had for the group that he once idolized, Jerrod wondered what Freddie did to afford his lifestyle. It was something he'd never even considered before, but he had a sinking feeling that whatever it was had illegal ties.

"You feeling a'ight, J?" Freddie put his arm around Jerrod and gave him a supportive pat on the back. "You mighty quiet."

"Yeah." Jerrod nodded. "I'm doing better."

Unconsciously, he squirmed a little in his seat. The brotherly touches of approval that Freddie gave had always made Jerrod feel special and accepted. Now, knowing what Freddie had done, being honored by the top dog made Jerrod feel like he was just as guilty as the others who had carried out the crime.

The whole reason Jerrod had joined this group was to prove that he wasn't the "punk" that his mother's cruel boyfriend labeled him. All of his life, he'd felt inferior, and acting tough was the only way he knew to hide his low self-esteem. Jerrod knew that becoming a big dog was one sure means of making the school kids respect him. Never in a million years did he consider the fact that Freddie and the other wannabe hoodlums were any more than just a tough act. Now the petty crimes and pranks that they pulled off in the past weeks had been nothing in comparison to what happened last night.

Now, instead of being afraid of what any of the other boys at school might do to him, Jerrod sat on Freddie's couch fearing what his own gang leader would do to him if he picked up on any trace of the thoughts in Jerrod's head. Jerrod wanted nothing more than to bow out and say he'd changed his mind about wanting to be a Doberman, but his heart pounded at the thought of what would happen to him if he did.

"You ain't said much about how we took care of Ms. Shepherd for you, dog," Freddie pointed out. "Did we do good or what?"

Tears burned in the back of Jerrod's eyes when he was forced, once again, to think about the horror and terror that his favorite teacher must have gone through. Ms. Shepherd had never done anything to hurt anybody. All the girls loved her, and all the boys admired her. She was always kind to her students, and sometimes she'd take the smallest of things and find a way to turn it into a learning experience for her students.

"I'm a little bit of all of you," she once said when her nationality was brought into question by one of the flirtatious boys that shared the class with Jerrod. "My father's parents are white and Creole, my mother's parents are Asian and African-American. I don't call myself any one of those things because I am *all* of those things. I am a woman of color."

"Did we do good or what?" Freddie repeated, snapping Jerrod from his stroll down memory lane.

"Yeah, man," Jerrod said in the most genuine voice that he could. "Y'all did real good."

"For sho'," Freddie said, proud of himself. "Ms. Shepherd's pretty hot, you know. I been wanting to hit that anyway. I guess I ought to be thanking you for giving me a reason."

Without warning, Jerrod jumped from the sofa and barely made it into Freddie's bathroom in time before his body began purging itself again. This time, the vomiting session was painful and rendered him almost too weak to stand. He sank onto his knees and held on to the sides of the commode for added support.

It was several minutes before he emerged and rejoined the others in the living room, but when he did, Jerrod heard Freddie continuing to use him as an example to the puppies who were struggling to make it to big dog status.

"See, that's why J ain't Puppy J no more," Freddie was telling them. "Y'all niggas see how sick he is? J ain't never let nothing or nobody stop him from being where he had to be and doing what he had to do. I'm gonna have to make him go home so that the rest of us don't catch that bug, but if I don't make him go, he'll be right here hanging with us. That's what you call dedication, mutts. J is a natural born leader, and by the time he's my age, he's gonna be doing even bigger and badder things than me. Watch what I say."

*"By the time he's my age, he's gonna be doing even bigger and badder things than me."* The words hit Jerrod like a ten-pound block of concrete.

When Freddie saw him standing there and suggested that Jerrod let him take him home, Jerrod jumped at the chance. Unlike the other times when Freddie or one of the other big dogs had driven him to the mouth of the Braxton Park subdivision, today's ride was quiet.

"Feel better, dog," Freddie said, pounding Jerrod's fist with his before letting him out at the corner. "See you tomorrow."

"For sho'," Jerrod mumbled.

It wasn't until he knew for certain that Freddie's car was out of sight that Jerrod sank onto the sidewalk and leaned his back against the fencing and cried freely.

For well over an hour, Elaine had been lying across her bed, trying to figure out how her life had gotten into such chaos and what she could do to make things better. When Colin and Angel brought her home after the hospital visit and she saw all three of Mason's vehicles parked in the garage and driveway, she had mixed emotions. In one sense, she felt it was good that he was home. That way, she could just lay all the cards on the table and whatever happened would happen. On the other hand, she felt overwhelmed and wished for some time to get herself mentally prepared before confronting Mason on their troubled marriage.

When Elaine found that he wasn't home, there was a sense of relief. She really did need time to get a game plan together. She couldn't just come out and blab about her illicit affair. Maybe the first thing for her to do would be to contact Dante and tell him that she couldn't see him anymore. She had picked up the phone and rehearsed everything she would say.

"Listen, Dante," Elaine said, holding the phone to her ear as if he was actually on the other end of the line. "I made a mistake. I never should have come to your house that day, and I never should have allowed myself to get involved with you. I just want you to know that I'm not blaming you for any of this. All of it is my fault. I fully accept that, but now I have to do what I have to do to straighten out this mess that I've gotten myself into. I promise that I won't give him your name, but I have to come clean with Mason. I just wanted you to know that I can't see you anymore. I just can't. I know I said some pretty bad stuff to you about my husband and my marriage, but the truth is, I love Mason and I want to give it one more try."

The whole spiel sounded acceptable to her, and since making the fictitious call an hour ago, she'd picked up the phone and dialed Dante's cell number three times, but only got his voicemail. Elaine wanted to put things to rest with Dante before her husband got home, but she didn't want to leave a message that the wrong person might have access to. It was just too dangerous. All of the events surrounding the double life that she had been living for the past four or five days had been dangerous.

*"You reckon whatever it is you doing to him, you'd be all right with him doing it to you?"* Essie's words posed

to her early this morning had been repeating themselves in her ears throughout the day. Even while she was cooking and enjoying the company of her neighbors, the words would resurface on occasion, forcing Elaine to face a reality that she didn't want to. She knew she would be beyond distraught if she found out that Mason was meeting another woman during odd hours of the day and night and giving himself to her.

Then she remembered Essie saying, *"If you can come out of your present, go back to your past and define the moment that things went wrong, with the help of the man upstairs, you can change your whole future."*

The bitter truth was, things had been dire in their relationship so long that Elaine couldn't begin to know where to start. The motivational tapes that she had been listening to for months told her not to ever look back. All she had to do was find the Guardian Of Divinity within herself and it would give her all she needed to move forward.

*"You need to gather all them tapes and throw that mess out the door."*

Elaine took a quick look around. That time, the voice was so clear that it seemed like Essie was right there in the room with her. The complete set of ten CDs had been kept on the shelf in Elaine's closet ever since she received the mail order delivery. The thought of how much money she'd spent on them made Elaine think twice, but she walked into the closet anyway and began reaching toward the far corner where she'd stashed the package.

As she tugged, another box fell from the shelf, scattering memories that she hadn't looked at in years. Elaine stared at the items for a moment and then sat on the floor of the closet and began gathering them. The colorful souvenirs that had been used to decorate the tables of the building where her wedding reception had been held were still in good condition after being stored away for more than seven years. Red ribbons that kept the napkins folded, silver sprinkles that caught the light of the candles and made each table look as though it was covered in diamonds, white matchbooks and place cards that guests could take home in remembrance of the happy occasion . . .

Elaine smiled as she thought about that day. She and Mason were married in one of the best-known churches in Dallas, Texas. They only lived there a year as a married couple before Mason lost his job and was offered a position in Atlanta, if they were willing to make the move. They talked about it and agreed to accept. For Mason, it was a chance to get out of the hole that being unemployed for three months had begun putting him and his family in. For Elaine, it was a chance to get away from her nagging mother-in-law and the rest of Mason's family. Moving and getting a new start seemed like the perfect idea at the time, but somewhere along the way, things spiraled downward and they never recovered.

Elaine shook her head in sadness and continued to sort through the items and put them back in the box where they had been. A few loose photos that had never been placed in their memory album were tucked in the box as well. She and Mason looked so happy then, and it wasn't just a show for the cameras. They *were* happy. Then came the multiple miscarriages, the long work hours and Mason's fascination with cars. Nothing had been the same since.

Picking up a folded sheet of paper that had al-

most escaped her eyes, Elaine opened it and immediately recalled it as the vows that Mason had written and recited to her at the altar on their special
day. At the top of the paper were written the simple
words, "I Do". Mason had never claimed to be a
poet, and his heartfelt tribute to her was the first
time he'd ever written a poem. That day, Elaine remembered it sounding like the best verse of poetry
she'd ever heard. Even now, when she read the senti-
ments for the first time in years, the rhythmic words
brought a flood of tears to her eyes.

*I'm so excited I don't know what to do*
*Just the mere thought that I'll be spending the rest of*
*my life with you.*
*This is the second greatest day of my life*
*Because we both know the greatest day was the day we*
*gave our lives to Christ.*
*Yes, right now my palms are sweaty and my knees are*
*shaking*
*But no matter how nervous I am this is our day in the*
*making.*
*I get to show and tell this world just how I feel about you*
*And yes, all the other times I say I love you; today it*
*comes in the form of "I Do".*
*I Do means I will always be by your side*
*I Do means I wear my wedding band with pride.*
*I Do means your tears are now my own*
*I Do means for you, I can't wait to get home.*
*I Do means now there are some things that I don't*
*I Do means next to God, you have everything I want.*
*So, today with my whole heart and the greatest of pride*
*I say these vows*
*And they hold the same value if we're standing together*
*or separated by miles.*

*They mean the same if we're low in finances or rolling*
*in wealth*
*They mean the same thing if you're feeling okay or hav-*
*ing problems with your health.*
*There are so many other things I Do means, but we both*
*know to put those words into action is the most impor-*
*tant part.*
*Now, it's my job to see how much happiness to you I can*
*bring.*
*So, starting this second, next to God, you are the most*
*important person to me*
*And because I gave God my soul; to my heart, you hold*
*the key.*

"Oh my God," Elaine gasped, using her arm to wipe moisture from her face. "That's it!" It all became clear to her in a way she'd never even imagined or considered. All this time she'd blamed her failed pregnancies, Mason's coldness toward her, and their constant fighting for the downfall of their once-happy marriage. It wasn't that at all. All of those things had just been results of the real issue. Essie was right. Nothing would be solved until the real issue was faced, and the truth of the matter was their marriage had begun to decline almost immediately after they moved to Atlanta.

But the relocation wasn't the problem either. The issue lay in what happened after they moved. In Dallas, Elaine and Mason were faithful worshipers at their church, often praying together as a couple even in their home. Both of them had been exposed to right, but somewhere along the way, they'd chosen to do wrong.

Elaine had looked into Mason's eyes as he recited his vows on their wedding day and she knew that he meant every word of them. But there was no way he could keep them when they both had drifted so far away from the foundation their marriage had been built on.

Gradually, they'd allowed work to take precedence over family. Mason had become too busy for church, and Elaine had allowed some motivational speaker that she'd never even met lead her to replace God with the G-O-D within herself. No wonder they had forgotten their vows. No wonder their lives were in such shambles.

Elaine scampered around the room, searching for her keys. Since Dante wasn't answering his telephone, she would have to make an impromptu visit to his home. Ending her affair with him couldn't wait another moment, and as awkward as it might be, giving him the axe was going to be the easy part.

The hard part would be facing the music with Mason, but she had to tell him the truth. He was a proud man, and she could only hope that he would be able to forgive her.

"Where are my keys?" she asked aloud. Remembering that the last place she'd seen them was on her computer desk, Elaine dashed out of the room and took the short trip down the hallway. She simply had to get to Dante and back home before Mason returned from wherever he'd gone. She needed to get home ahead of him so that she could set the stage for her apology.

"Oh, my—"

The shattered computer brought Elaine to a standstill. The hardwood floor of her office was covered in glass. Her first instinct was to think that their house had been burglarized, but the picture before her made no sense. Why would someone break into their house, steal none of their valuables, and destroy her computer? Taking slow steps, she walked across the glass and turned the power off on the surge protector her computer was plugged into.

"What happened here?" she whispered, seeing her file drawers open and important papers scattered.

"I did it."

Startled by the voice that sneaked up behind her, Elaine let out a yelp and turned to face her husband. Mason stood in the doorway wearing a torn shirt, dirty jeans, and a large bandage above his eye. Elaine was almost sure those were stitches that she saw peering from under the bandage, and she was even surer that those were tears that suddenly glossed his eyes as he stared directly at her. "Mason, wha . . ." She stepped closer to touch him.

He immediately stepped away and one single stream fell down each of his cheeks. "How could you?" he whispered.

Elaine immediately knew that he had found out about her transgressions. She wanted to say something, but in all honesty, there was nothing she could say in her own defense.

"How *could* you?"

# Chapter 17

### *Thursday Night: 10:18 P.M.*

**"M**aybe we shouldn't."

Those were the words that Colin had whispered over an hour ago when Angel began caressing him in ways that made her desires unmistakable. It wasn't that he didn't want to, but Colin was fearful. The doctor had delivered the words that Essie had already predicted—The baby was fine. Austin had settled in Angel's birth canal, he'd said, and because of it, the infant didn't have the freedom to move as before.

Colin was overjoyed when the sounds of his child's heartbeat radiated throughout the office during the unscheduled checkup. The ultrasound that followed verified the doctor's suspicions that Angel's body was getting prepared for labor and delivery. When Colin conveyed the news to the women in the lobby who awaited an update, Essie, Jennifer, and Elaine celebrated as if the pregnancy were their own. Knowing that their baby wasn't injured or dead brought Colin overwhelming relief, but it was what the doctor said after Angel's pelvic examination that heightened his apprehension about physical intimacy. That, and the memories of the day before.

"Mrs. Stephens, you have already begun dilating. You're at two centimeters." The doctor removed the latex gloves from his hands. "We're looking at the possibility of you having your new addition anywhere within the next ten days."

"But I'm not due for another month," Angel responded, her voice saturated with concern.

"Well, the fall didn't cause any physical harm to your son, but it's possible that it may have contributed to his premature movement into the birth canal. The upside to this is that his being born a little early isn't reason for worry. You didn't know this, but on your last visit, I made a note in your chart that we might need to schedule you for a cesarean. From the looks of things, if we were to wait until your due date, there was a good chance that your baby would have been quite large, perhaps too large to take a chance on you, as a first time mother, delivering naturally. If he comes within the next week or so, you should be fine with the vaginal delivery that you prefer."

Colin and Angel left the hospital thanking God for answered prayers and apologizing to each other for the inconsiderate things that were done, said, and even thought, throughout the ordeal

As they prepared for bed and Angel exited the bathroom, still wet from her fresh shower, Colin watched and admired her. She carefully dried herself before dropping the towel to the floor and proceeding to moisturize her skin with the fragrant lotion that he loved to smell against her flesh. Her silhouette was magical, and although he had seen her hundreds of times before, tonight he saw her differently. Angel wasn't just his wife anymore; she was also the mother of his child. An appreciation for that hit him in a way that it never did before.

Angel turned and caught him staring as he sat on the side of the bed. Colin teased her with his eyes, and she returned the favor by flashing him a shy, but approving smile. When he beckoned for her, she approached, but not before picking up the remote and activating their stereo system. Maxwell's "Whenever, Wherever, Whatever" began to play, and the lyrics were almost as stimulating as the kisses that Angel placed near Colin's ear.

It had only been a couple of days since they'd made love, but it felt like forever.

Colin succumbed to her demands as she pushed him back onto the mattress and his nostrils soaked in the smell of the ointment that she had used just moments earlier. He endured the sensual agony of her soft, playful kisses for as long as he could, and then Colin firmly gripped the back of her neck with his hands and held her lips to his, releasing repressed passions that she had ignited.

As they lay wrapped in one another's embrace, Colin shifted his position, and in the process, his knee bumped the base of his wife's stomach. "I'm sorry," he said, reaching for her abdomen. "Are you okay?"

"I'm fine, Colin. It's okay; really," Angel responded just before delivering a kiss to his lips.

"Wait," Colin whispered as he pulled away. "Maybe we shouldn't." Thoughts of the scare they'd just had sparked more fears. They had dodged a frightening bullet once. As much as Colin wanted to be with his wife, as much as he knew she wanted to be with him, it wasn't worth the gamble. Not tonight anyway. There was no rush. This bedroom was their heaven, and he had his personal angel. They had a lifetime to make love under the moonlight, go to sleep, wake up and start all over again at the rising of the sun.

Colin ran his fingers through her thick, wavy hair and watched the strands fall against the side of her face. Angel was disappointed, but she understood just like Colin knew she would.

They lay in each other's arms, caressing one another, listening to their favorite music and talking about their exciting future for an hour before Angel drifted off to sleep.

Last night's sleep deprivation began to take its toll, and Colin's eyelids began to feel as though they were being forced closed by some invisible power. Just as he was giving up the fight to stay awake, he felt a nudge against his thigh. His eyes flew open and he looked at Angel's stomach, which was resting against his leg. Of all the movements he'd felt from his son over the last five or six months, that one meant the most of all.

Essie looked at the clock as she walked out of the kitchen after finally putting away all of her dishes. It was ten-thirty, ninety minutes past her bedtime. This week had been one for the record books. She'd gotten less sleep than she'd been accustomed to, but felt more energized and more fulfilled than she had for a long time. Putting the last of those dishes away reminded her of the time she'd spent with her neighbors today. Sharing all of her cooking secrets with them felt good, and seeing them all smiling, talking, and laughing together was a welcome change from the quietness that generally reigned in her house. The time had gone by at a rapid pace, and it wasn't until everyone had gone their separate ways that Essie realized that Jennifer, Elaine, and Angel had practically spent the entire day with her.

But as wonderful as those hours made Essie feel, nothing could top the magnificence of the moment Colin walked into the waiting area of the doctor's office and announced that his and Angel's baby was fine. Essie knew he would be, but hearing it was as much of a relief to her as she knew it was to them.

She picked up the woven pink-and-blue blanket and admired it for a moment before folding it and placing it in the middle of the sofa. Sounds from the outside caught her ear, and she stood motionless, hearing footsteps crossing from the pavement into the grassy area in front of her house. Those were Jerrod's footsteps, and just as he had done for the past three nights, he was once again getting home before the curfew his mother had set in place. Essie was glad that he was doing better, but in her mind, a fourteen-year-old boy needed to be inside well before eleven o'clock.

A peculiar quietness made her pay even closer attention. She had heard his approaching steps, but Essie never heard him walk up his front porch or let himself in the house. It wasn't like Jerrod to linger on the outside. She walked to her front window and used her finger to make a small division in the closed blinds. In the lighting provided by the lamp over her door, she could see the boy sitting on the bottom step of her porch. Essie watched for a few minutes, waiting to see if he was just taking a rest, but when Jerrod wrapped his arms around his knees and hung his head, she knew something was wrong.

"Hey, sugar," she said as she walked out onto the porch and stood. "What you doing out here in the dark all by yourself?"

"Waiting for you," Jerrod said, lifting his head.

"Sho' 'nuff?"

"Uh-huh. I knew you'd come out if I just sat here for a minute."

Essie chuckled and then sat in her usual rocking chair near the door.

"How do you do that, Ms. Essie?" Jerrod stood and walked up the steps to sit on the floor of the porch by her feet. "How do you hear stuff that don't nobody else hear and know stuff that don't nobody else know?"

"It's a gift from God," she answered. "But the good Lord don't tell me everything. Some things I need to be told just like everybody else."

"Like what?"

"Like, why you sitting out here in the dark waiting for me?"

Jerrod turned and looked away, staring into the empty street that ran in front of the houses on Braxton Way.

Essie waited patiently. She knew he'd talk when he was ready.

"If I tell you something, do you promise not to tell my mom?" Jerrod finally asked.

"I can't make that promise, baby. Your mama might need to know, and if she needs to know, I would hope that you would tell her yourself."

Jerrod shook his head and then turned his eyes back to the street. "She won't understand. She'll just start yelling at me and stuff, and I just don't want to hear all that right now."

"I'll tell you what," Essie said. "What if I promise you that I won't let her yell at you? Would you tell me then?"

"How're you gonna promise something like that? When my mom gets mad, she yells and can't nobody stop her. She don't listen to nobody; she just yells."

Essie reached down and patted Jerrod on the head. "Why don't we try it and see. You tell me what's on your mind, and I'll keep my promise."

"I'm in trouble, Ms. Essie," he said after a momentary silence. "I'm in trouble, and I don't know what to do."

"What kind of trouble you in?"

"I joined this gang at school and I thought they were cool and all, but today our principal gave the whole school a note to give to our parents. One of our teachers got hurt real bad last night, and I just found out today that the boys in my gang did it."

"You know that for sho'?"

Jerrod nodded. "They told me."

"Did you report it?"

"Ms Essie, it's a gang. You just don't rat on a gang. They'd kill me if I went and told on them. Plus, I'm scared that I'm gonna get in trouble too if it ever gets out that the Dobermans did it."

"The Dobermans? Baby, why would you want to be in a group that's named after a dog?"

Jerrod shrugged. "It's just a name."

"Umph." Essie grunted, deciding not to press the issue. "So tell me this: Why would you be in trouble if you didn't take part in what was done?"

" 'Cause they did it for me," Jerrod said. "They

raped and beat Ms. Shepherd because she kept me after class on Monday."

"Raped?" Essie stopped the rocking motion of her chair and sat up straight in her seat. "Them boys raped a teacher? Lord have mercy. Didn't I tell you just the other day that people ain't your friends if they doing things to get you in trouble?"

"I didn't know they would do something like that."

"But you knew they had you stealing from your mama."

Jerrod looked up at Essie and swallowed.

She could tell that he was surprised to know that she knew. "When they had you stealing from your mama, you should have cut them loose right then and there. Now, y'all might not even have enough food in the house to take you through the month, and your phone might be in danger of being shut off, and you sitting here worried 'bout whether or not your mama gonna yell at you?"

"She's always—"

"Boy, let me tell you something," Essie said, her voice firm but wrapped with concern. "I grew up in a house with two older sisters, and my parents didn't believe in yelling. You know why? 'Cause they let the switch do the yelling for them. How many beatings have you gotten in your lifetime?"

"I've been hit before."

"I ain't said nothing 'bout being hit. I'm talking about a good old-fashioned, pull-your-pants-down butt-whipping with a leather belt or a switch that you ain't even had the time to pull the splinters off of."

Jerrod sat in silence.

Essie reached down and lifted his chin so that he

looked directly into her eyes. "You know why y'all got gangs and all this other mess in the schools that wasn't nowhere to be found just a few years ago? 'Cause the government done come in and took prayer out the schools and then they told parents that they can't raise their children no more. 'Cause now, y'all can cuss out a teacher, but they can't do nothing to y'all or else they go to jail. 'Cause everything is called abuse now where it used to be called discipline. My mama beat me when I needed to be beat; and you know what? It didn't feel good. It ain't *supposed* to feel good, but it made me think twice about doing that same wrong again. All the children in my neighborhood got beatings, and sometimes it was the teachers and the neighbors that beat us.

"There was a widow that lived in the house beside us and she had two little boys and she would ask my daddy to come over and bring his belt when they got out of line. Chile, sometimes my daddy would just beat them for what he knew they was gonna do later. Every Sunday, right after prayer meeting, they got a beating so they would remember not to cut up in school the following week. And you know what? It didn't kill them. It didn't even hurt them. Both of them boys grew up to go to college and be somebody. They loved my daddy 'til the day he died, and they made their mama real proud. And it was all because somebody loved them enough to raise them.

"I ain't saying your mama don't love you, baby; 'cause she do. I'm just saying she been so busy working, trying to buy you stuff you don't even deserve to have and then crying when you was cutting the fool, that she forgot to raise you. I guarantee you, if she had a beat yo' behind all them years ago, you wouldn't be in no gang today. Now, there's some teacher out there that done been disrespected in the worst way by a bunch of hoodlums and you all mixed up in this mess.

"Jerrod Mays, Ms. Essie is *very* disappointed in you. You know why? Because I love you and I *know* you somebody special. You gonna be somebody one day, and all of this that you letting go on in your life is just evil trying to take you where God ain't never meant for you to go. I ain't gonna let it happen, baby. Your mama ain't gonna let it happen either. You gonna be somebody; you hear me?" By the time her mini-sermon ended, Essie was in tears.

Seeing her broken heart put Jerrod in tears too. He sank his head and cried heavily as he sat at her feet.

"You stay right here," Essie said.

Getting up from her chair, she walked into the house and pulled a tissue from the box on her table on the way to her bedroom. After drying her eyes, Essie kneeled beside her bed and lifted the comforter. From between her mattresses, she retrieved a red-and-white bank envelope that contained several twenty-dollar bills. Drying her eyes with her hands, Essie counted out the thirteen bills and then tossed the empty envelope in a nearby garbage can. She'd had Colin make a stop by the bank this afternoon just for this purpose.

When she walked back onto her porch, Jerrod was still there, using the sleeves of his shirt to dry his face. "I'm sorry, Ms. Essie," he said.

"I know you are, but there's somebody else that deserves your apology way more than me."

"Yes, ma'am," Jerrod whispered, once again returning his eyes to the porch beneath him.

"You know what, sugar?" Essie took her seat again. "You been so busy trying to be a man that you ain't enjoyed a day of being a boy. Your mama ain't never had the chance to show you how much love she got for you 'cause you too busy pushing it away. Starting today, I want you to promise me that you gonna make an effort to change all that. Can you promise me that you'll try?"

He nodded. "Yes, ma'am."

"I'm gonna hold you to that; you hear me? I don't care what happens from this day forward. I want you to know that Ms. Essie loves you, and all I want from you is for you to love your mama and grow up to be the somebody that I know you can be." Essie reached down and took Jerrod's hands in hers.

When she released him, he looked at the folded bills, and then back at her.

"You gonna give that to your mama and tell her that you sorry that you took it in the first place."

Jerrod rose to his knees and threw his arms around Essie and held on tight. "Thank you, Ms. Essie. I promise I'll pay you back. I'll mow your yard this summer, take out your garbage, wash your car, whatever you want me to do."

Essie laughed as he finally pulled away. "No you won't," she said. "If you do what I done asked you to do, it's already paid in full. All I want from you is for you to love your mama, get your schoolwork done, and grow up to be a proper man. No more disrespect and disobeying, no more running the streets late at night, and no more fooling with that gang."

Jerrod's eyes dropped back down. "I don't know how to get out, Ms. Essie. I wish I did, but once you're in—"

"Don't you worry 'bout nothing, sugar. Consider yourself out. You might be scared of them boys, but I ain't."

"Ms. Essie, they'll hurt you too. I don't know what I'd do if they hurt you because of me."

"Mark my words, baby," Essie said, cupping his concerned face in her hands. "Them boys ain't no match for me and the good Lord; so you ain't got to worry none about that. Now, get on home before the clock strikes eleven, unless you planning on sleeping on my sofa again."

Jerrod hesitated, and Essie smiled, knowing that there was a part of him that wanted to spend the night on her couch.

"G'on now," she said.

Jerrod leaped from her porch in a single bound and ran to the house next door to let himself in.

# Chapter 18

## *Friday Morning: 2:12 A.M.*

Elaine lay in her bed contemplating what she should do next. Just a few minutes ago, she'd heard her front door open and close and then she heard keys drop just before the setting of her house alarm. After walking out nearly six hours earlier, Mason was home. His return was a pleasant surprise. Elaine had prepared herself to spend the night and maybe even the rest of her life without him there. She had breached their wedding vows in the most horrific way, and as strained as their marriage was, she couldn't see Mason forgiving her for this indiscretion any time soon, if he could forgive her at all.

Before she went to bed, she read the poetic vows again. Yesterday, while they were cooking at Essie's house, Essie had told her and the other women how she had a favorite letter that her husband wrote to her that she read every night before going to bed. She said it kept Ben close to her heart. When Elaine read Mason's vows before getting into bed, she couldn't help but wonder if his written words were all that she would have of him from now on. His walking in the house had provided a bandage for her bleeding heart, but she speculated how long it would be before he'd walk out again; for good.

From her room, Elaine could hear shower waters running from the guest bathroom down the hall. They had a restroom that was attached to their bedroom, but Mason had opted for the other one. At one moment, she could hear her husband release a loud, agonizing moan. The shower waters, no doubt, had hit a bruise or a sore muscle and caused him pain. It was almost enough to make Elaine burst into tears.

The house they shared consisted of two bedrooms, but the second room had been converted into an office space for her, and the floor was still covered with broken glass. Maybe the lack of sleeping options would be enough to drive Mason into the room with her, but as hurt and angry as he was, Elaine didn't hold on to much hope. Mason would sleep in one of his vehicles before lying next to her; and she knew it.

After the shower was turned off, she could hear him moving about in the living room. Now, all was quiet. Elaine sat up in her bed and strained her ears, hoping to detect some sound or motion that would give her an idea of what he was doing. What she wanted more than anything was to be given a chance to talk to him. She needed to tell Mason how sorry she was and how much she regretted the way she had hurt him. If Elaine thought there was any chance that he would listen to her, she would march right in there and make her plea, but before he stormed out earlier, she had seen the angry tears in his eyes and heard the hurt in his voice. Perhaps she should just wait and allow everything to settle naturally.

Ms. Essie had talked about the power of prayer, reminding Elaine that nothing or no one could take the place of the one and only living God. There was no Guardian of Divinity within her that held the key to happiness. Elaine hadn't been happy in years, and that should have been enough of a hint for her to know that she was looking for help in all the wrong places. But she just kept ordering more CDs and listening to more speeches about how to find the higher power in herself instead of seeking help from God. Now, her life was in an even bigger mess than it ever was in before and because of the choices she'd made, Elaine feared that she was about to lose the only man she genuinely loved.

Tonight, before going to bed, she'd done something she hadn't done in years. She prayed. Just the act of kneeling and trying to open a line of communication between God and her was tedious. Elaine didn't feel worthy, and she saw no reason why God would ever listen to any of her petitions. In fact, as far as she was concerned, she was getting exactly what she had coming and didn't deserve to be helped. She had closed the door on God a long time ago and hadn't talked to Him in so long that she wondered if He even remembered she existed. But God must have heard her. One of her requests was for Him to send her husband home, and although it was after two o'clock in the morning, Mason arrived.

Realizing that her husband's return had been an answered prayer, Elaine was also forced to face the fact that her request didn't stop there. She'd promised God that if He sent Mason back, she would talk to him and beg on her knees for his forgiveness, if that was what it would take. Now that he was home and lingering somewhere just outside their bedroom door, Elaine wanted to take it all back. She didn't want to be made a fool of. What if Mason laughed in her face or told her where she could go? She'd be humiliated.

*No more humiliated than he must have been when he found out that you were cheating.*

Elaine knew that her conscience was right. This was no time to try to protect her selfish feelings. She had committed the crime, and now it was time to face her judgment. If he laughed or cursed her to her face, she deserved it. At least here, there was no audience like the one that she was sure had gathered when Mason walked down to Goodyear to confront Dante. No one other than she and Mason would be present to see whatever embarrassment she could possibly be in for. But no doubt, plenty of people had seen Mason take the blow that delivered a gash over his eyebrow.

"Okay, God," Elaine whispered, "I know this isn't going to be a walk in the park, but all I ask is that You please just don't let him leave. I can take anything else except losing him right now, please." She wiped away the onset of tears.

Having stated her plea, Elaine pulled her legs from under the bed covers and brought herself to a standing position. Slipping on her robe, she took a deep breath and then began taking slow steps toward the door. Halfway there she stopped and rethought her strategy. Untying the belt of her robe, she let it fall from her shoulders and onto the floor. Elaine was wearing a short, silk, red gown that Mason had always loved seeing her in. Wearing it tonight may have been a cunning tactic, but she needed all the help she could get.

In the living room, Mason sat with a large blanket separating him from the leather that covered the couch. He stared at the water that bubbled in the large fish tank that was positioned against the wall next to the loveseat across from him. Staring at the fish that swam freely in the water had always offered a sense of serenity to him on days and nights when he and Elaine fought. Tonight, the calm scenery did nothing.

Maybe he shouldn't have been surprised by what he found out. After all, his marriage had been on the decline for years now. Here it was, a few days shy of April, and he could count on one hand the amount of times this year he and Elaine had been intimate. He should have known that a woman who had once been as sensual as his wife wouldn't just settle for a sex life as inactive as theirs had become.

When Mason was straddling Dante's torso and clawing into his neck, nearly cutting off his flow of oxygen, the man swore that his relationship with Elaine had just started this week.

"Yeah, right."

As Mason mumbled the words, he angrily pounded his right fist into his left hand and then winced from the sharp pain that followed. That was the fist he'd used to punch his wife's lover in the jaw.

In the story she was writing, Elaine described Dante as pure muscle and it was only barely an overstatement. Even his jaw felt like it was made of muscle and Mason was sure that the punch had hurt his knuckles far more than it had hurt Dante's face.

Strength for strength, Mason was no match for the man who had been sleeping with his wife. One swing from Dante was all it took to draw blood from the cut he'd opened over Mason's eye with his fist. For the first time in his life, Mason literally saw stars. Behind the cheers of his co-workers, Dante dragged him through the oil-riddled repair shop like he was a weightless rag doll. It took the blow of a hubcap that Mason grabbed from the display shelf to knock the man off his feet, which gave him the opportunity to get the grip on Dante's neck.

By the time the other workers stepped in to pull the men apart, the authorities that had been called earlier had arrived, sirens and flashing lights surrounding the building. Both men had been tossed in the back of separate police cruisers, but when the storeowner chose not to press charges, they were released to medics who carried them to the hospital to care for their injuries.

Mason hadn't seen Dante since the ambulance he had been put into pulled from the Goodyear parking lot. The gash Dante gave him required six stitches, but Mason had comforted himself by conjuring an image of his opponent with a knot the size of Texas in the middle of his forehead where the metal hubcap had landed.

Massaging both his fist and the scrapes that his arms suffered after the protective covering of his shirt had been ripped away, Mason shook his head. The last time he'd been in a fight of that magnitude was ten years ago, and as he recalled, that fight was over Elaine too. He'd gone to the *Dallas Observer*, where she served as a staff writer, and taken on her boss, who had made an inappropriate pass at her the day before. For that one, he spent the night in jail and then was sentenced to two hundred hours of community service. In hindsight, Mason knew that he could have gotten a much worse deal as a result of the brawl with Dante. He had been lucky. Or maybe somebody up there was looking out for him. The last thought brought Mason's eyes to the ceiling, but the sound behind him quickly caused him to look in the direction of his bedroom.

"Can we talk?"

The lights in the living room were off, but the lamp from the bedroom was on and it cast a glow on Elaine as she walked from the room whispering her request.

Mason's eyes immediately locked on her gown. He hadn't seen that one in a long time, and it seemed to fit her curves differently than it had before. *When did she get so fine?* Mason had to remind himself that he was angry with her so that he could successfully force his eyes away and re-align his thoughts.

"I ain't got nothing to say to you, Elaine."

"Okay, then. Just let me talk and you listen."

"You ain't got nothing to say to me either."

Mason expected her to walk away and disappear on the other side of the bedroom door, but she didn't. Instead, Elaine came and sat beside him on the sofa, clutching a piece of folded paper in her hands. Immediately, Mason got up and relocated to the love-seat on the other side of the room. From there, he could see the light reflecting off of her legs. They looked shapelier than he remembered. An image of Dante touching them while he ran his hand up her thighs flashed in Mason's head and replaced the attractive picture that had begun to form.

"Okay, I deserved that," Elaine said.

Laughing in disgust, Mason said, "No, Elaine. You deserve a lot worse than me moving to another seat!" He swore as he took a jab at the arm of the loveseat, sending a sharp pain through his hand and up his arm, causing him to curse again.

"Mason, I'm sorry."

"Are you, really? Are you sorry that you let him bang you, or just sorry that you got caught?"

"I was going to tell you . . ."

"Oh, yeah, I'm sure you were, Elaine. I'm sure you were going to come out and admit to me that you've been cheating on me. Do you *really* expect me to believe that?"

"No, I don't expect you to believe it, Mason, but it's true. I spent the day with Ms. Essie and she had prayer with me and—"

"So the whole world knows about this? You told Ms. Essie, but I had to find out by reading your little sex chronicles?"

"I didn't tell Ms. Essie. She doesn't know what I was doing; at least I don't think she does. She just had prayer with me and a couple of the other girls who live in the neighborhood today. She made me see and understand that what I was doing was wrong. I was trying to hurt you, Mason. I was trying to get back at you for ignoring me and spending all your time with your friends and your cars."

"Oh, so now this is my fault? You're gonna turn this around and blame me for you spreading your legs all over town? Don't you *dare* try and make me feel guilty, Elaine! I'm not the one who turned you into a ho!"

His words cut into her like a razor-sharp machete. Mason watched as she broke into tears and hung her head in unmistakable shame. He hated that seeing her tears made him want to cry too. He hated that he wanted to go over and hold her in his arms. He hated that he wanted to apologize for referring to her in such a demeaning manner, but as much as he wanted to, he wasn't about to take it back; not after what she'd done.

"Go to bed, Elaine. Just go to bed and leave me alone."

"Please, Mason," she begged.

"What do you want me to do?" Mason yelled as he stood to his feet and flung his arms in the air in indignation. "I just got beat up by a man who's been sexing my wife, Elaine. What do you want me to do, huh? I spent an hour in the back of a cop's car like a common criminal and then six hours in a hospital getting tetanus shots and sewn up all because you did what you told me, at the start of our relationship, you would never tolerate from a man.

"So you did it to hurt me. Well, congratulations!" Mason said, glad that the darkness hid the tears that had begun streaming from his eyes. "Congratulations, Elaine. You got your wish. I'm hurt. Are you happy now? What else do you want from me?"

"I want to start over, Mason," she said as she stood, too. "I want us to go back to when we used to be a family. I want us to pray together again and go to church together and just spend time with each other. I want us to talk to each other and make love to each other and show love for each other like we used to. I want to go back to *this*." She opened the paper in her hand and dropped it on the sofa. "I want you to believe me, Mason. I really am sorry and I really was just getting ready to end it and confess everything. I know I did wrong, and I'm not trying to blame you. I take all the blame, and as much as it hurts to hear, everything you said about me is true. But I promise you it will never happen again. I love you and I've never been unfaithful to you, Mason, not until this week. This week, I just lashed out in the worst way and I'm sorry. Can't you forgive me?"

Mason stared at her in silence for a moment. As much as he didn't want to, and as angry as he still was, he believed that Elaine meant every word she'd just said. Still, there was a part of him that couldn't stand the sight of her right now. All the images were still too vivid, and his bruises were too fresh for him look the other way.

"If it were me who fooled around on you; would you forgive me?"

"I don't know," she whispered tearfully.

"Well, I don't know either, Elaine. So, you're asking way too much of me right now. All I'm asking from you is to be left alone. Considering the circumstances, I think you're the one who owes me right now. Can you do that for me?"

Elaine slowly turned away. Although she closed the bedroom door behind her, he could clearly hear her crying on the other side.

Mason walked back to the blanket-covered sofa and picked up the paper that Elaine had dropped earlier. Reaching for the lamp beside him, he turned the switch and looked at the poem that he didn't even know he had kept. Through the tears that ran from his eyes, he read his own words, reread them and then read them again before turning off the light and stretching his sore body across the couch.

# Chapter 19

## *Friday Morning: 10:15 A.M.*

"Ms. Essie?" Jennifer walked outside of her house and saw her neighbor reading as she sat on the porch. "You got a minute?"

"Girl, what you doing home? Ain't you got no job no more?"

Jennifer walked down her steps and joined Essie on her porch. She sat in the vacant chair and stared straight ahead at the empty street. "You gave him the money, didn't you?"

"He didn't ask for it, if that's what you're worried about." Essie closed her Bible and placed it on the floor beside her.

Jennifer turned to face her and smiled. "I know. He told me everything when he came home last night."

"Everything?" Essie removed her glasses from her face.

Jennifer could tell that she was trying to figure out if she actually knew the whole story about the gang involvement.

"Yes, ma'am. It was the first time in years, maybe even in his lifetime, that Jerrod and I really talked without me screaming at him or him screaming at me. I can't believe I let things get so out of hand. He told me that he was going to do better from now on, and you know what . . . I believe him."

"I believe him too," Essie said.

"This whole gang thing has me worried though. I tried to keep him out of school today, but he was determined to go. Ms. Essie, I'm scared. I was too upset to go to work. I want to go out there to the school to make sure he's okay, but—"

"Ain't no need, sugar," Essie told her. "I been up since six o'clock this morning taking care of that mess he got mixed up in. I stopped Jerrod on his way to the bus stop this morning and got him to write down the names of all them boys that was involved in hurting that teacher. Then 'bout an hour later, after I had done talked to the Lord, I called the police and told them what I knew."

Jennifer's eyes grew wide in a mixture of surprise and fear. "Ms. Essie, that's a gang. Those boys are liable to come out here and set all our houses on fire just to be sure they got the right one."

"You know, they have this thing called anonymous," Essie said calmly. "You can call the police and fix it so that they don't have your name to give to the news folks or nothing. So don't nobody never know that you was the one who called, unless you tell them."

"That's what you did?"

"Sho' did." Essie nodded with a laugh. "I was listening to the local news about an hour ago, and the police done already been out there to arrest them too. A couple of the younger boys, Jerrod's age, done already confessed and told the police that one of the older boys made them do it."

Jennifer was too upset to watch television this morning, and upon hearing Essie, her initial response was one of relief. However, another terrifying thought bombarded her mind as soon as Essie completed her last sentence. She asked, "What if they name my baby in all this mess?"

"You ain't let me finish," Essie said. "The Lord works in mysterious ways. On the news report, they said that soon after the boys were arrested, that teacher come out her coma and named the same boys that I did. Jerrod's name wasn't nowhere in the mix. God done gave that boy of yours another chance, and this time I think he gonna do good with it."

Standing from her seat, Jennifer walked over and embraced Essie. "Thank you so much, Ms. Essie. I don't know what me and Jerrod ever did before you came in our lives. Thank you for everything."

"I always said timing was everything," Essie said after she was released. "Seem like we should have been met since we live right next to each other, but the good Lord knew when you would need me the most; and you know what else? He knew when I'd need you the most too."

Jennifer took a step back. "Need *us*? You don't need us, Ms. Essie. All I've done and all Jerrod has done is dump all our problems on you."

"Baby, you and Jerrod gave Ms. Essie some usefulness and some excitement. When you get old like me, you like to know that somebody needs you. This week done been full of action for me, and in the middle of it all, I was able to help some nice people and make some good friends. It just proved that what my pastor preached on last Sunday was the God-in-heaven truth. It pays to love your neighbor, and sometimes they ain't the only ones that get rewarded by the love that you show. I can't tell you the last time I was this happy. So, yes, ma'am," Essie assured her, "you and that boy of yours did a lot for me."

Instead of going back to the chair that she'd abandoned, Jennifer chose to sit down on the porch next to Essie's chair. There was something about her neighbor; the closer she was to her, the safer Jennifer felt. Her eyes dropped to the Bible that Essie had been reading. She picked it up and smoothed her hand over the worn leather cover. She looked up when she heard Essie's voice again.

"Now, when them boys come up for trial, Jerrod might get called on to testify, but the same God that's keeping him out of juvenile hall right now is gonna keep him then too. I ain't worried one bit, and I don't want you to be worried none either, you hear me?"

Jennifer nodded.

"God gonna be with him. And when they throw the book at them boys, they gonna be locked up so long 'til they ain't even gonna remember their own names by the time they get out, let alone Jerrod's."

The porch was quiet for a moment, and then Essie spoke again. "Well, look who's coming. Am I 'bout to be blessed with a house full again today?"

When Jennifer followed the direction of Essie's eyes, she saw a woman walking up the street, dressed in jeans and a striped shirt. It was Elaine. After their time together yesterday, seeing her was like seeing an old friend.

"I guess she ain't running today," Essie said.

"Probably all that macaroni and cheese she ate yesterday." Jennifer laughed. "She's probably still too stuffed to exercise."

Both Essie and Jennifer were laughing as Elaine crossed the grass and walked toward them.

"Are y'all talking about me?"

"Course we are," Essie said. "Come on up here and join us."

Quietly, Elaine sat on the top step and then turned to look at both of them.

Jennifer immediately knew something was wrong, and she knew that if she had picked up on that realization, then Essie probably had it figured out before Elaine even left her house.

"I think Mason's gonna leave me," Elaine said, trying hard to hold back tears.

Jennifer's hands covered her mouth in shock. She remembered Elaine mentioning the day before that her and Mason's marriage was in trouble, but Jennifer didn't think that it was so far gone. As a matter of fact, when they were sitting in the waiting room of the hospital, Elaine had talked about how she was going to make some changes and get her marriage back on track. That was also when she promised Essie that she and Mason would join her in church on Sunday. She seemed so sure that she could patch things up, and Jennifer couldn't stop wondering what had happened so suddenly to change everything so drastically.

"What makes you think he's leaving?" Essie said, posing the question that Jennifer didn't feel comfortable enough to ask.

"It's my fault, Ms. Essie. If he leaves, then I don't have a soul to blame but myself. My parents taught me right from wrong, and I was an honor student from kindergarten all the way through twelfth grade. I can't believe I let myself do something so stupid."

Her tone was grave, and although she didn't go into any details, Jennifer was almost sure that she wasn't wrong in thinking Elaine had gotten involved with another man. She had that frightened look of a cat caught in the headlights of an oncoming car. Jennifer had seen that look twice in her lifetime, but it had been on men that she'd dated and trusted. When she'd discovered their unfaithfulness, they had that same look of entrapment.

"All of us done did stupid things in our lives, sugar," Essie said. "That's why God spends so much time forgiving us."

"It's not God I'm worried about right now, Ms. Essie. I know He's forgiven me. I prayed so hard last night until I started feeling like a piece of Heaven had come down and took residence in my bedroom. But as much as I knew that God had forgiven me and that He was there with me, I needed Mason to be there holding me in his arms too. I miss him already, and he hasn't even officially left me yet."

"He wasn't at home?" As soon as Jennifer asked the question, she wondered if she was being too forward.

Elaine answered without hesitation. "He was home," she said with a nod. "He just couldn't stand to look at me, talk to me, or sleep with me, that's all."

"Give him some time, baby," Essie said. "He'll be all right. He gonna hurt for a while, and things between the two of you gonna be strained for a while. But God's gonna fix it, and when He does, it's gonna be better than ever."

"I wish I could believe that, Ms. Essie." Elaine shook her head in doubt. "I mean, I didn't just mess up a little. This wasn't just some fender-bender. What I did is like a forty-car pile up on I-285 during rush hour on a rainy Monday morning."

"Dang," Jennifer whispered. Now she had no doubt that another man was involved.

"Honey, Jesus ain't no shade-tree mechanic," Essie said, unaffected by Elaine's analogy. "He can fix a totaled car just as good as He can fix one that got a scrape on the bumper. And unlike ordinary mechanics, when the Lord fix something, it's just as good as it was before it ever got wrecked."

Jennifer looked at Essie and smiled. Not since her grandmother had she known a woman with as much love and wisdom as Essie. She knew just what to say, how to say it, and when to say it. And the best part of all was that when she said something, you could almost bet your paycheck on it.

Elaine forced a smile through glassy eyes. "I have to believe that, Ms. Essie."

"That's right," Essie replied with a nod of her head. "You believe it. God ain't never failed me, and if you believe Him, He won't fail you either."

The porch became quiet for an extended moment. Then Elaine spoke again and abruptly broke the silence. "I'm gonna write a book on you, Ms. Essie."

Essie burst into laughter, but Elaine's expression remained serious.

"A book about what?" Jennifer asked.

"About everything," Elaine said. "I was thinking about it this morning when I got up and was getting dressed to come here. I have to get a new computer, first, but when I do, one of the first things I'm going to do is get in touch with some of my contacts at one of the publishing houses that I've written short stories for and tell them that I want to write a novel. I'm almost sure I can sell the idea on them."

"Girl, ain't nobody gonna buy no novel 'bout no old lady who sit on her front porch reading and knitting," Essie said.

"But, Ms. Essie, you do a whole lot more than that," Jennifer said. "I think that's a great idea."

"And all of our stories are gonna be in it," Elaine said. "I'm gonna write about me and Mason and Jennifer and Jerrod, and even Angel and Colin. I'll change all of our names so nobody will know who the book is really about, but all of us will know. What do you think, Ms. Essie? Would you mind?"

Jennifer was as excited as Elaine. "Please, Ms. Essie. She'll even put Mr. Ben in there and tell everybody how much you love him."

"Sure will," Elaine agreed.

"Honey, you ain't got to ask my permission. If you want to write a book 'bout me, then you go right ahead. Ain't much to tell as far as I'm concerned, though. I'm just Ms. Essie, that's all."

"What's going to be the title of it?" Jennifer asked.

"I don't know," Elaine responded thoughtfully.

"How about *The Women of Braxton Park*," Jennifer suggested. "You know, kind of like that Brewster Place novel that Oprah turned into a movie back in the eighties."

"If Mason doesn't leave me, I'm gonna title it *Ms. Essie: Miracle Woman*."

All three of the women laughed heartily, but Jennifer could see that Elaine was still worried about the future of her relationship. Her laughter was just a means to try to cope with the unknown.

The yell came from the distance. "Doesn't anyone work in this neighborhood anymore?"

The women turned to see Angel crossing the street from the corner of Braxton Circle. "Who's paying the bills around here nowadays?" she asked.

"Wobble yourself on over here and have a seat, chile," Essie called back.

As she neared, Elaine and Jennifer stood and helped her up the stairs. Angel sat in the chair that Jennifer sat in earlier.

"How you feeling?" Essie asked.

"Fat. But my baby is alive. I could feel like the Goodyear blimp and I'd be okay," Angel said. "What are you all doing over here?"

Jennifer noted a scowl cross Elaine's face when Angel said the word *Goodyear*. She wondered if she'd gotten bad service at the store, but Jennifer chose not to ask any questions, since she always went to the dealership to service her Toyota.

"Well, you know I always love having you over," Essie said, "but I could ask you the same question. It ain't Wednesday, and it ain't Saturday."

"I know." Angel rubbed her stomach. "I just felt a strong urge to come and see you today. You were on my mind so much that I was worried for a minute, but I see you're in good hands."

"Yeah, I'm in good company, but I'm still glad you came by."

"Maybe you can help us, Angel," Jennifer said. "You've known Ms. Essie longer than the rest of us. Elaine is going to write a book about her, and we were trying to think of a title. What do you think?"

Essie shook her head and chuckled.

"That's great," Angel said. "Are you really going to do it?"

"I sure am," Elaine said. "Any ideas for a title?"

Angel placed her hand under her chin and thought deeply.

"She might be the wrong one to ask," Essie said. "When she was a little girl, I had to take a switch to her behind a time or two. I don't know if I want her naming a book about me or not."

While the women laughed, Jennifer tried to picture Angel doing anything to deserve the aid of a switch. Maybe that's the reason she was so refined and had captured the heart of a great guy like Colin. Maybe it was because she had been put in line whenever she stepped out. Jennifer couldn't think of a time when she'd physically punished Jerrod with anything more than her open hand. Most times he didn't even cry, and by the time he was five, he was starting to hit back. If she had to do it all over again, things would be done differently. Jennifer wouldn't dare abuse him like her parents did her, but she would be the parent that her son needed for all those years.

"Well, she's always saying, 'Timing is everything,'" Angel said. "Name it that, or maybe something else that has to do with time. That seems to be her favorite thing."

Jennifer looked at Elaine, and they exchanged glances of approval.

"I like that," Elaine said.

"Yeah." Jennifer nodded. "It's got to be something about time."

To add irony to the conversation, the clock chimed inside of Essie's house and she immediately stood. "Well, y'all can sit out here flapping your gums if you want. But speaking of time, it's eleven o'clock and Bob Barker is about to walk through some curtains to give away some prizes. Y'all can either come on inside with me for lunch, or stay out here. Don't make me no never mind."

By the time Essie had smoothed the bottom of her dress, a familiar vehicle rounded the corner and captured all of their attention. They stood silently and watched Mason's BMW pull to the curb and park. He didn't get out of the car, but the tinted window on the driver's side descended.

Jennifer noted Elaine's demeanor. Her laughter was gone now as she watched, along with the rest of them, as her husband removed his sunglasses.

"Well, hey, baby," Essie called, breaking the silent tension. "We 'bout to go inside to get some lunch. There's plenty if you want some."

Mason shook his head. "No, thank you, Ms. Essie. I was just getting ready to see if Elaine was free to come home for a little bit, but if you're busy—"

"Naw, sugar, we ain't busy." Essie almost pushed Elaine down the steps as she nudged her to leave. "She can come back and eat anytime. I'm sho' she'd rather be with you anyway. She was just talking 'bout how she missed you."

Jennifer was almost sure that she saw a smile tugging at Mason's lips, but he refused to allow it to develop fully.

Elaine turned before walking down the steps. "Thank you, Ms. Essie," she whispered just before placing a kiss on her cheek.

"G'on and get your man, girl," Jennifer whispered to her. "We'll keep our fingers crossed."

"And our knees bent," Essie added.

Even after Essie and Angel walked into the house,

Jennifer stood on the porch and watched Elaine get into the car with her husband and drive away. Although she had a lot going on in her own life with her son, who wasn't completely out of trouble yet, Jennifer unselfishly closed her eyes and said a quick prayer just for Mason and Elaine.

# Chapter 20

## *Friday Afternoon: 12:02 P.M.*

Toby Simon had been the only one, other than Jerrod, who hadn't been accused by Ms. Shepherd and picked up by the police. The two of them weren't present the night that the attack took place. Jerrod saw Toby sitting alone in the cafeteria during lunch and walked over and sat next to him. They exchanged glances, but the boy almost immediately looked away and began eating in silence.

Jerrod wondered if Toby was as frightened as he was when the emergency announcement blasted over the intercom for everyone to remain in their classrooms and in their seats until instructed otherwise. The school day had barely begun when it happened, and although Jerrod was sure that Essie had already made good on her promise, his heart pounded and he looked as bewildered as all of the other students when they saw the swarm of uniformed policemen taking quick steps up and down the halls. They were clearly on a mission.

*Please, God, please, God, please, God.* Those were the words that kept repeating through Jerrod's mind as he sat at his desk praying that the policemen wouldn't come into his class to collect him along with the others. Sweat leaked from his pores so heavily that he could feel his shirt beginning to cling to his back.

For almost a full hour, the students of Alpharetta High were on lockdown, and it wasn't until Principal Wright's voice echoed over the speaker system again, giving them permission to resume as normal, that Jerrod was able to exhale. It felt like he'd been holding his breath for the entire ordeal.

Even now, as he brought his milk carton to his lips, Jerrod could see the trembling of his own hand. There was no one that he could comfortably talk to about what had happened, except Toby, and as shell-shocked as he looked right now, that didn't seem to be a good idea either.

"Hey, Jerrod!"

The sudden call of his name startled him, and Jerrod nearly dropped his milk carton, spilling some of the liquid as he steadied his hand and looked behind him. It was T. K. Donaldson, his gym teacher and the head coach of the track team. Next to Ms. Shepherd, Coach Donaldson was his favorite teacher. Jerrod picked up his napkin and wiped the splattered milk from his hands and then turned to face the oncoming instructor again.

"Hey, Coach D," Jerrod said.

Coach Donaldson was one of the coolest teachers Jerrod had ever had in all of his nine years of public schooling. He seemed more human than most teachers he'd sat under, and the coach knew how to make his class so enjoyable that it didn't really seem like a class at all.

The name T. K. Donaldson was an esteemed one at Alpharetta High. He'd graduated from the school some years ago and still held the school record for the 100- and 200-meter races. Coach Donaldson was a remarkable basketball player as well. His jersey was retired, and one bearing his number hung in the gym, along with two others, representing the school's most outstanding past players.

Coach Donaldson's best-loved sport was track though, and his most valued achievement was being chosen to try out for the 1992 Olympics. An injury in the qualifying meet shattered his dreams, but he had so many high school and college trophies and medals on the shelf in his office that Jerrod figured he probably didn't even miss the one he didn't get.

"Remember how you told me that you wanted to be on the track team next year?" Coach Donaldson asked.

"Uh-huh."

"Well, I think we might be able to make room for you."

Jerrod could hardly believe his ears. "For real, yo?"

"Hold up, now." Coach Donaldson held up his hands to contain Jerrod's escalating excitement. "All of this hinges on conditions. I was looking at your grades. You're gonna have to work a lot harder on your academics. Track is cool, but you've got to get it up here too." He pointed to Jerrod's forehead. "I need you to pull up those low C's, and that D that you got in Math is just totally unacceptable. If you prove to me, between now and the end of the school year, that you can substantially improve all those scores, then the spot is yours. You don't have to become an instant honor student, but you've got to make an honorable effort."

Jerrod was a bit embarrassed by the tears that burned in his eyes, but he was too excited to be overly concerned with them. He accepted the handshake that Coach Donaldson offered and then gave him a quick embrace.

"Are you up for the challenge?"

"For sho'!" Jerrod said. "I can do this. No problem."

"I know you can," Coach Donaldson said as he stood to leave. "If I didn't think you could, I never would have laid it out there for you. See you in class later."

"A'ight. Hey, Coach!" Jerrod called, stopping his teacher in his tracks.

"Yeah?"

Jerrod stood and walked closer. "You still stay after school to practice shooting hoops in the gym?"

"Sometimes."

"Are you staying today?"

Jerrod saw an inquisitive look in his coach's eyes. He knew the man was wondering why he had asked such a question.

"Do you need me to for some reason?"

"If you don't mind, I just need to talk a minute, if you got one to spare."

"Sure, partner," he responded with a pat to Jerrod's shoulder. "Can you meet me on the court at four?"

"For sho'," Jerrod responded with a nod. "Thanks, Coach."

"Don't thank me, li'l man," Coach Donaldson said

with a teasing laugh. "You betta come with your game face on, if you know like I know."

"Oh yeah?"

"For sho'." The coach pointed at the teenager and then turned and walked away.

Nearly two hours had passed since he picked Elaine up from Essie's house, but Mason had said very few words. His wife was surprised to find that he'd gone and purchased her another computer system, and she'd thanked him more than once.

"Yeah." That was all the response that Mason could come up with.

Together, they had cleaned up the glass that was still covering the hardwood floor in Elaine's office. After sweeping, they vacuumed and then mopped the area to be sure that there were no particles left behind. Taking apart what was left of the destroyed computer was a time-consuming task and the first thing Mason and Elaine had done as a team since they'd played and won a scaled-down version of *Fear Factor* on the cruise three years ago.

Having worked with computers in his early career life, Mason was familiar with putting them together and could usually do it in no time. However, his body's lingering soreness made the job a bit more challenging than normal. Every time he moaned as a result of discomfort, he could see the guilty regret in Elaine's eyes. He threw in a couple of extra, unnecessary grunts just to add to her remorse.

"Thanks, Mason," she said when he plugged in the last connection and powered up her new flat-screen model.

"Yeah," he responded, pulling away from the hand she'd placed on his arm.

Mason could feel her eyes on him as he walked out of the room, leaving her to admire her new system.

Purchasing the computer for her was a hard choice to make. Mason knew that in a day or two, Elaine would've gone and gotten another on her own. Her job required her to have one, so it would have been replaced whether he'd done it or not. For some reason, though, he felt like it was his duty to replace it.

Sitting on the sofa to remove his shoes, Mason's mind wandered to the day's happenings. He had gone to work as normal, but upon seeing the fresh stitches and reading the label on the medication that he had to take, his boss made the decision to give him a few days off to recuperate. A few of his work buddies had asked about the nature of his injury. Too proud to tell them that his wife had been getting her needs met by another man, Mason told them that he'd been in an accident the day before. He failed to tell them that the accident involved Dante's fist running into his face.

After he left the job and was headed home, he felt a sense of guilt. Why, he wasn't sure, since Elaine was the one to breach their marriage vows. Although Mason couldn't understand the feeling that engulfed him, he couldn't shake it either. That's when he got off at the next exit and headed toward the bank to get the cash he would need to purchase the system. The events afterward led him to believe that all of it happened for a purpose.

Elaine entered the room. "Are you off from work?"

"Yeah," Mason said as he removed the second shoe from his foot and dropped it to the floor.

"Do you want me to fix you something to eat?"

"No."

Mason momentarily froze when his wife sat next to him, but in no time, he was on his feet and moving in the direction of the other side of the room.

"Mason, don't . . ."

"Don't *what*?" he barked.

Elaine folded her arms in front of her and lowered her head. He saw tears drop from her eyes onto her lap. A moment later, she looked back at him. "Are you gonna leave me?" she whispered. Her voice trembled, and she appeared to almost be afraid of the answer she might hear.

Mason stared at her and then turned and faced the fish tank beside him. "I don't know," he said. "I don't know about anything anymore, Elaine."

"I'll do anything, Mason. Whatever I can do to make it right, just tell me, and I'll do it."

Mason turned to face her and laughed, but there was no amusement in the expression on his face. "You can't do anything to make this right, Elaine. Don't you see that? The only thing you could do to make it right would be to erase the fact that it ever happened in the first place, and you can't do that. See, that's the thing about doing stuff; once it's done, it can't be undone. I can go out there and get in my car and drive to the end of this street, but even if I turn back around and come home, that doesn't undo the fact that I drove to the end of the street. So, calling it off with that man is fine and good. Never seeing him again is fine and good. But won't none of that erase the fact that you gave him . . ."

Mason stopped and dropped his body into a

seated position on the couch behind him before burying his face in his hands. Just talking about it made his head throb in the area where the stitches were. He took a deep breath and then looked across the room at Elaine as she wept. "This morning when I woke up on that sofa, I was all set to pack my bags and get out. I even called Extended Stay America and made reservations for a week to buy myself some time to get a more permanent place to stay."

"Mason, no," Elaine pleaded softly.

"Then I messed around and went to the bank to withdraw some money and ran into a friend of yours named Colin somebody."

"Colin Stephens?"

"Yeah." Mason nodded. "He just kind of struck up a conversation with me while I was standing in line. He told me he and his wife were expecting a baby in the next week or so, and I told him that me and mine were getting a divorce. I figured it was safe to tell him. I mean, what were the chances that he'd know you? He told me his wife's name, and I didn't know her, but when I told him your name, guess what?"

"I'm beginning to see what Ms. Essie means when she talks about timing," Elaine said.

"What?"

"I just met Colin yesterday," Elaine explained. "If you had run into him at any point before today, he probably wouldn't have known who I was either. You told him about us?"

"He asked me to come with him to his office and I did. We talked for about an hour, I think. He thinks I should stay and work on it." Mason could see renewed hope in his wife's eyes when he said those words, but he continued before she had a chance to speak. "I just don't know, Elaine. I don't know if I can do this. I can't live every day of my life having flashes of you with another man. How am I supposed to ever make love to you again knowing that somebody else done been there with you? You know, Colin had prayer with me and he said the day will come when it won't hurt so bad, but he ain't never been where I am. I don't think this kind of pain ever goes away."

"I was so busy trying to hurt you when I did what I did that I never even considered the possibility that I'd be hurting me too," Elaine said. "I've just been so stupid. I think that anything that happens to me as a result of what I did is a deserving punishment. And I could handle any of them, Mason, except you leaving me. I couldn't handle that."

Mason leaned forward on his elbows and placed his hands under his chin, almost as if he were about to pray. Leaving her would be just as unbearable for him as it would be for her, and he knew it, but he wasn't about to verbalize his thoughts. Besides that; no matter how unbearable leaving Elaine might be, staying with her and being forced to constantly re-live the memories had the potential of being more intolerable.

"Where did you find my wedding vows?" he asked, deciding to take the conversation in a different direction.

"On the shelf in the closet with some of our other wedding keepsakes."

"What happened to us, Elaine? What happened to the man who wrote those vows and the woman who cried when she heard them for the first time?"

"He started working long hours and buying stuff he really couldn't afford, and she got her dream job, but couldn't have the baby that he wanted. So she started acting out and being stupid. I'm sorry that I can't give you the babies that we planned to have, Mason. I'm sorry for everything."

Mason's first instinct was to tell her that her not having a child didn't bother him, but he knew that Elaine would see right through his lie. For years now, he'd been allowing calls from his mother, who often belittled Elaine for her inability to carry a child full-term, and seeing his brothers with their sons and daughters always left him feeling like there was something missing in his life. Maybe the reason he couldn't shake the guilt that he felt inside was because Mason knew that he carried some of the blame. Yes, Elaine was wrong for finding attention and gratification in the bed of another man, but taking an honest look at the root of the problem, Mason knew that he had been purposefully doing callous things to indirectly punish her for the spare bedroom that was decorated with a computer, bookshelves, and file drawers instead of nursery items.

"It's not your fault that you can't have kids, Elaine. There are other options, you know." Mason couldn't believe the words that came out of his own mouth. He'd always said that he'd give no thought to adoption. He wanted a child that he'd fathered and that was that. From the look on Elaine's face, he knew she was equally surprised.

"But the baby issue and the car issues are just a part of it and we both know that," Mason continued. "You were right when you talked about the need for us to get back to our spiritual roots. Colin said that you promised Ms. Essie that we'd go to church with her on Sunday. Maybe we can start there."

"Thank you, Mason!"

"I'm not making any promises, Elaine." He held his arms out in front of him to stop her from running toward him for an embrace. "This is a long, *long* way from being resolved, and only time will tell if we can survive this. I'm not talking about a week or a month either. You're going to have to give me time, and I don't need you sweating me about anything, including when I'm going to move back in the bedroom. So, if my not having sex with you is going to send you down to the automotive shop, then tell me now so I can get out."

"No, no," Elaine assured him. "It won't. I can wait."

"For now, that sofa is my bed. The only promise I can make to you is that I'm gonna try. That's as good as it gets right now."

"That's more than I deserve," Elaine responded, new tears rolling down her cheeks. "That's good enough."

# Chapter 21

## Friday Afternoon: 6:08 P.M.

"*It's time to sing and rejoice. Lift up your hands in praise. Hallelujah, glorify the Lord in all your ways. It's time to dance and shout, in the name of the Most High God. It's time to dance and shout, in the name of the Most High God.*

"*One glad day, He's coming back, and we'll live forever more. What a glorious day when we go back with the Lord. It's time to sing, rejoice, praise, dance, and shout . . . hmmm . . .*"

The lyrics that Essie started out singing faded into a hum as she sat on her porch and looked at the children playing in the open field across the street. It was only a matter of time before a home would be constructed in that spot, taking away one of the only wide, grassy spaces in the area where the children could convene on afternoons like today.

"Why'd you stop singing, Ms. Essie?" Jennifer asked as she walked out onto her porch next door.

"Mostly 'cause that's as much of the song as I

know. This visiting choir came to our church and sung it a while back. I ain't no singer no way. Now, them sisters of mine could sing up a storm. They'd have all the church folks shouting on Sunday morning. Felt like them old wooden floors was gonna cave in under all that dancing." Essie chuckled.

"Well, could they cook like you?" Jennifer asked. "I smell your food all the way in my house."

"Y'all welcome to come over for dinner if you like. I got a hen in the oven, got some rice and gravy, squash casserole, and some turnip greens. Made some banana pudding too. It's plenty of it."

A dark grey Range Rover rounded the corner, and the horn blew just before Colin stuck his arm out of the open widow and waved.

As soon as his vehicle made the turn onto Braxton Circle, Essie sat up straight in her seat. "I wonder if Angel done cooked already? I got more food than a little up in that kitchen of mine. If you and Jerrod come over and I can get them two over, then maybe I won't have so many leftovers to store in the icebox."

"That sounds almost as good as that food smells," Jennifer said. "I hope Jerrod gets home soon. He called earlier and said he was being counseled after school. I thought that was a good idea, so I told him it was okay. But the longer he takes to get home, I'm starting to worry. I hope he don't say too much to the wrong person and end up getting himself in trouble."

Essie stood from her chair and brushed her hands over her dress. "Oh, he's fine. He'll be home directly. You just sit right there, and I'm gonna go in the house and give Angel and them a call."

Walking inside, Essie took a quick look at her

grandfather clock and then headed straight to the kitchen to turn down the temperature of her oven. By the time Angel and Colin got there, she would be ready to set the table. With her calling the police on this morning and now calling the Stephens, Essie's phone got more use in the last few hours than it had for the past few days.

Getting Angel to come over didn't take much effort. When Essie called her, she agreed to the arrangement before the offer could be fully extended. It would only take fifteen minutes, Angel said, for them to arrive.

Based on her track record for tardiness, Essie figured that they'd be there in thirty. Just as she was about to go back onto her porch, she turned back around, placed her glasses back on her face, and picked up the telephone book.

This time, she got the man of the house.

Mason answered the phone, but politely turned down the offer to join them twice before Essie convinced him otherwise. She could decipher from his tone that he really didn't want to be bothered, and on most days, Essie wasn't pushy or insistent with matters such as this; but today, she wanted to bring all of her old and new friends together. Getting them out of their separate environments and bringing them on common ground seemed to be the order of the day.

"Well, if the good Lord willing and the creek don't rise, we gonna have a family reunion going on over here this evening," Essie said, walking back outside and finding that Jennifer had moved from her own porch and taken a seat on hers.

"They're coming?" Jennifer asked.

"And Elaine and her husband too."

"Ms. Essie, where are you gonna seat all of us?" Jennifer asked with a laugh.

"Chile, it's a whole heap of space in that house. I can fit five at my round table in the kitchen; plus I got a sofa, a loveseat, and a chair in there. I got plenty of room for y'all, so you let me worry 'bout all that."

An early-model white Corvette with a heavy-sounding engine pulled into the subdivision and then eased to a stop in front of Essie's house. She narrowed her eyes, trying to see what unexpected company had arrived. The doors opened, and Jerrod jumped out of the passenger side as his teacher stepped from the driver's seat.

"Oh, my," Jennifer said, just above a whisper.

Essie turned and looked at her, noting how Jennifer smoothed down stray hairs that had wandered away from her neatly pinned ponytail. Chuckling to herself at her neighbor's adolescent-like actions, Essie walked to the edge of the porch to meet her guests.

"Hey, Ms. Essie." Jerrod trotted up the steps and bent down to deliver her a warm hug.

"Hey, baby," Essie said, kissing the cheek he offered before releasing him. "And who is this handsome young man you done brought to my house?"

"That's just my coach." Jerrod laughed. "That's Coach Donaldson. We just call him Coach D."

Coach Donaldson walked up the steps and reached for Essie's hand. "I'm pleased to meet you, Ms. Essie. I've heard quite a lot about you today. I feel privileged to make the acquaintance of such a remarkable woman."

Essie stepped closer, avoided his outstretched hand, and hugged him firmly around the waist. "Well, any man who can sweet-talk Ms. Essie like that gets to have a little bit more than a handshake. Nice to meet you too, sugar."

From behind her, Essie heard Jennifer cough and clear her throat.

"Jerrod, where are you manners?" Essie said. "Ain't you gonna introduce your teacher to your mama?"

"Oh, yeah. This is my mama," Jerrod said. "Ma, this is Coach D."

Placing her glasses back on her face for a clearer view, Essie watched as the tall, good-looking man stepped in front of Jennifer and offered his hand. Essie wasn't sure if she'd ever seen Jerrod's mother wear a prettier smile than the one she flashed for the coach.

"I'm Jennifer Mays," she said. "It's nice to meet you. Thank you so much for the giving of your time to Jerrod."

"Jerrod's a good kid," the coach responded, still holding her hand. "I told him that anytime he needed to talk, I'm here."

"I appreciate that more than I can tell you, Coach Donaldson."

"T. K.," he corrected, their eyes remaining locked.

"Well, now, T. K.," Essie said as she tugged at his arm so that he would look in her direction. "It *is* okay if I call you T. K. too, right? I mean I just want to make sure, seeing as how you didn't give me that same option."

"Oh, yes, ma'am," he quickly said. "You're welcome to call me T. K. as well."

"Me too?" Jerrod asked with a sly grin.

"I don't think so," Coach Donaldson replied, "but nice try."

"T. K.," Essie said, turning his attention back to

her, "in just a few minutes, we were all gonna sit down to dinner. Would you like to join us . . . I mean, unless you have other plans with your wife and family?"

"Uh, no, ma'am. I'm not married, and I have to admit that whatever you're cooking in there smells a whole lot better than the hotdogs I was planning to eat. But I'd just hate to be so last-minute."

"Aw, c'mon, Coach," Jerrod urged. "Ms. Essie's cooking is da bomb!"

"Jerrod and his mama will be joining me," Essie said, knowing that saying so would be all the encouragement he would need.

"Oh," T. K. said, looking back at Jennifer and smiling. "Well, if it won't put you through any added trouble."

"No trouble at all," Essie said. "Make yourself comfortable. Jennifer, you'll keep him company, won't you? Jerrod, why don't you come in and wash up so you can help Ms. Essie out. We got a few more coming, so I need your extra hands."

While she put the final touches on dinner and showed Jerrod how to properly set a table, Essie could hear pieces of the conversation taking place just outside her door. She heard the coach filling Jennifer in on some of what he and her son had discussed. He bragged on Jerrod's courage to report the gang and seemed assured that all of what had happened was just what Jerrod needed to nudge him in the right direction. Essie smiled as she listened. She couldn't agree more.

"I'm gonna be on the track team next year, Ms. Essie," Jerrod said with beaming pride in his voice.

"Sho' 'nuff?" Essie replied

"Yes, ma'am. Coach D said if I bring my grades up, he'd save a spot for me."

"Well, you make Ms. Essie proud, you hear me? Just like I told you last night, God got something great for you. You study hard and remember to pray. Them teachers out there ain't gonna know what to think when they see your new grades. I ain't got no doubt at all. I know you gonna do good with your grades, and I know you gonna be something else on that track team."

Just then, Essie heard laughter on the outside. Jennifer and T. K. seemed to be enjoying one another's company.

Essie looked at Jerrod. "How you like your coach?"

"Coach D? He's the coolest teacher at Alpharetta High. Now that Ms. Shepherd ain't there, he's my favorite teacher. Well, really, he was probably my favorite all the while. He just ain't as pretty as Ms. Shepherd."

"Ms. Shepherd is doing better, I hear," Essie said.

"That's what they told us at school today. Coach said he'll take me out there to see her on Sunday if Mama will let me go."

"Oh, I think your mama will be just fine with that."

Noises on the outside increased. Essie wiped her hand on her apron and looked out the front window just in time to see Angel and Colin climbing the stairs to the porch. Jennifer was introducing T. K. to them as though she'd known the man for more than just the last twenty minutes. Before she stepped away from the window, Essie also saw Elaine and Mason's BMW approaching and parking in front of Jennifer's house.

"Okay, baby, how you coming with them napkins and silverware?" Essie asked Jerrod. "I think everybody 'bout here now."

"I'm done with those. I just need to put these glasses on the coffee table for whoever is gonna sit out here."

Essie walked to the refrigerator and pulled out a large pitcher of fresh-squeezed lemonade that she'd mixed earlier in the day. She walked around the table and filled each glass and then gave the pitcher to Jerrod so that he could do the same for those on the living room coffee table.

As though she thought she might have forgotten something, Essie walked into the kitchen and counted every serving dish that she'd placed out on her countertop, making sure that everything was in order for all her guests to prepare their own plates. Once she was satisfied that everything was perfect, she walked to the front door.

"Dinner is served," she said, opening the door so that they could enter. "Y'all know where the bathroom is. There are some fresh towels on the counter. Wash up and come on back so the food won't get cold."

"Ms Essie, it smells good up in here," Colin remarked when he kissed her cheek before helping Angel down the hall.

After they all had had their turn at the sink, they returned to the living room, where Essie and Jerrod were waiting.

"I just want to say thank you to all of you for accepting my invitation to dinner," Essie said. "Y'all sho' do know how to make an old lady happy."

Like a chorus on cue, everyone began talking at once, telling Essie that she was the thoughtful one and the one who deserved to be thanked.

Essie laughed and then gestured for them to quiet down. "Then I reckon we all just made each other happy, and that just makes it all the better," she said.

Without further words, Essie reached out her hands, and everyone else did the same, linking with the person beside them, until they had formed a complete circle. Devoid of any formal prelude, Essie bowed her head and began praying.

"Lord, before we do anything else, we just want to say thank You. Thank You for life, health, and strength. Thank You for family and thank You for friends. Lord, I thank You for every miracle that is standing here in my living room, 'cause whether we know it or not, You done did some mighty works just among us few. Thank You for Colin and Angel and for protecting little Austin Benjamin during the fall. He could have been cut off, but You spared his life and we know it wasn't nobody but You, Lord. Thank You for rescuing Jerrod and saving his mama from heartbreak. As bad as it was, it could have been worse. You might not have come when we wanted You to, but You was right on time. Thank You for healing Elaine and Mason's marriage and proving that ain't nothing too hard for You. We speaking it by faith 'cause You said in Your Word that we could and ain't nothing too hard for You. And thank You for T. K. He might've thought he come by here just to bring Jerrod home, but, Lord, You know that it ain't by chance that he's here with us this evening. He come for a purpose and we thank You.

"Now, Master, we thank You for this food You done blessed me to share with my friends and we ask You to bless this fellowship. No matter what happens from this day forward, don't never let this circle be broken, but let us hold up one another and love one another in the same way that You loved us . . . in Jesus' name. Amen. Y'all help yourselves and eat up."

In her mind, it was a simple prayer, but Essie watched as nearly all of her dinner guests reached for the box of Kleenex that she kept on her coffee table before gathering in the kitchen.

When she set the table, she pictured seeing Mason, Elaine, Colin, and Angel sharing the dining room table with her, and Jennifer, T. K., and Jerrod in the living room. Instead it became a seating arrangement separated by gender. She sat at the table chatting and laughing with Angel, Elaine, and Jennifer, while the men and Jerrod sat in the living room, where they could eat and watch a basketball game at the same time.

It was the same game that Jerrod had stolen the money from his mother to buy the tickets for two of the Dobermans to attend. Unfortunately for them, Freddie and his crew wouldn't be able to watch it tonight.

# Chapter 22

## *Saturday Morning: 1:15 A.M.*

Nearly two hours ago, Essie had said her prayers for the night and read Ben's letter before getting into bed. Although she lay with her head propped against two pillows, the letter was still in her hand and she was wide-awake. It had been a full day, and as tired as she thought she should be after entertaining guests until after nine o'clock, Essie felt surprisingly rested. With the exception of Angel, who sat on the sofa with her swollen feet perched on her husband's lap, the women had helped her clean the kitchen. Jerrod pitched in and vacuumed the crumbs that the men had clumsily dropped on Essie's living room carpet during their energetic, but fruitless, cheers for the home team.

"That boy done come a long way from where he was just a few days ago," Essie mumbled to herself. She thought of the fourteen-year-old and smiled.

She was grateful for the good appetites that her

neighbors had brought with them. Because of it, there was very little food to put away. Almost everybody came back for seconds, and the men even scraped the pots for a third helping of the meal that they couldn't stop raving about. All that was left of the banana pudding were smudges of the meringue topping that had stuck to the sides of the glass dish.

Not since Ben was alive did Essie feel so useful and so loved. She could hardly wait for Sunday morning to arrive when she'd be able to look around in the pews at the Temple of God's Word and see all the people whose lives she'd touched, as well as those who'd touched hers.

She had put last Sunday's message to the test and would be able to testify to the fact that loving those people who lived around her enough to reach out and give them hope was a powerful thing. Now, Essie felt as though she knew a little of what Ben must have felt when he was out on the battlefields fighting for the hopes, dreams, and freedoms of others. In a way, she'd just done the same thing by sharing her wisdom, her experiences, and her love for Christ with the folks in Braxton Park. She knew that there were others that needed to be helped too, but for now, Essie felt contented knowing she had reached out to all of those that God had placed in her heart.

"Ma?"

Jennifer heard the call just as she was about to close her son's door after peeking in on him. Not being able to see his features through the darkness, she assumed he was asleep. Jennifer flipped the switch on the wall, and Jerrod squeezed his eyelids together from the blinding overhead lights. "Why are you still awake?" she asked. "It's one-thirty in the morning."

"Couldn't sleep," he answered as he moved into a seated position.

Jennifer looked around her son's room and grinned. She couldn't recall the last time his bedroom looked so neat. He'd put away all the clothes that were tossed on the floor and on nearby chairs. All of his shoes were in the closet where, for years, she'd been begging for him to place them, and his video games were tucked neatly in the drawer beneath the television stand.

"You like?" Jerrod beamed, holding out his arms and gesturing like one of the paid beauties on Essie's favorite television show.

"I like!" Jennifer nodded. She walked to his bed and sat on the edge of it. "Looks like a whole new room."

Jerrod sat in silence for several minutes, but Jennifer knew that there was something that he wanted to say. She smiled as she looked at him, his eyes staring into the bedspread. For the first time, she could see a little boy inside of him, a little boy hesitant to talk to his mother for fear of what she might think or do. Jerrod had never confided in her before, and the times that he'd spoken to her in the past were in a manner that showed how little he cared about what she thought.

Jennifer reached out and touched his knee. "What is it, Jerrod?"

He shrugged, and after a moment of silence said, "I'm just sorry for everything, that's all."

"I know you are, sweetheart. You told me that when we talked last night, and I know you meant it.

You don't have to keep apologizing. I'm sorry too. I mean, you won't tell me what I did to make you feel you needed to lash out, but whatever it was, I can't tell you how I wish I could have a chance to do it over."

"It wasn't what you did, Ma. It's what you *didn't* do."

Jennifer braced herself. When Jerrod chose not to go into details with her about this the night before, in a way she was relieved. Not knowing meant that she didn't have to face her failures in motherhood. Now that her son seemed prepared to open up completely, Jennifer felt unprepared to hear what he had to say.

"I was mad, Ma," Jerrod continued. "I guess I didn't really know that I was so mad, but I was. I was mad about that dude you dated when we were still living in the projects."

"What dude?"

They'd moved from public housing for the last time less than two years ago when she graduated from DeVry University and got her present job as the personal secretary to the vice president of an insurance firm in Buckhead. For the first time in her life, she was able to afford the luxury of working just one job, and the expenses of living in a comfortable home where she didn't feel she was sharing her space with others who she could hear breathing just on the other side of the thin walls that separated their units. Before her graduation, they'd always lived in one area or another that catered to people on public assistance. Jennifer had dated several different men between the time her son was born and when he turned twelve years old, so Jerrod was going to have to be more specific than what he'd told her so far.

"I don't remember his name, but it was when we lived in South Carolina. He hit me for scratching his ride, and you were standing right there and saw him, Ma."

It was almost embarrassing, but Jennifer couldn't immediately recollect his name either. They hadn't lived in South Carolina in almost ten years. "I recall that, Jerrod. I laid into him big time. You don't remember that? I pushed him away from you and told him not to ever hit you again."

"Yeah, but he kept coming back, Ma; and *you* were the one who let him come back. You cooked dinner for him the next day, and I had to sit across from him and look in his ugly face at that gold-teeth grin while y'all laughed and flirted like everything was cool. It was the same man that jacked me up by the collar of my shirt, called me a punk, and smacked me in the face. It was like you chose him over me, Ma. When you let him stay, it was like you chose him over me."

Jennifer felt miserable. She'd forgotten the incident a long time ago, but somehow Jerrod, barely three when it happened, not only remembered it, but accurately recalled every detail. To know that something she'd considered so insignificant had affected her son to the point of following him through life, nearly landing him in the prison system, was heart-wrenching. Jennifer's lips trembled as she choked back an outburst of tears. Feeling Jerrod's hand on top of hers did little to ease her heartbreak.

"I know you didn't mean to hurt me, Ma," he said. "Well, at least I know that now. When me and Coach D talked after school today, he made me realize that as a man, I got to own up to everything I do. Even if you did mean to hurt me, I can't live my whole life doing crimes and making other folks' lives miserable and then trying to blame it on something that happened when I was just learning to ride a tricycle.

"Coach D said I couldn't grow up like that. He said black men today are doing all kinds of stuff and blaming it on how white folks held them down way back in the day. He said we got to come up out of that and make our own way. We're just as good as every other man. We ain't got no excuses, and on Judgment Day, God ain't gonna say, 'Oh, okay, a'ight, dog. I understand you lived like crap and didn't make nothing of the life I gave you 'cause the white man discriminated against your people. You cool. Welcome on into Heaven and put on your shouting shoes.' "

In spite of her tears, Jennifer burst into laugher. "T. K. told you that?"

"Yeah. He went through some stuff when he was a kid too. Just like me, he ain't have no daddy, but he had a strong mama." Jerrod then added, "Just like me."

Overcome with emotions at her first time hearing her son describe her in such a positive manner, Jennifer leaned in close and pulled Jerrod into a tight hug. Essie was right all along. She did have a good kid.


Elaine looked at the empty space beside her in the king-size bed that she and her husband had shared for seven years. The bed had never seemed as large or as empty as it did for the last two nights. In spite of that, tonight she'd seen a light at the end of the dark tunnel encircling their marriage. Last night, Mason wouldn't even come into the room, but tonight he did. He even took his shower in the master bathroom instead of down the hall. It was a small step, and even though it may have even been a simple coincidence, Elaine couldn't help but find a glimmer of hope in it.

Generally, she shut down her computer at eleven and was in bed by midnight, but it had been closer to one o'clock when Elaine turned in tonight. Not much time was spent on writing. True to her word, she e-mailed a publisher, pitching her idea to write a story based on Essie's life. It would be Monday before they saw it, but she wanted to get it done tonight. Elaine was confident that she'd be able to sell them on the storyline. Nobody in her right mind would turn down the opportunity to publish a love story like Essie and Ben's. And with all the drama that she, Mason, and their friends added, it was destined to be a bestseller. Elaine was excited to get started, but winning her husband's trust and affection was priority.

Since Mason wouldn't be lying next to her, she wanted to spend as much time with him as she could. While he sat up and snacked on roasted peanuts, Elaine sat on the sofa across from him and pretended to be interested in the old western movie he'd chosen to watch. It wasn't until she saw him fluff his pillow and stretch out on the couch that she said goodnight and walked across the room toward her open bedroom door. Mason wasn't aware of it, but in her side vision, Elaine saw his eyes following her. The white silk gown she'd cleverly picked from her closet almost seemed to shimmer in the lighting that the television cast on her. It was like bait, dangling in front of the eyes of an endangered animal. Elaine wanted him and found some satisfaction in knowing that, in spite of the lingering hurt and anger, Mason wanted her too. But she'd promised him that she wouldn't push and would give him space. If that was what he wanted, then it was definitely not too much to ask. But Elaine decided that while she waited, she'd find subtle ways of reminding her husband what he could have whenever he was ready. She wouldn't rush him, though. Some things were just worth waiting for.

"Like Ms. Essie says," Elaine whispered as she smoothed her hand over Mason's side of the bed, "timing is everything."

She was already dreaming about the night when Mason would decide to move back into the bedroom with her. But even more important than that, she was ecstatic that he'd agreed to give their lives a fresh start, beginning with Sunday service with Essie and the rest of their newly made friends. It had been years since they'd been to church, and until she found the tucked away wedding vows, Elaine had lost her appetite for worship. Now, she was anxious to get there, knowing that, somehow, just taking the first step would be all that was needed to get them back on the right path in every aspect of their lives.

This last week had been an enormous wake-up call. Elaine's mind reverted back to details that she'd given no thought to before. Essie's warning about being careful of vicious dogs, the bizarre sounds of barking that she'd hear periodically in the middle of the day with no dogs in sight, the erroneous teachings on the motivational CDs, the timing of Dante's entrance in her life—all of it had been a trial and she had failed miserably. She had to reach the point of losing everything before she could see her own foolish ways. In Elaine's mind, this had to be what the bottom of the barrel felt like.

Still, as she finally drifted off to sleep, she understood that it had all happened for a reason. If this was what it took to get both her and Mason's attention, then Elaine couldn't have any regrets. In a sense, she felt that she was flirting with the man of her affections again, and soon he would ask her on a "first date" that would begin a whole new relationship. And now that she and Mason were finally reaching the point of understanding the vows that he'd spoken to her, it was only a matter of time before she would be, in every way, with the man she loved.

"Well, I guess you got over your fear of me being two centimeters dilated," Angel said through heavy breaths.

Colin laughed. It really was his intent to wait it out, but tonight the craving for his wife was far stronger than his objective. "I'm sorry," he whispered.

"I'm not."

Angel had been complaining throughout the day of back discomfort, so Colin was hesitant to even make a move toward her. He didn't verbalize his desires, but his wife read the signals well and accommodated him. Her loving left him without strength.

Slipping his arm under her neck, Colin struggled to pull Angel closer to him. She laughed at his feebleness as she moved over and placed her head on his chest. Perspiration caused several strands of her hair to stick to the side of her face, which he moved with his fingers.

He kissed the top of her head. "It's two o'clock in

the morning," Colin said. "Most people are 'sleep and look what you're doing.".

"Look what *I'm* doing?" Angel said through a laugh. She raised her head and looked at him.

Colin pulled her back to his chest and stared up at the ceiling as he felt his heart beating against Angel's ear. With his eyelids quickly getting too heavy to keep open, Colin enjoyed the feel of Angel's hand caressing his chest as he drifted off.

"Colin!" His wife's voice jolted him into an upright position, and the heart that was just returning to its normal rhythm felt as though it was going to burst from his chest.

"What, baby, what?"

Angel was staring down into the bed sheets, saying nothing.

Colin reached over and turned on the bedside lamp. Following her eyes, he noticed the sheets beneath them becoming saturated.

"It's my water," Angel told him. "The baby's coming, Colin. Austin . . . he's coming!"

Jumping from the bed, Colin tried to remember all of the things they'd learned in Lamaze classes. "Okay, baby, breathe." He started demonstrating the short pants that they'd been taught.

Angel laughed. "Sweetie, I'm not hurting yet. I don't even know if I'm in active labor. I just need to get up and get a bath."

"A bath?" Colin, amazed at Angel's calm demeanor, wasn't at all sure that they had time for that.

She walked into the bathroom and turned on the shower while Colin ran around the room in circles, getting dressed and forgetting everything that they had rehearsed. He stopped and closed his eyes while he took deep breaths and tried to calm himself.

"Okay, Colin, your wife and your son need you," he said to himself. "You got to calm down and think."

Walking to the closet, he retrieved the packed suitcase and opened it to be sure everything they needed was still inside. When he picked up the book that Angel had packed away, the letter he'd written to his unborn son fell out. As he reread the words, Colin remembered the overwhelming joy he'd felt when they got the news of Angel's pregnancy. It was hard to believe that it was seven months ago.

"You okay?"

Colin looked up. Through his tears, he saw the blurred image of Angel wrapped in a towel and standing in the doorway of their bathroom. He nodded. "I'm better than okay, baby."

When she stepped close enough, he pulled her into his arms and held her there.

Angel kissed his lips and then walked toward the phone. Colin knew, without asking, that she was calling Essie.

As he finished getting dressed and laid out Angel's clothes for her, he listened to the excitement in his wife's voice while she told the woman that she was on her way to the hospital. From where he stood at the foot of the bed, Colin could hear Essie's response. She was excited too.

"I knew I couldn't sleep for some reason," he heard Essie exclaim. "That was the good Lord keeping me awake so I could get this phone call! When li'l Austin Benjamin come out, you make sure you kiss him and tell him that Ms. Essie loves him to death, you hear?"

"Okay, Ms. Essie." Angel laughed. "But you'll get a chance to tell him yourself if you come to the hospital. And even if you don't, your house will be the first place we stop on the way home in a couple of days."

"Yeah, but by then your mama and Colin's mama and a hundred more people would have been up there to kiss him. I want mine first. You do what I say, you hear? Get my kiss in soon as that boy hits air."

"Yes, ma'am. I love you, Ms. Essie. Thanks for everything."

"You ain't got to thank me, sugar. You know I love you and I'll do just about anything for you. Now get on to that hospital before you drop that load on your bedroom floor."

By the time Angel got off the phone, Colin was fully dressed and had everything ready to go. Angel put on the dress he'd chosen for her and then smiled as she walked past him and out of the bedroom. "You ready?" she asked.

As they neared the front door, Colin turned in the direction of the baby's room empty for months as the couple waited for their special day. "Wait," he said. "I've waited nine months to do this." Colin picked up the telephone and punched in a few codes to change the outgoing message.

"Hi. You've reached the home of Colin and Angel Stephens. Sorry I'm talking so fast, but my wife's in labor, and I have to get her to the hospital. So if you have a message for me or for her or for our new son, Austin, you can leave it at the beep. Peace and God bless."

Angel laughed at his satisfied grin.

"Now, I'm ready."

# Chapter 23

## Saturday Morning: 3:00 A.M.

Jerrod's eyelids flew open and he sat up straight in his bed. He was almost sure that he'd heard a grandfather clock chime, but it couldn't be possible. There was no way he'd heard Essie's clock from inside his bedroom, and certainly not loud enough to have awakened him. He looked at the digital clock on the dresser beside his bed. It read three o'clock. It was eerie, to say the least. The clock next door chimed on the hour, but it just wasn't possible that he'd heard it. Maybe it was a dream. He tried to lie down and go back to sleep, but the drumming in his chest got faster and harder.

Climbing out of his bed, Jerrod walked into the living room and looked out the window that faced Essie's house. As normal, the house next door was dark, with the exception of the light on the front porch. When Jerrod released the blinds and stepped backward, he noticed his hands trembling.

"Ma!" he called as he ran and knocked on Jennifer's bedroom door. "Ma!"

"What?!" he heard his mother say in a frantic voice as she was jerked from her sound sleep.

Brisk footsteps were followed by the quick opening of her door. Jennifer stood there with several clumps of hair sticking from her ponytail, looking like she had been terrorized by an alien during her sleep. "What is it, Jerrod? What's wrong?" she asked.

"Can I go over to Ms. Essie's house?"

"Can you do what? Do you know what time it is?"

"I know it's after three, Ma, but I just need to go and check on her. I'll be right back."

Jennifer grabbed him by the arm as he turned to leave. "Jerrod, what's wrong with you? You can't go over there at this time of night. You can check on her in the morning."

"Can I call her then?"

"Jerrod, what's wrong with you? Don't you know that when you call old people at crazy hours like this, they immediately think something is wrong? You'll scare Ms. Essie half to death, boy. You can't do that."

"Please, Ma. I think something's wrong."

Jerrod watched as his mother looked at him in bewilderment. He didn't know how to explain his feeling, but he just felt like something wasn't right. His terrified look was enough to make his mother walk toward the telephone.

Jennifer picked up the telephone book and found Essie's listing. She dialed the number, and from her quietness and the look on her face, Jerrod knew that she wasn't getting an answer. Before his mother could stop him, he ran for the front door and set off the house alarm, opening the door without first punching in the code.

Jennifer disarmed the unit.

As Jerrod rang Ms. Essie's doorbell and pounded on her front door, he could hear his mother coming behind him.

"Stop it, Jerrod!" she whispered harshly. "You're gonna wake up the whole neighborhood."

She held both his hands in hers to prevent him from any further knocking, but Jerrod could see in her eyes that she was convinced too that something was out of sorts. Jennifer stared at the door for a moment, giving Essie time to answer. When the quiet continued, she turned back to her son. "Run down to Ms. Elaine's house and get Mr. Mason. Tell him we need his help. Hurry!"

Mason turned over on the sofa and placed the pillow over his head, but the noise wouldn't go away. By the time he sat up and realized that the pounding wasn't in his dream, but at his front door, Elaine was rushing past him, bundled in his bathrobe. "Who is it?" she called.

"It's Jerrod, Ms. Elaine. Please help!" he shouted from the other side of the door.

Mason jumped from the sofa and moved Elaine's hands as she attempted to unlock the door. "Hold on a minute, Jerrod," Mason said through the wood that separated them. "Turn off the alarm," he told Elaine.

Once he heard the beep that cleared him to let Jerrod in, Mason opened the door and caught the boy in his arms as he fell into the house, breathing heavily. "What's wrong, Jerrod?"

"It's Ms. Essie . . ." Jerrod panted. "She-she won't open her door, and she won't answer her phone. Something's wrong."

Elaine immediately picked up the phone and gave all the information to a 911 dispatcher. Although the distance to Essie's house was short, the three of them climbed into Mason's BMW and sped down the road, ignoring the neighbors on both sides of them who'd heard the commotion and had come out on their porches or peered out of their windows. The car had barely come to a stop in front of Essie's place when they jumped out and ran up the porch steps to meet Jennifer.

"She's still not answering," Jennifer said.

"Did anybody call Angel?" Elaine asked.

"No. I'll go look up the number and call." Jennifer ran down the steps and back toward her own house.

"What kind of locks does she have on this door?" Mason clenched his teeth as he bore the pain of slamming his still sore body against the wood to try to knock it in.

Jerrod joined in, helping all he could, but the door wouldn't budge.

Minutes later, Jennifer returned. "I called Angel," she reported. "The machine said that she was in labor and she and Colin were gone to the hospital. I called T. K. too," she added. "He's on his way. He said he'd be here in about ten minutes."

"Angel's having the baby?" Mason asked.

Jennifer nodded. "Yeah."

"Stop, stop." Mason pulled Jerrod away from banging his body against the door. "Maybe she's at the hospital with them too. If Angel is having a baby, isn't it a pretty good guess that they picked up Ms. Essie on the way?"

All of them exchanged glances as the sounds of sirens neared.

"Oh, my God," Elaine said.

"Oh, Jerrod," Jennifer whined.

"No," Jerrod said, shaking his head adamantly. "She's in there. I just know it."

"Well, it's too late to back out now," Mason said.

Two police cars, an ambulance, and a fire truck pulled into the neighborhood, waking everybody within listening range.

An armed officer walked up the front stairs with his right hand cautiously on his holster. "We got a call of an unresponsive elderly woman?"

"Uh, yeah," Mason said, trying to find a way to tell the policeman that it had all quite possibly been a terrible mistake.

"Who made the call?" the officer asked.

Elaine raised her hand like a student in grade school. "I did."

"Where is the subject in question, ma'am?"

Elaine's eyes widened. "Well, actually . . ."

"She's in there, but she's not waking up." Jerrod pointed toward Ms. Essie's front door.

At the direction of the officer, Mason, Elaine, Jennifer, and Jerrod stood back and watched as the people in authority got the door open with the speed of professional burglars. At first, all of the adults were so sure that the police would find no one inside that they stayed out on the porch and awaited the scolding they would get for being nosy neighbors.

"In the bedroom!" one policeman's voice rang out.

Upon hearing it, all of them rushed inside and

stood in the doorway of the master bedroom while the paramedics repositioned Essie's body and put an oxygen mask over her face.

"We have a weak pulse," one of the medics said, while the other supplied air to the mask, using a manual hand pump.

"Ms Essie!" Jerrod yelled as he lunged from his mother's arms and jumped onto the bed beside her. "Ms. Essie!"

"Jerrod!" Jennifer called through her own tears.

"Come on, man." Mason grabbed Jerrod and pulled him away. "Let them do their thing. It's gonna be okay."

"Take him out of here," the police officer ordered.

"He's fine," Mason assured him. "I got him. Let him stay."

From the officer's expression, it was obvious to see that he didn't think the child's staying was the best idea, but he didn't insist any further. For several minutes they worked toward reviving the woman, who seemed to just be in a deep sleep.

The policeman who'd ordered Jerrod's removal approached them with a pen and tablet in his hand, asking questions about Essie's health. "There are no signs of trauma," he said. "So whatever caused this is natural. Any heart problems that you are aware of?"

Having just spent an extended amount of time with her a few hours earlier, all the gathered friends could tell the officer was that Essie's health appeared to be exceptional, especially in light of her advanced age.

"Jerrod? Jennifer?"

Dressed in a pajama shirt and a pair of jeans, T. K. appeared in the doorway.

Jerrod instantly tore away from Mason and ran into his coach's arms.

"What happened?" the coach asked as he saw the action that was going on by the bedside.

"We don't know," Jennifer told him. "Looks like Ms. Essie just stopped breathing in her sleep."

"Start CPR!" one of the medics suddenly yelled.

Having been trained in CPR as a part of his job as track coach, T. K. Donaldson knew that more was going on than the attempt to restore breathing. Full CPR was only needed when a heart had stopped beating as well.

Just like the others around him, he stood helplessly and watched. For several minutes they pumped Essie's chest and breathed into her mouth, and when they stepped away, all of Essie's friends knew she was gone.

"Ms. Essie!" Jerrod flung himself back onto the bed and laid his head on Essie's chest and cried.

This time no one tried to stop him, and as the medics gathered their equipment, the other neighbors approached for one last look at the woman who had been instrumental in changing all of their lives.

Mason reached forward and used two fingers to completely close Essie's half-open eyes and then hesitantly placed his arms around Elaine when she broke into heavy sobs, allowing her head to rest against his neck.

"She looks so peaceful," Jennifer said, using her hand to wipe away the water from her own face.

"What's this?" Coach Donaldson reached down and gently tugged at the papers that Essie held in her hand.

All of them looked at the faded words for a moment before they realized that it was the letter that Essie had talked about so fondly.

"Go'n and get your man, Ms. Essie." Jennifer's voice quivered as she whispered the same words she'd said to Elaine just a day earlier.

Jerrod climbed from the mattress, and from the chair beside the bed, he picked up the beautiful design that Essie had knitted. For a blanket that had been made for no special reason, it sure had helped them through some of their most difficult times. Walking around all the grown-ups, Jerrod opened the blanket and spread it out over Essie's body.

"Time of death," the medic said, "three fifty-seven a.m."


"It's a boy!" The doctor held up the crying infant and watched closely as Colin cut the umbilical cord. Using a suction device, the doctor cleared the child's nostrils and mouth.

The nurse, who had assisted in the relatively quick labor and delivery process, wrapped the pasty baby in a hospital blanket and laid him next to Angel's heart.

As though he knew he was in his mother's arms, Austin quieted and rested against her.

"Time of birth," the doctor announced, "three fifty-seven a.m."

With tear-filled eyes that matched those of her husband's, Angel immediately lowered her lips to Austin's forehead and delivered the requested kiss. "That's from your great-grandma Essie," she said. "She told me to tell you that she loves you."

# 3:57 A.M.

## (The poem that inspired the book)

It's like an alarm clock that instantly goes off inside
   me
But there's a craving for you that just won't let me
   sleep.
I'm tossing and I'm turning, trying not to awake
   you again
I know I've already awakened you three times this
   week; today is only Wednesday and here I go
   again.
But your loving . . . I just can't seem to get enough
Somehow, your loving is more than a necessity,
   your loving is a must.
It's 3:57 a.m. and, baby, I'm craving you so bad it's
   beginning to hurt.
I know in a few hours we'll have to get up and go to
   our jobs, but I'm going to have a serious problem concentrating at work.
Am I fienin' you? We both know the answer to that
   question is YES.
Now don't make me pull out medical reasons for
   needing your loving . . . my hypertension or relieving stress.

I'm only trying to awake you so I can put you to
  sleep.

Now, you know how good we sleep after we've
  made love although sometimes we get a little
  hungry and you want something to eat.

You said I have carte blanche with you. It's 3:57
  a.m.; can I cash in on one of those favors?

I don't know how many more favors I have, but
  that's not important now; I'll worry about that
  later.

But isn't it ironic, playing on the radio right now is
  our favorite song.

Maxwell is singing like I've never heard it before:
  "Whenever, Wherever, Whatever." Let's see if
  we can have a marathon and go to the break of
  dawn.

I want the sun to rise with our bodies entwined.

Baby, I want our hearts and souls so close that your
  thoughts are mine.

I can hear the rain beginning to fall; doesn't it
  sound like an orchestra on our roof, playing?

Or does the rain sound like we're at the opera with
  an Italian woman singing about our passion and
  we understand every word she's saying?

Baby, sweetheart . . . it's 3:57 a.m.

Baby, all I want to do is make our bedroom your
  heaven.

Is that all right?

# Discussion Questions

1. Who was your favorite character, and why?

2. What did you think of Essie's reasons for never remarrying after the death of her husband?

3. Were you able to grasp the significance of the woven blanket?

4. Something that happened in Jerrod's preschool years paved the path that he chose to follow in life. Do you feel that this could be the issue with some of today's troubled youth?

5. What are your thoughts on the way Elaine handled her rocky marriage?

6. If the result of the fall had turned out differently, do you think Angel and Colin would have remained a loving couple? Why? Why not?

7. One of Essie's favorite quotes was, "Timing is everything." Do you agree or disagree with this sentiment?

8. Which one of the characters and/or situations could you most identify with?

9. If you could change or rewrite one of the circumstances in this story, would you? If so, which would it be, and why?

10. What kind of emotion(s) did the ending draw from you?

# About the Authors

## Hank Stewart

**Hank Stewart** is a highly acclaimed poet and self-published writer who is a catalyst for action and a messenger of hope. He considers spirituality, history, and love as his major influences for delving into the world of literature.

Hank released his first book of poetry, *The Answer*, in 1993 and followed up with a second book, fittingly titled *Second Chance*, which was written to reveal the Savior to lost souls and to rejuvenate the Christian experience. In 1996, Hank wrote his third book, *Be Still and Know . . .* , a religiously conscious collection of works focusing on the power of prayer and the importance of spiritual guidance.

A devoted Christian, Hank believes that a firm spiritual foundation can help an individual remain true to the mission of life and success. Therefore, he incorporates this belief in his poetry by encouraging people to move to new emotional heights and spiritual levels.

Over the past ten years, Hank Stewart's poetry has

afforded him many opportunities, including working on programs with prominent officials such as former Vice President Al Gore, and honoring the mother of the Civil Rights Movement, the late Rosa Parks, with a special poetic dedication. Mr. Stewart has recited his works for Reverend Jesse L. Jackson Sr., Atlanta Mayor Shirley Franklin, and Dr. Joseph E. Lowery. He also presented Mr. Carl Ware of The Coca Cola Company a special piece of his work. He's appeared on platforms with Tavis Smiley, Michael Vick of the Atlanta Falcons, the late Reverend Hosea Williams, the late Johnnie Cochran, and the list goes on and on.

In addition to all of his other credits, Hank is a founding member of "Five Men on a Stool," a highly successful contemporary R&B/jazz ensemble, accompanied by a touch of spoken word. This Atlanta-based phenomenon, with its captivating yet indescribable mix of talent, repeatedly performs before sold-out crowds in the southeast and beyond.

Born in Jacksonville, Florida, Hank now resides in metropolitan Atlanta. He is the father of one son, Austin Stewart.

# Kendra Norman-Bellamy

West Palm Beach, Florida native, **Kendra Norman-Bellamy**, is the third child born to Bishop H. H. and Mrs. Francine Norman. She attended, and graduated with honors from, Valdosta Technical College in Valdosta, Georgia, where she received an Associate of Applied Technology degree. Her love for words began with writing poetry as an elementary school student and blossomed into novel writing in the late nineties.

Now, an award-winning, national bestselling author and motivational speaker, Kendra began her career as a self-published writer. Her debut novel was released in August 2002 and was nominated Best Christian Fiction release of that year. Since that time, Kendra has been blessed to author several books, many of which have graced several national bestseller lists, including, *Essence*, Wal-Mart, Black Expressions, and more.

In addition, Kendra is founder and president of KNB Publications, LLC, an independent self-publishing house set in place as a vehicle to help aspiring writers reach their goals of becoming published authors. She serves as a columnist for *Global Woman* and *Hope for Women* magazines, a contributing staff writer for *WOW*, and the editorial consultant for *Booking Matters* magazine. She is also Georgia-area coordinator of ACFW (American Christian Fiction Writers).

Aside from her literary endeavors, Kendra is also an AFAA Certified Group Fitness Instructor, trained in teaching Step Aerobics, Kickboxing, Body Works, and Total Body Conditioning.

With a God-given talent for the pen, Kendra is pursuing a full-time career in writing faith-based novels that tell stories of human love, drama, and passion in the Christian community.

Kendra resides in metropolitan Atlanta with her husband, Jonathan, and daughters, Brittney and Crystal.